VAMPIRES, SAINTS, AND Lovers

JULIA
PHILLIPS SMITH

VAMPIRES, SAINTS AND LOVERS
By Julia Phillips Smith

Cover Design and Interior format by The Killion Group
http://thekilliongroupinc.com

PRAISE FOR VAMPIRES, SAINTS AND LOVERS

"This book is savagely beautiful. Can she write fight scenes in all their bloody, violent glory. Puts the monster back into vampire." - Melissa Bradley, *Melissa's Imaginarium*

"Dark, compelling, intriguing, a fresh and dramatic take on the vampire genre that will hold you spellbound." - Anna Campbell, *Publisher's Weekly's* Top 100 Books pick for *Captive of Sin*

"A triumphant novel that will leave readers breathless. Julia Phillips Smith is destined to become the next superstar of the vampire genre." - Julianne MacLean, *USA TODAY* bestselling author

DEDICATION

Though words are my tools in trade, I've never found any to truly express the depth of my gratitude for our friendship.

So I shall simply say – this book is for you, Connie.

ACKNOWLEDGMENTS

First, I want to thank my husband Brad. His unwavering belief in me kept me going when putting two words together was more than I could handle.

My gratitude goes out to Natalie Hallett, who came to speak to my writers' group and introduced us to NaNoWriMo. A 50,000-word month-long writing marathon seemed so crazy to me, I just had to do it. Without that challenge, my vampire character Peredur would never have come to me. So Natalie, thanks!

To the White Point Beach brainstorming session that solved my initial story issues: Stella MacLean and Lori Robitaille, I'm so grateful for your help in getting this story on the right track.

I would like to thank several groups of critique readers whose feedback shaped this book: Kelly Boyce and Pamela Callow, who read an early version of this story; Tara MacDonald, Caroline Ruyle, Travis Cody, Paulette Phillips and Michelle Helliwell—all of your comments brought the story to another level entirely; and finally, to Shawna Romkey and Julianne MacLean, whose later critiques of my manuscript truly helped me to see from a clearer vantage point.

To my editor, Pat Thomas – the remarkable care you invested in this book made all the difference.

To my cover designer, Kim Killion – a very great pleasure to have your work gracing my cover.

Finally, to my cousin Julianne MacLean, whose belief in Peredur has been a beautiful thing to behold.

1

Near Caer yn ar-Fon, 577

Peredur coughed up blood.

Moans hung in the autumn air as women picked carefully between the tangled embraces at their feet. He could only watch them pass. A spear pinned him to the ground as the sun made ready to set without him.

His lips fought to form the name of his beloved. *Tanwen.*

"No..." forced its way out as a sigh, sending more blood to bubble up. The sticky smell filled his nostrils. This wasn't happening. Not to him.

A voice beside him prayed in sobs for deliverance. Another voice whispered to be forgiven. 'God,' Peredur longed to scream out. But not to beg.

A grimy face loomed over him, searching for signs of life. Peredur lay in outrage as the ragged man frisked him for valuables. He heard the snick of his own knife leaving its sheath at his ankle. His body jerked as every last bit of silver ornament was cut from his clothing.

A grasp of his hand – only to have the rings pulled from his fingers – gave Peredur the strength he needed. He grabbed the vulture's wrist as if it would prevent the last of his breath from passing through clenched teeth.

"Holy Mother!" blurted the man, drawing back. "Save me!"

The man wrested himself free, taking with him the ring once given Peredur by his father.

"God," Peredur whispered, choking horribly on blood. He knocked his head backward into the ground. The battle against this latest band of Irish raiders had been Peredur's final grab at loot for his wedding coffer. On his return, he was to formally ask for Tanwen's hand.

Whispered prayers surrounded him, unrelenting and pathetic. He would ram those prayers down all their throats if he had a chance. His life had amounted to nothing but this monumental joke; his fury smoldered as the horizon lit to an impossible red.

A row of birds perched on a limb along the forest's edge, staring down at the littered battlefield.

God! I curse you!

Peredur flailed his hand against the mud, his legs stiffening. The image of Tanwen rose in his mind as if gesturing to stop him from forming those words. But he would not be stopped.

I curse you for this day!

An irresistible dragging sensation upon his soul made him thrash to hold on.

"I curse you, God!" he rasped.

A figure appeared just as Peredur's body seized with a powerful shudder.

No battlefield scavenger, he stood tall and powerful, a black silhouette against the blue of nightfall. Kneeling beside Peredur with easy grace, he gazed down upon him like a carrion bird.

"Peredur of Gwenedd," he said.

He should be terrified. He should be begging at long last – begging for mercy. On the brink of hell, the only thing Peredur could muster was the gob of blood he spat in disgust.

What do you want of me? Peredur's lips no longer formed words.

Barely flinching, the stranger wiped an elegant hand along his soiled cheek. Peredur watched as the man licked the blood from his fingers as one would lick honey.

I offer you another chance at life, the being said, though the words merely rumbled in Peredur's head.

Peredur started to smile but had no strength to finish it.

Do you want another life? the voice persisted. *I can give you a new life.*

Another life? He just wanted his old one back again, to hold Tanwen in these useless arms. If he said yes, would Tanwen be returned to him? That's all he wanted – Tanwen, to feel her embrace one more time.

I want her... Peredur's thoughts were barely thoughts anymore.

Do you want another life? the voice repeated.

Tanwen...

Another life? the voice persisted.

He could barely hang on to the word...*yes...*

Something sharp pressed hard on his neck. Peredur's blood surged away as though ripped from his veins.

His vision swam, then cleared enough to behold a figure bent close as though in a lover's embrace. The thing's teeth were at his neck. New pain blossomed where the fiend bit deeply.

So he was in Hell. This must be the very first of an eternity of torments.

Tanwen. All I wanted was one last glimpse of your eyes looking into my own. For that I cursed God. And for that I am damned.

The being cupped Peredur's head in an iron grasp. He was like an infant, held in his father's battle-worn hand. The figure looked down and Peredur saw two pale eyes gleaming from the shadowy face.

"Peredur." Such a voice.

Though Peredur lay at the mercy of a fiend here in this first hour in Hell, he couldn't remember ever having felt so contented.

"Do you want another life?" the demon whispered, so enticing.

Am I not claimed by death?

"You can still be spared."

A tongue licked his throat up to his ear, sending a shiver to erupt over his skin. *Who are you?* Peredur asked.

"I can yet send you to God," the stranger said.

The night lost some of the clarity that the demon's bite had bestowed. Stars seemed to buzz around Peredur like flies. He must be finally slipping away.

The demon's face drew close, ghastly and pale. The creature's eyes took on a lurid glow that cast fear like a rock into Peredur's gut.

I have come for you, Peredur, the demon said. *I was sent to call you to the Brotherhood.*

Peredur heard the horrible sucking noises coming from the wound in his chest. *Who sent you?* His wheezing body could not go on much longer. There would be nothing for this stranger to gather up for his brethren.

When you cursed Our Father in Heaven, you yourself called me here.

Will you turn me into a demon? The fiend stretched its body to lie beside Peredur.

All I ask is whether you desire another life, it whispered in his ear.

Chills swept over him, and Peredur shut his eyes against an unbearable tugging on his soul. *Would I have cursed Him if I had not wanted to live?* Peredur turned his head away from the being, but it read his thoughts. There was no escaping it.

The demon curled itself around Peredur like a man about to take a woman. Iron hands bent Peredur's head to the side, exposing his neck. Terror burst through Peredur as it had never done on any battlefield – not even this day's.

Live, then.

For a brief instant Peredur saw impossibly long pointed teeth between the demon's lips. Then his mouth opened wide in a silent cry of horrified shock as the fiend clamped its teeth down deeply into Peredur's flesh. His life force gushed from his body, convulsing him like one demented while a sound like sea birds hung in the air overhead.

2

Near Yn Wyddfid

The path before her shimmered, as tears balanced on her lashes, refusing to fall. Fighting for breath, she discovered her feet had carried her to a spot on the crag overlooking the bay. Dampness hung heavily on the breeze, beading on her hair and woolen robe. She felt awash in tears, inside and out.

They finally seeped in an unbroken stream from her eyes. She might have thought her heart broken, if she had a heart left to break. Sea birds glided between the rocky coast and the surf, crying out her anguish with their shrieks.

Why?

Why had she loved such a proud man? Peredur never listened when she'd told him he was all she needed. He kept leaving her to fight the raiding Irish. To win a name for himself, he'd said, so her father would agree to a match.

Where did that leave her? *Betrothed to a corpse.*

Sobs punched their way through her chest at last. Tanwen curled into herself, clutching tight with arms that could not stop the mourning. She heard painful cries and wondered where they came from, even as her throat ached and tears spilled down over her jaw and chin.

This couldn't be real. He was too powerful, too swift, too expert a fighter to go down to a spear. Even so, she couldn't see anything except his green eyes staring through her, felt nothing but the whisper of his breath on her neck as they embraced.

The man was mistaken. Peredur was alive somewhere. He couldn't be gone.

Then why was she tottering on rocks slick with mist? Why did she want the pain in her chest to stop squeezing? Why hadn't Peredur arrived at her father's door, as promised, to ask for her hand?

Wiping a sleeve across her face, Tanwen emerged from the darkness of shock to feel a presence behind her. Expecting her brother, sent to fetch her back, Tanwen turned to behold Cavan, the son of the village wise woman.

His pale gray eyes gazed upon her as though he knew what lay screaming in her heart. She almost went to him, but stood there, shaking her head, her tears starting anew. "It can't be! It can't be true!"

They stood for a moment before Cavan gestured to a large boulder behind them. "Come and sit with me awhile."

Tanwen moved as though she were a carved wooden figure in her baby sister's hand. Cavan helped her to sit.

"It's true, Tanwen." Something in his tone made her look up. Cavan turned a small object over in his hand. Her gaze came to rest on the silver ring he held in his fingers. The ring which Peredur's father had given him.

She looked up into Cavan's eyes. "Where did you get that?" she demanded.

Something lurked behind his gaze, something he fought against and blinked away. "A peddler sold it to my mam yesterday. When she held it in her hand, she saw it all before her. Everything that happened. She asked him where he got it and he gave her a story. It didn't matter. She knew."

Tanwen stared at Peredur's ring and fought the urge to grab it out of his hand. Cavan must have sensed how she felt. He held it out and dropped it into her outstretched palm.

As soon as the metal touched her skin she saw the ring being slipped from Peredur's cold hand. The reality ripped a gasp from her throat. The ring nearly tumbled onto the scraggly brush at her feet.

This time Cavan wrapped his solid hands around hers, ensuring her grip with his own. Tanwen sagged until her forehead touched her wrists. If Cavan were not here she would pass out. The crying started again. This time she could not listen to it as though it came from someone else. She would not be holding her beloved's ring if he still lived.

She'd yet to pledge her fidelity to Peredur before the village, but she'd said it often in her heart. God knew her pledge to be true. He knew that today she became a widow.

3

Peredur drifted toward consciousness. His first night in the mead hall as a youth had been easier than this. He blinked the fuzziness away.

Peredur saw several men concealed by shadow. Watching him.

Suddenly the images of the battle he'd just fought reared up in his mind. Peredur started and made to rise.

"Take it slow." He knew that voice somehow.

Peredur looked across the murky space to the man who had spoken to him in his mind. He was a huge muscular fighter. Peredur still could not place him.

Then he remembered. This was no man. This was a fiend sent by the devil to fetch Peredur into Hell. He pulled himself into a crouch, recalling with a catch in his breath that he should not be able to move like this. His hand groped for the hole in his chest.

A glance confirmed it. His patched tunic showed where the spear *had* pierced his body. Yet now he lived. His bludgeoned shoulder now worked. His father's ring was missing from his right hand.

"Will you tell us your name, Brother?" the fiend asked.

"Why do you call me that?"

"You have been called to join with us. Tonight you will become the newest member of our Brotherhood."

Peredur looked carefully at the other figures. Clearly they were all warriors of some sort. All were fit, strong, experienced. They regarded him with the same appraising glance he gave them.

Who do you serve? Peredur wondered aloud.

The men looked at each other. Peredur stood, feeling the strength in his legs when he knew there should be none. He faced the one who had come to him as he lay dying.

"We serve the Brotherhood," the demon said finally.

"Fighting monks, are you?" Peredur scoffed.

A few derisive laughs met his challenge. Peredur stole a glance or two at rocky walls that could only place them in a cavern. No entrance was visible in the unfamiliar light – its source he could not make out.

"You are safe," the fiend assured. "No one will find us here."

"Who would be looking for us?" Peredur asked in a tone laced with warning.

"All men look for us after a time."

"Why?" Peredur felt an ominous foreboding that emanated from almost exactly where the spear once jutted from his chest.

"Let us say that those who are hunted, rightly fear the hunters."

The memory of this demon's tongue along his cheek sent shudders through Peredur. "These hunted men," Peredur began, his voice cracking, "what are they accused of?"

"It is not for the brethren to bring criminals to justice. Though we doubtless encounter some, all the same." The fiend nodded to one of the others. Two of this strange brotherhood departed, while the others exchanged knowing glances. Then all that remained gazed upon Peredur.

"Why was I chosen?" he whispered.

"For the same reason we all were." The demon smiled with a look that was nearly kindness.

The missing brethren returned with a third person in tow. A young fellow not much beyond boyhood, the youth appeared dazed and unsure of his surroundings. Eyes which did not truly see seemed to train their inward gaze upon Peredur.

The demon moved imperiously toward the young man. No one could refuse such authority. The boy stood expectant, if wary. Taking his hand as if the youth were a woman and the fiend a dance partner, the demon paraded him back and forth for a few moments, whispering something to him as well. The fiend stepped back, still holding the youth's hand.

The boy stood as if awaiting orders. The others all stood with barely concealed anticipation, looking to the newcomer for the next move in this chilling ceremony.

Peredur shook his head, no. The demon nudged the youth forward.

Unable to prevent himself from advancing, Peredur took up his role as though he knew what should happen. He recoiled from the ideas that crept through his mind.

The brethren moved imperceptibly forward, surrounding Peredur and this lamb offered up. With their approach, a horrible chill crept further along his spine.

"No," Peredur whispered, shaking his head against it. "Please."

The demon looked directly at Peredur. When his own blood had smothered him on the battlefield and he could bear it no longer, this fiend had bored the same eerie gaze directly into Peredur's frenzied brain.

The demon now pressed on the boy's shoulder, urging him to sink to his knees. Something began to pulsate in Peredur's veins. A desire he could not place moved through him – compelled him to step toward the boy.

The slightly distant gaze in those young eyes unnerved Peredur much more than if terror had washed across that fresh face. Something very near to panic grew stronger and higher in Peredur's chest. Still, he moved closer.

The demon tipped the boy's head back, exposed a neck that strained at the unnatural angle. A rush of ecstasy burst through the dread that had built up inside Peredur. All of a sudden he knew what he was being asked to do.

With a sinking heart, Peredur looked to the demon for confirmation. The reassurance in the fiend's face sent tremors coursing all through Peredur's body. He heard the near-moans of anticipation in the brethren surrounding him.

Go on, he heard in his mind. *Take him. Enjoy your first.*

He knew he smelled saliva, though until this moment that humble substance hadn't demanded any notice. Some of it was his, most belonged to the others in the cavern. He was suddenly privy to the various states of mind of the six other members of the brethren.

Peredur gazed down at the kneeling youth. What disturbed most was not the sudden ability to feel the pulsations of the boy's every heartbeat. Peredur could now smell and hear the boy's blood as it surged with life just a few membranes away from him.

He closed his eyes, trying for one last desperate moment to fight this all-consuming desire to unite with that blood. He remembered his own blood in his mouth as he coughed it up at the mercy of the spear.

Peredur's eyes opened to look down on the slightly bewildered smile of the boy.

There was no cry at all when Peredur sank his teeth into the boy's neck and tasted the red joy at last.

Power burst into every part of him as he swallowed deeply and drank again. He felt submerged in bliss. Nothing in his old life compared to this. *Nothing.*

A wounded moan finally escaped the boy's throat. Peredur pressed his mouth further against the boy's soft yielding flesh. A short struggle ensued. Very short.

Peredur surfaced from the depths of that first taste. Satiated and dripping with contentment, he found the other brethren circling close, closer than they'd been so far. Again he smelled their saliva and knew their terrible hunger. He stepped aside, releasing the boy who drooped and crumpled forward onto the floor of the cavern.

Within a heartbeat the six descended on the youth, still full of luscious pulsating riches. A single cry of pure terror pierced the night. Then all was still, save for feeding sounds of the brethren.

Peredur swayed and sat heavily. He felt dizzy with unaccustomed strength and satiation. He watched as the others devoured the unfortunate until he was nothing but a shell. One of the brothers dragged the source of their feast out of the cave.

The rest turned to regard Peredur, their eyes alight with gratitude. And something else. A hunger, still – for more.

The demon, in all his terrible splendor, strode forward to stand before Peredur. His face lit with a sinister smile. Raising a hand to indicate the newest member, the fiend said to the six, "Behold your brother."

He swept his hand wide to include the others. "Behold these, your brothers. They have given freely of their blood to waken you from the sleep that transformed you. You have taken your first life and shared that freely with your brothers. Now..." The demon stepped closer, moving smoothly behind Peredur.

"The final step in your rebirth," the demon said. Iron hands placed themselves upon each of Peredur's shoulders. "The brethren will taste of your essence and share with you this final act of Becoming."

He wondered, too late, what this essence could be that he must share. The demon pulled him to his feet in a smooth motion, as if Peredur weighed no more than an afterthought. The others closed in. The demon's grip tightened, pulling Peredur's arms behind him.

"I asked if you wanted another life," the fiend whispered in Peredur's ear. Two of the brethren knelt and sliced open his leggings, while the demon helped to pull his tunic off. Sharp nails dragged across Peredur's flesh. He bucked and twisted, but the demon and brethren held him fast. Mouths descended on the beading lacerations, licking up the precious blood.

A groan escaped him. The power so newly won from the feast flowed out of him and into the others, racking his body with weakening shudders. Each of the brethren sighed or moaned his pleasure, like kings sipping the blood from Peredur as from jewelled goblets. His energy ebbed so completely he sagged forward, hanging from the demon's grasp.

The brethren raised him in the air. They turned him about in a slow arc, kneeling as one before the demon. Peredur was displayed and presented like a stag before a feast.

The fiend stepped forward into Peredur's field of vision. *Such a being.* Power emanated from him in his every gesture. He smiled upon Peredur.

"Before I take your gift of brotherhood to myself," he said, "I bow to your offering and receive it with humble thanks." He swept forward in an elegant reverence. Raising his arms like a druidic priest, the demon cast his eyes to heaven. "You gave Yourself freely, offering to us what You held most dearly. You asked in return that we love one another as You loved us."

Was this demon addressing the Roman God? Did he have no fear? Perhaps there was nothing to fear when the worst had already happened.

Pure crystalline dread took hold of Peredur now. He fought to get his breath. Dangling in the grip of these beings, offered up to this demon with the blood of that boy still sweet on his lips, Peredur feared for what remained of his soul.

The fiend knelt before Peredur, who hung now in the brethren's grip so that he faced the cavern floor and regarded the bowed head of the demon.

"In our hour of death," continued the demon, "when we most needed Your Presence to guide us Home, each of us cursed You instead." The dread in Peredur's gut grew worse. The brethren holding him in their grasp shuddered – as if they felt it, too.

Without warning, Peredur saw in his mind's eye a series of battlefield deaths, each one featuring a member of the Brotherhood:

One fell to a battleaxe hurled from such a distance the fighter hadn't seen it coming.

One was thrown from a tower and impaled on a tree.

One slipped from a ship's wreckage within sight of the shore – unable to cling with numbed hands any longer.

One writhed in the grip of poisoned wine, served by an ambitious captain on the eve of battle.

One shook with fever caused by festering wounds and was left for dead by his own retreating force.

And the last, Peredur saw the death of the demon himself.

The demon had secretly loved the daughter of his king. He'd been unable to keep one look of longing from others' notice – and for that he'd been forced to watch her submit to cruel punishment. Then he was sent to the battlefield stripped of shield and blade with the knowledge she would be married to another. The curses that man had flung toward God!

Peredur's own surely paled in comparison.

He looked down now upon this demon, upon his bowed head, and Peredur was filled with a curious compassion for this Brother. Those slow deaths were injustices for fighting men such as these. As shocked as he was by the curses he'd heard in his mind when he witnessed their demises, he could blame none of them.

The kneeling fiend continued, "We humbly beseech Thee, oh God, to accept this new member into Your Brotherhood with our petition for forgiveness."

"Forgive us, oh God," the others intoned.

The demon raised his head and looked directly into Peredur's face. The suffering, the longing Peredur saw there took his breath away.

Spreading arms wide to encompass them all, the fiend said, "Now you have seen us in our hour of damnation." Peredur realized the demon no longer addressed the Roman God, but Peredur himself.

"God, in His mystery, did not banish us to reside in the fires of Hell. We are instead compelled to walk amongst the living, though we no longer live as mortals. And as you can clearly see, we are not dead."

Peredur felt a ripple of unrest run through those who held him.

"You have shared your blood freely with the Brotherhood," the demon continued, "as they have shared with you. In this way you are welcomed to this life."

Peredur wondered just how freely he'd shared, when it was the brethren themselves who'd cut into his thighs and torso, helping themselves to his blood. Then he recalled the delirious joy that had filled him as he'd sunk his teeth into that poor boy's neck. Now the thought of it made him hunger for more.

The memories of each warrior's death swiftly pummeled him again. His body twisted as they buffeted his consciousness. Worst of all was the image of that woman writhing under her mistreatment in the tormented memory of the one who knelt before him. Peredur and the demon locked gazes.

Inhaling sharply, Peredur saw the lovers' reunion in his mind. The demon had joined with her after his transformation. Somehow Peredur knew that revelation was true.

Tanwen.

The fiend nodded. If Peredur shared his blood with this last of the brethren, he would one day hold Tanwen in his arms. For that he would gladly face this between-worlds' purgatory. For Tanwen he would face anything.

"Peredur of Gwenydd." Solemnly, the demon at his feet addressed him. "Do you give freely of your blood? In so doing, you will seal your fate to that of this Brotherhood."

He felt the stirring amongst the others – a profound anticipation. "I asked once before," Peredur insisted. "I must know. Who do you serve?"

"The Brotherhood," they answered in one confident voice.

"You merely serve yourselves?" Peredur persisted.

"The Brotherhood serves Him Who made us." The demon gazed patiently at Peredur.

"To what purpose?"

"Who can say what purpose God sets down for us?" the fiend said.

Peredur looked again into those pale eyes that returned his gaze openly. *What other option did he have?*

"I can yet release you from this life," the fiend said, as though he'd just read Peredur's thoughts.

"How?"

"None must join the Brotherhood who do not wish it."

"If I don't join with you?" Peredur asked.

"Instead of merging your blood with mine," the demon explained, "I would devour you as we did the boy."

The only thing that seemed real to him was the borrowed memory of this demon and his wronged beloved. To reunite with Tanwen was all that mattered. He would give himself to this demon and pay whatever price was required of him.

Peredur took a deep breath. "I give myself freely."

A sigh of joy escaped each one who held him. Peredur raised his head and saw an irresistible smile creep over the lips of the demon. An expression of gratitude filled his eyes before they began to glow in a hellish way.

Peredur felt their tightening grip upon him. He tried to still himself but couldn't stop from rearing back against the others as the demon lay on the cavern floor directly beneath him. Peredur hung suspended over the fiend, whose gaze bored deeply into Peredur's own. In a swift movement the demon drew a sharp nail across Peredur's chest.

The cut bit. Peredur felt a wave of disorientation and moaned. His blood dripped quickly onto the waiting lips of the demon. Peredur kept his eyes open even as his head swooned. The demon closed his, threw his head back as if in rapture and bared his teeth. They gleamed white between the glossiness of Peredur's blood.

He writhed in their hands as the brethren growled their approval. The demon put his fingertips gently against Peredur's wound, tracing it. Then, taking a small white amulet from where it was concealed beneath his tunic, the demon pressed it against the wound, smearing it with blood. Opening his mouth wide, he collected the blood and swallowed, laughing throatily. He looked up once more – this time into Peredur's very soul.

He knew that the demon saw Tanwen; that the broad bloody grin was for her. Peredur's feet touched the ground as the brethren finally lowered and released him.

He sank to his knees, breathing heavily.

The demon raised himself to kneel as well. He took Peredur's face in his hands. "Welcome, Brother. I am Melnak."

Peredur tried to speak but could not find the words. Finally he managed, "What have I become?"

"Vampire," Melnak replied, voice thick with emotion. "You are now a vampire. Welcome to our Brotherhood."

4

The wise woman's son walked Tanwen to her father's hut, one arm solidly around her. Tanwen had never spent more than a few moments in his company before today, yet today he had been a comfort to her. She would always be grateful to him for that.

Before they got too far from the rock they'd sat upon, her brother appeared on the path. He followed along behind as their father must have told him to do. A little ways along and they met up with her two youngest sisters near the bottom of the hill. Before too long they resembled nothing more than a small procession.

Her mam and another sister waited in a heap of dismay on a bench outside the hut. They rose as Tanwen approached, while her father darted into the doorway. Something about his urgency made her stop in her tracks. New tears began.

"I can't go home," she said.

Cavan pressed his mouth like a kiss near her ear. "Yes, you can," he whispered.

Tanwen squeezed the ring in her hand until the edges bit. She took a deep breath, nodded and covered the rest of the space between herself and her home. As she neared, Cavan's arm slipped away and she walked the few steps to her father alone.

His eyes filled with sadness. It gave her strength to see her tada's pain through her own. He would have been proud to stroll across the village green in the presence of their kinsmen and friends to present her as Peredur's bride. That was all she needed at this moment.

She unrolled her fingers, revealing Peredur's ring sitting in her palm like a promise kept.

Tada inhaled sharply. Tanwen looked up and felt an unfamiliar closeness to her father. He looked over at Cavan, who stepped forward and bowed.

"You brought this to her?" Tada asked.

Cavan nodded, explaining how his mother had come to possess it. Tada reached for his pouch of coin. "How much did she pay?"

"Oh, no, sir. This is a gift. For Tanwen."

"Come, Cavan," Tada snapped. "This is no time to quibble."

Tanwen turned and saw Cavan's normally pale cheeks flush pink. "The ring is a gift for your daughter, sir."

She looked back at her father in time to see the shock register in his eyes. A chill went down her spine. The wise woman's son was stating his intentions. He meant to court her.

Tanwen looked again at Cavan, as she had never done before. He had always been such a handsome lad. In fact he'd merely lived up to the name his mother had forseen would fit him so well. The girls in the village always liked to catch his eye and giggle, Tanwen herself among them.

No one would take the wise woman's son for a husband. His mother lived on the edges of their village in more ways than one. Everyone sought her out when ill or in pain, but feared the very healing powers she possessed. Cavan's future was tainted by association.

His gaze now sought hers. There really was intention there, but of what design there was no telling. He'd pulled a veil of protection over his emotions, as he always did with his winks and smiles. But today there was no twinkle there.

"Mam," Tanwen said, turning to see her regarding Cavan with distrust. "Do you have any cakes prepared?"

Mam nodded, then gestured for the daughter closest to the door to run and fetch some. No one spoke nor moved as they waited for the cakes to be brought. Cattle lowed in discontent over in the meadow.

Tanwen's sister re-emerged from the hut with a woven basket containing three honey cakes. She paused, but made her way to Cavan and made the offering. Cavan took it with a slight smile at her sister, who blushed and returned to her mother's side.

"To thank your mam," Tanwen said, "for thinking of me."

Cavan turned to her, his cool gray eyes snapping with unaccustomed ferocity. "It is her way. She holds all of the village in her thoughts. 'Tis not why she sent the ring."

"We are grateful, all the same," Tada said, moving forward to stand beside Tanwen.

Cavan took a last look at her, his gaze lingering as he bowed to her father. Then he turned and strode across the meadow and out of sight.

Tanwen looked up at Tada. So many feelings seemed to wash over his normally stoic face. She placed a hand upon his cheek, rose on her toes and kissed him.

5

Peredur needed less time to recover from this latest feeding. With only one day's rest he was up and ready and heading outside the cavern.

Melnak stood near the entrance speaking with Sigbjorn and Brude. All three turned as Peredur approached. The moonlight shone strongly upon their faces, hiding their eyes in shadow. For a moment he couldn't tell if they wanted him to join them or whether he intruded.

As he neared the rather formidable trio, he sensed the same readiness in his muscles as when preparing to fight. It was almost as though a part of him expected an ambush. He never failed to heed that feeling.

Yet he decided to assume friendliness until things suggested otherwise. Brule was the first to smile and Peredur smiled back.

Sigbjorn faced Peredur squarely. "Tonight we'll begin your training. We'll soon need you to accompany us."

Peredur looked at the other two, his master who wasn't a master, and the Pict. They returned his gaze easily but left him with the lingering impression of trickery. It was unsettling to be suspicious of his new brethren. He had nothing with which to compare this distrust, having enjoyed loyal friendships in his mortal life. But he knew his own gut feeling and would never doubt it, whether he was man or vampire.

Peredur merely replied, "I would like that."

Sigbjorn grinned in his broad manner. He nodded and turned, and Peredur knew he should follow. He fell into step behind the Norseman while Melnak and Brule flanked him like guards.

They made their way into the forest that swallowed them like a leviathan. Spruce boughs ushered them in, rustled with their passage, then fell back as though no one had passed.

Peredur marveled again that he could see through this gloom so effortlessly. Sigbjorn's golden hair gleamed white in the moon's glow. Deer paths called like beacon fires.

Soon they arrived at a clearing by a narrow lake. When they'd left the trees and Peredur detected moist air rising off the water, he felt lightheaded. He shook it off as the others stopped along the shore.

He could see that the others felt the queasiness, as did he. Why should they stop here if something made them all feel uneasy?

Melnak answered his question with, "You may never have been bothered by water when you lived as a man, but as a vampire your first lesson is to avoid it."

He gestured for Peredur to sit on a large outcropping of rock, nearer the forest's edge than the lake. With every step he took away from the water Peredur felt noticeably stronger. He turned and sat as instructed.

Melnak began to disrobe. His body was very fit though unscarred. Jagged white lines should have told their tales of Melnak's warrior life from long ago. Peredur couldn't help but stare.

Glancing down, he searched for the scar design carved into his arm by the swordmaster when he was a boy. Nothing but smooth white skin remained. None of the nicks, gouges or marks from his lifetime of meeting blow for blow remained upon him any longer.

Brude attended Melnak like a servant would, despite this being a brotherhood without masters. Melnak may forbid it, but it was his own presence that dictated such reverence. Peredur felt vindicated.

When Melnak was stripped bare, his mentor faced Peredur as though clad in regal robes. "Watch carefully, that you may remember and take heed," he warned.

Melnak looked once at Sigbjorn, then turned and strode into the water. When he was chest deep, he turned and gazed back at Peredur. His face was drawn and he seemed on the verge of collapse.

Brude and Sigbjorn exchanged glances. The Norseman loosened something from his belt – a rope – that he began to uncoil. Peredur felt their alarm rise sharp as shouts.

Melnak swayed faintly in the water, losing his footing to slip beneath the surface to his shoulders. Sigbjorn hoisted the rope to throw it.

Melnak managed to raise a hand to stop him, his teeth chattering with misery. Brude shifted weight back and forth, like a hound held back from the hunt. Sigbjorn cocked his arm back, rope ready to throw.

Peredur could feel his master's strength ebbing, an even more profound weakening than his own on the night when the brethren had cut into him and fed. He pushed up from his seat on the rock, trying to use his will to send energy toward Melnak.

The vampire's eyes finally closed, his body threatening to sink beneath the water's still surface. Brude looked sharply at Sigbjorn.

"Throw it!" the Pict whispered hotly.

Sigbjorn rocked backward for momentum, then extended his arm fluidly. The rope snaked forward over the water, hitting the surface with a slap. It landed within arm's length of Melnak, but at this point Peredur doubted his master could lift his arm to grasp it.

Brude looked over at Sigbjorn, shaken and frustrated. The Norseman waited for an endless moment, then drew the rope back in and pulled it, dripping, from the water. He calmly readied his arm again and threw the rope.

This time it nicked Melnak's temple. The vampire's eyes opened and he groggily focused on the rope.

Grab it, they all three urged him.

Melnak moved but slowly, as though the water were thick mud and he was trapped in its grip. He managed to wrap his fingers around the rope, but Sigbjorn waited until they could all see Melnak grip it before the Norseman began gently pulling.

Brude dashed toward the shoreline, swerving erratically the closer he got to the water. Melnak struggled to keep his head above the surface, somehow managing to keep his fingers locked around the rope.

Sigbjorn pulled and steered with the rope as though trying to land an enormous catch. Close to shore, Melnak tipped forward, face first, letting go of the rope. Brude dashed into the water, plunging in for several steps before falling sideways. But he righted himself and pitched his hand down to grab Melnak by the scruff of the neck. Brude grabbed the rope himself as he fought the effects of the water sapping his strength.

Guiding Melnak by the shoulders, Brude worked as swiftly as he could with Sigbjorn, whose practised motion on the rope pulled Melnak free of the water's grip. Their leader who was not their master flopped like a fish upon the grass.

Brude sank to his knees, water pouring off him in rivulets. He tried to help Sigbjorn with Melnak but was succumbing to the water-drenched tunic and leggings. He crumpled to the grass in a soggy ball.

Peredur found himself at Brude's side before he realized he'd even moved. Dropping to his knees, he began peeling off the wet tunic. The water touching his skin stopped his fingers from working when he commanded them to pull and tug.

Risking a glance to his left, he saw Sigbjorn rolling Melnak onto his side, patting his face rapidly. Melnak's eyes were closed. To Peredur, he looked too pale and still.

Brude began shaking. Peredur turned his attention back to the Pict, but his brain seemed not to focus well. *What had he been about to do..?*

Peredur grit his teeth and stared hard at the sodden wool and his two hands, willing them both to move. Brude's arms twitched as he tried to help. But they would not obey him.

Out of the corner of his eye, he saw Sigbjorn throw off his own leather doublet and tunic. Bunching the linen in his meaty fists, Sigbjorn rubbed it over Melnak's glistening skin.

Brude grunted with effort as his hands finally grasped hold of his tunic. Together Brude and Peredur peeled it over the Pict's head.

Brude sighed with relief but still shook. As he pushed at his leggings, Peredur looked down and saw that the Pict wore shoes that laced all the way up his calves to his knees.

Heart sinking, Peredur scrambled to the Pict's feet and began the torturous job of unlacing the ties. After only a moment of trying, Peredur knew he could not make his fingers work to free his brother.

His hand moved to his own calf for the short knife that should be strapped there, but it had been taken after the final battle that claimed him.

He looked over to the Norseman but he was immersed in his efforts to dry Melnak off.

Peredur remembered his own wolfish teeth that only seemed to appear at feeding times. With those he could bite through those laces in a snap. Raising his forearm,

Peredur gnawed sharply at his skin. In a moment the blood began to bead there.

He felt it start, the fangs descending as the smell of his own blood filled his nostrils. He pressed his arm to his mouth and tasted the glorious drops, sweeter than any honeyed wine.

Buoyed by that mouthful, Peredur bared his fangs and bent low. The laces gave in to his bite, first one leg, then the other. He swiped at the loose ties like a dog digging for a bone.

Sigbjorn knelt beside Peredur and pulled off one shoe while Peredur yanked at the other. He was glad for the Norseman just then. It took the two of them to roll the wet leggings down Brude's thighs and pull them, still wet and clinging, free of his feet.

Sigbjorn reached his hand palm-up toward Peredur, who gave him his own tunic as soon as he could shrug it off his shoulders. The Norseman wiped it vigorously over Brude's clammy skin as the Pict lay shivering on the wet grass.

Peredur had only wet his tongue with a few drops of his own blood, but it had been enough. He crawled along Brude's prone form, then crouched beside his head.

Peredur saw that the small tear he'd made in his own flesh wouldn't do for what he had in mind. Inhaling deeply, he brought his arm up to his mouth and plunged his fangs deeply into the wound.

The pain of it sharpened his mind like a slap. Blood welled into his mouth. Although it was his own, it sent a ripple of strength through his weakened muscles.

Cupping his brother's head in his other hand, Peredur moved his arm into position before Brude's chattering lips. Brude stirred as the scent of it revived him, even before the blood was taken on an inquisitive tongue.

Peredur could feel the strength returning to the Pict as he held him. He coaxed him to taste again.

Brude did what he was bid, then Peredur dragged him off the wet grass so he could recover himself. Sigbjorn nodded and hooked his arms beneath Melnak's, dragging him to drier ground.

Sigbjorn sat in a heap next to Peredur, panting. Peredur felt the Norseman's gaze upon him as he crawled to Melnak's side and offered his arm to his mentor's lips.

Melnak's eyes were closed, but he too seemed to react to the smell of blood. Sigbjorn joined them and lifted Melnak's head to meet the offering.

Peredur's head swam as Melnak drank deeply. Peredur braced himself with his other arm against falling backwards, feeling his lowered energy dip even further.

Melnak released his mouth from Peredur's wound and opened his eyes to gaze intensely into Peredur's own.

"Some would find fault that you don't listen when I tell you to sit and watch." Melnak's weakened voice broke the silence.

Sigbjorn chuckled wryly.

6

How many days had she been followed everywhere by her sisters, her brother? Would she be given any peace?

Tanwen shuffled through the tall grasses edging the stream on the far side of the meadow, a sack of clothes to wash clasped to her hip. Her sister Meira forged ahead, looking back to hurry Tanwen along. Why did Mam keep her on such a short tether? It made no difference only days ago, when food held no taste and sleep eluded her. This morning was a different matter.

If she could shove Meira into the stream and take off running into the forest for an hour or two, would it be worth the furor it would cause with Tada?

Tanwen actually contemplated it as Meira crouched on the bank to open her own sack of clothes. The water wasn't too deep here. The bottom wasn't terribly rocky. The water rolled and tumbled past, luring Tanwen with its promise of change.

She would give anything to alter her existence. The waiting she'd done while Peredur fought had seemed bearable when his return had waited for them both. Now there seemed to be no use in washing up, dressing, pulling a comb through her hair. Chewing. No use for any of it. Any reason to wake up in the morning was gone – along with Peredur.

Meira scrubbed her clothes upon the washing rock in a curve of the stream, looking over her shoulder now and again at Tanwen. Meira seemed very put upon this morning. Probably wished her sister was gone as much as Tanwen wished it. Taking a very deep breath, Tanwen stepped onto the bank to open her sack.

Untying the bundle, Tanwen plunged her hand into the folds of wool and linen. A forgotten pin still clasped on her father's tunic sliced the skin along her forearm. Gasping in surprise, she pulled her arm toward herself, making yet another slice above the first one.

She sat clutching her arm, watching the blood bead slowly at first, then well clearly along both cuts. Before she knew it, Meira grabbed her arm and dropped to her knees beside her.

"What have you done?"

Tanwen wrenched away from Meira's grip. "There's a pin in there, what do you think?"

Meira's face had lost its color. "You want to leave us. That's what I think."

Tanwen fumbled for a rag in the folds of her gown. "You'd be right." She found one and flicked it open with a shaky hand. "How I long to be gone from here." She pressed the rag over the cuts and felt the throbbing begin.

Tanwen glanced again at her sister. Tears were forming in Meira's eyes. "Why, Tanwen? How could you want that?"

"How can I not want it?" Tanwen demanded, surprised at how much her heart crushed inside her chest. "He was my love, and he will never come back to me."

"But we are your family, Tanwen. We love you."

Tanwen could see the hurt in her sister's eyes. If Meira loved her, why couldn't she also feel the weight of Tanwen's loss? "Someday your own love will come for you, Meira, and take you from us. And that day will be your joy. Even though we love you, we will mourn."

Meira nodded but tears still dropped from her lashes.

"Your love is still out there to ask for your hand," Tanwen continued. "Mine is gone."

"Say you don't wish to join him," Meira pleaded.

"I can't. I do wish it."

Meira's hand covered her mouth as she shook her head. "God forbids such things."

"He took Peredur from me, Meira. He must expect it."

"You mustn't tell anyone else."

Tanwen lifted the rag to see the red smear across her skin. It gave her a strange comfort to know that her numbed body could still bleed. Replacing the rag, she looked again at her sister. She saw Meira's fear but didn't want to acknowledge it.

"Tell Tada what you think, then. Let him beat me. I won't care." And at that moment, she didn't.

"I'll never tell."

Tanwen sighed. It would almost be better if she would. These cuts had wrung some feeling from her at last. Perhaps her father's reaction could bring her back from this horrid nothingness.

But the paleness of her sister's face wrested away that reverie and its allure. "There's a pin in the sack, Meira. That's all."

Meira nodded. She glanced down once at the rag, sidling again toward her washing on the bank. Tanwen lifted the rag and saw the bleeding had stopped. She bent and took the sack, gingerly shaking out the contents to prevent another encounter with the errant pin. When it flashed in the morning sun, Tanwen smiled to see that it was Tada's circle clasp.

Of course it was Tada's. Even his ornament carried out his will.

7

Melnak sent the others away once they'd returned to the cavern. Peredur watched as the brethren retreated into the darker spaces. Of late, they'd given him wider berth, he noticed.

Peredur moved closer to Melnak when he was bid to do so by a nod. The vampire was fully recovered, which in itself was impressive. Melnak regarded Peredur with an appraising eye as he sat on the floor of the cavern beside his mentor.

"That was to be your first lesson, Peredur, but you've taught all of us instead."

Peredur's brow hunched in confusion.

"That is the first time a novice has interceded on my behalf." Melnak smiled subtley with his eyes.

"Do you mean the rest could watch you suffer like that? And do nothing?" Peredur's tone scoffed that the others he'd come to know could be so callous.

Melnak gave the slightest nod in apology for the others. "This is the first time a novice has acted so decisively on my behalf. Not only on mine. Brude's as well."

Peredur did not know what to make of that. In his mind's eye he saw a flash of Melnak sinking below the lake's surface.

"But to sit and watch..." Peredur began.

"I'd given the order to sit and watch. These are fighting men, remember. They are used to following a commander's orders."

"I am loyal, brother." Peredur wanted that made clear, at least.

"I don't doubt that you are. And yet when presented with the task of watching me struggle in the lake, you flouted what you had been told to do."

Peredur lowered his gaze. This had been his first test. In truth, he had been instructed to watch, not to act. A stirring of anger bubbled up in his chest.

The others had not acted but had obeyed when all their instincts had likely been the same as his. He knew from several fighting engagements that it was essential to stick to battle plans when all appearances begged otherwise.

"What gave you the idea to use your own blood to revive us?" Melnak asked, true curiosity in his voice.

Peredur couldn't keep an embarrassed smile from flitting across his face. "I was too weak to untie Brude's laces. I needed to get all his clothes off and dry him as Sigbjorn had done with you."

Melnak regarded him but said nothing.

"I knew if my teeth were long I could..." Peredur gestured to where the fangs appeared and continued. "The only way I knew to make them grow was the longing for blood feasting."

Melnak nodded appreciatively.

"I just chewed at my skin till I broke it. Once I tasted blood, the fangs grew. Then I bit through the laces and freed Brude from his leggings."

"Ah." Melnak considered Peredur's tale for several moments. "You have taught us all with your actions tonight."

"In what way?" Peredur asked, not eager to hear the answer.

"It isn't every man or vampire that can think on his feet or take charge when the need arises."

The newest of the brethren looked over to where the others had retreated into the shadows. Then he looked back at the master who claimed not to be one. "Be straight with me," Peredur demanded. "Either I disobeyed you or I didn't. Either I passed this first test, or I didn't. Which is it?"

Melnak smiled again, more obviously this time. "Were you in command of men at your last battle?"

Peredur thought back to those men to whom he'd answered, and then to the ones to whom he'd barked orders. "Some," he replied.

Melnak nodded.

"You've told me there are no masters here," Peredur clarified.

"And there are none."

Peredur bit back his response but looked Melnak in the eye. There was only amusement there.

"You have left your old life behind in more ways than can be apparent so soon," Melnak explained. "I can hear the unspoken 'My Lord' whenever you address me. Be assured I am not that."

"Yet all defer to you."

"For my experience only. We are a collection of equals, Peredur. Brethren. We serve together and we serve each other."

Peredur could not make out the meaning of this response to his actions by the lake. The more Melnak said, the more muddied it became.

"Then my assuming leadership is not what you were hoping for?"

"It's not a matter of what I hope, Peredur."

"The brethren, then," Peredur said hotly.

"Think," Melnak said simply. "What would a group of equals want with one who shows leadership?"

"A leader is not welcome among equals."

"Is he not?"

Peredur could take it no longer. He stood. He felt like an arrow primed against a straining bow. "How is it your answers to me are not answers?"

"Are they not?"

Peredur turned away, unable to proceed against such evasiveness. After a moment to collect himself, Peredur faced Melnak once more. Melnak patted the floor of the cavern where Peredur had just been sitting.

With lips pressed tightly together, Peredur sat as he was bid by the equal who was lord of the vampires. He kept his gaze averted, partly to show the deference Melnak rejected, partly to hide the frustration that put Peredur at a loss.

"What would a group of equals want with one who shows leadership?" Melnak asked again.

Peredur sighed sharply. Was he trying to unbalance him so that they fought? Perhaps the first test was over and they were on to the second.

"Humility?" Peredur offered. He punctuated this with a direct look into Melnak's eyes.

The older vampire's raised his eyebrows. "You continue to surprise, Peredur. In fact, the Brotherhood operates best when all practice humility. But that was not what I meant."

Peredur's heart swelled with expectation. Did this mean Melnak would finally explain himself?

"What do men look to leaders to give them?" Melnak persisted.

Swallowing disappointment, Peredur fought to calm himself. Melnak would not be finished with him until he'd overwhelmed him with riddles. But Peredur had no intention of being bested. "Direction," he put forth.

"Would that not be a benefit to us?"

"At times," Peredur replied with his own half-answer.

Melnak's lips twitched. "When we encounter our cousins, the true vampires, I can assure you knowing our direction is essential to survival."

Peredur again heard the reference to these cousins of theirs. "Are we, of this brotherhood, not vampires, truly?"

"Let me say, for now, that we are vampires when compared to men, but members of the Brotherhood when up against true vampires."

Peredur decided not to press this. He saw how Melnak parceled out information like honey bits given to a fussy child.

"When you first meet with these, our cousins, it will no doubt remind you of your first impression of me as a demon," Melnak continued. "Only, then it won't be an impression."

Peredur looked off into the shadows, wondering if any of the brethren watched or if they'd truly left him alone with Melnak. He couldn't feel them there.

"Next time we encounter them," Melnak went on, "it will be a comfort to know there is one among us who will not hesitate, who will do what must be done, who will share of his own blood for the sake of his brother."

Peredur turned, looking this inscrutable being in the eye. There was no mockery there. Only gratitude and respect.

Nodding his acceptance of both, Peredur rose and left his mentor for some time to ingest all of this. He left the cavern and walked among the trees, and this time no shepherd came to guide his way back.

8

Tanwen sat in the crisp autumn sunshine on the bench outside the hut. She twirled a spindle in one hand, guiding the wool with practiced ease from the basket to her left. Her sister Meira sat beside her, combing the wool before placing it in her own basket. When Meira looked up and blushed, Tanwen followed her gaze to see the blacksmith's son approach.

Rhodri moved with swaggering grace. He glanced only briefly at both of them, avoiding eye contact as he passed, nodding instead at Gareth, who sharpened tools across the yard.

"Is Andras about?" Rhodri asked.

"He's down in the meadow," Gareth said, gesturing with the whetstone, "mending the fence."

Rhodri nodded, striding off with his head down in thought. Tanwen's breathing turned shallow, her hands chilling beyond the bite of the autumn morning. *Strange.* She looked at Meira, whose gaze followed Rhodri, her brow pinched with worry.

Tanwen forced herself to take a deep breath. She twirled the spindle vigorously, guiding the wool into a strand of yarn and as it lengthened, looped it into the basket beside her. Whatever Rhodri's business with Tada, it most likely had to do with Meira. It was understood in the village that Rhodri had taken interest in Tada's second eldest daughter.

Then why did Tanwen feel so unsettled all of a sudden?

Meira waited until Rhodri was out of sight. Then she put down the wool comb and stood. "Gareth, go on. Find out what they're saying."

Her brother gave her a look that held both affection and exasperation. His whetstone scraped methodically along his iron blade.

"Don't torment her," Tanwen said. Her spindle twirled back and forth, her fingers gathering and gathering the strand. It didn't keep her from glancing toward the meadow. Why did men always wander off to talk about anything important?

"Tada's mending the fence," Gareth said. "There's no place to hear what they're saying."

Meira started toward the door of the hut, then turned and began following Rhodri's trail herself.

"Meira," Tanwen called.

Mam appeared in the doorway. "You're finished with the wool?" she asked.

Meira gestured at Gareth. "He won't find out what's going on."

"Going on where?" Mam asked, seeing only two daughters and a son at work.

"The blacksmith's son came to see Tada," said Tanwen, nodding in the direction of the far pasture.

"Gareth, go to your father," Mam said.

He rose from his work impatiently, dropping the tool and whetstone onto the stool he'd been using.

"Don't argue," Mam continued. "If there's business being discussed, you need to hear it."

"If there's gossip, you mean," said Gareth.

"Go and join the discussion," Mam said. "You shouldn't need me to remind you. You're not a child any longer."

Gareth started to speak, thought better of it and glanced at Tanwen for support. Her brother was right, of course. But so was Mam. How else were they to find out anything?

When she didn't respond, he turned his gangly body toward the meadow behind the sheep's pen. Gareth trudged across the yard and out of sight, clearly in no hurry to do Mam's bidding.

"Why wouldn't Rhodri look at me?" Meira asked.

"Perhaps Tada makes him nervous," Tanwen said.

"Tada approves of him, doesn't he?" Meira turned to Mam.

"Don't put the cart before the ox," Mam said. "Sit and finish your work. Keep your thoughts on what's in front of you."

"He's never acted this way before," Meira continued, as though to herself. "We haven't quarreled."

"Meira," Tanwen interrupted. She held the wool comb out until her sister focused on it. Giving one more look toward the spot beyond their sight line where the men had gathered, Meira moved reluctantly to join Tanwen on the bench.

Certainly Rhodri would appear nervous if he'd come to ask Tada what they all expected. He must have come here to offer for Meira.

Tanwen forced herself to watch the spindle as she moved her fingers with practiced grace. There was no need, of course. She'd been doing this since she was a girl. But if she kept her eyes on her work, she wouldn't have to see how pale Meira had grown. She wouldn't have to watch Mam casually take up the woolen yarn from Tanwen's basket, winding it around and around into a skein when she had her own work to do inside the hut.

So much had changed with the turning of the leaves. Tanwen had thought her sister was sheltered by the warmth of Rhodri's affection. A different possibility sent a wintery blast through Tanwen's heart.

Meira was only the second eldest. Before she could marry, the eldest daughter must be wed. Tanwen was the eldest, and her promised husband could never claim her.

Could Rhodri?... As the blacksmith's son had passed them he'd barely glanced in Meira's direction.

Tanwen wished Gareth would hurry back. She longed for his return until she caught sight of him loping back over the rise of the meadow. Then her breath caught in her chest and she dropped the spindle, overcome by escalating fear.

Gareth approached his mam and sisters with a dragging step, his eyes downcast, his cheeks mottled red with foul temper. He picked up his whetstone and blade with exaggerated motion. Then he sat and started back at his sharpening.

Meira glanced at Mam in confusion. Mam put one hand on Meira's arm and stopped any question with a look.

Tanwen tried to pick up the spindle again, to still her unease with activity, but her hand groped blindly. She couldn't look away from Gareth's face, half hidden by a shock of dark hair. There was a feeling in the air that whispered 'doom.'

She'd felt it before, on the day when the fighter from the warband brought the news of Peredur's death. Tanwen's mouth went dry.

Mam walked across the yard until she stood before Gareth. Meira joined Tanwen on the bench, sidling very close.

Gareth shook his head at the question hanging unsaid. He should be taunting Meira about Rhodri. Instead it looked as though he longed to throttle someone.

"What did you learn?" Mam asked.

Gareth scraped the blade along the whetstone. Tanwen's stomach tightened.

"Gareth, I'm speaking to you." Mam's tone betrayed her own unease.

He stopped working and looked up. His hazel eyes crackled with outrage.

"Something is wrong," Mam said.

Gareth looked over at Tanwen. She saw a warning wash over his features. Meira slipped her hand over Tanwen's and squeezed.

"Rhodri came to offer for Tanwen," Gareth said, his words crashing into her chest like a fall from a great height. She looked at Meira, who had already withdrawn her hand from Tanwen's.

Mam slapped Gareth hard, the sound cracking through the air like a tree splitting in a storm. His head rocked from the blow and he nearly lost his seat. Meira gasped.

"I sent you to learn to be a man," Mam said, "to join in with your tada when the villagers come to discuss business. And you come back to us with cruel, childish jests."

Gareth stood then, staring at his mam, unflinching.

"Why would you say that about Rhodri?" Meira asked.

"You should know that Tada's agreed to Rhodri's offer." He looked at Tanwen, his gaze dark with disapproval.

"Why would he do something like that?" Meira said, her voice catching.

Gareth shrugged, still looking at Tanwen. But she'd caught sight of Tada and Rhodri strolling up over the rise, their pace unhurried. Meira choked out a sob and ran into the hut.

Rhodri stopped when he caught sight of his former intended fleeing inside. Tada said a few words to him, clasped him by the arm and then turned toward the hut. Rhodri looked over at Tanwen, his familiar features suddenly revealing the stranger he must always have been.

Tada and Rhodri conferred then, until Rhodri stepped away, nodded to Tada and walked quickly along the edge of the yard, skirting them all. He made his way to the road and disappeared into the cover of the trees.

Tanwen turned back to see Tada entering the yard to join them. He glanced at Mam and then at Gareth, who lowered his gaze. Then he addressed Tanwen.

"There has been an offer made for you, daughter," he said.

Tanwen set down her spinning and stood. She turned and walked away from all of them.

9

The next lesson was very straightforward. Peredur was woken early and led into the sunlight the following day until he passed out.

He came back to his senses under Wladyslaw's watchful eye. Peredur felt an instinctive urge to sit up as he would have done in the presence of a commander in his old life. Having once enjoyed the highest rank of all the brethren when he had been a man, the Polanie's smallest gesture still radiated authority.

Peredur fought the urge to show deference, realizing this was all part of the trials.

Equal brethren. Equal brethren. He closed his eyes. Inhaled deeply.

Wladyslaw touched Peredur's shoulder, in the very spot where it had been bludgeoned on the battlefield. "Don't hurry it," the Polanie said.

How ill Peredur felt.

The water sickness was very different from the sun sickness. Peredur didn't forget that sunlight could actually kill him in this new vampire life.

It had not taken long for Peredur to succumb. Once down, he was pulled into shadow by a rope already tied around his chest. The others dared not risk even minimal exposure if they were to look after him in the sun's aftermath.

Now he lay back on the cavern floor, safe within its cool earthiness. He could actually feel the presence of the minerals in the ground beneath him, and knew somehow that the earth already acted as a tonic for him. Where the water had worked upon his muscles and skin, making any movement impossible, the sun had worked upon his head and the borrowed blood within his veins, heating them both. He could not get any thoughts to settle in his mind, his blood pumping too fast until he lost consciousness. All in a much swifter manner than the water sickness.

Even now he felt the bleary haze of fever. He opened his eyes and fought to focus them. With his body feeling runny like the upturned contents of someone's stomach, Peredur forced himself to focus on the former *szlachcic* – his people's name for nobleman.

He thought of the blood that would revive him out of the stupor. Reading his thought, Wladyslaw explained, "I cannot offer you sustenance, Brother."

He placed a hand, for a little longer this time, on Peredur's arm. "This feeling is what you must experience. You will learn to cope with it in time."

Peredur closed his eyes against this unwelcome news.

"I have the unhappy task of instructing you through this transition, Peredur."

He opened his eyes again, urging himself to see this brother closely.

"Unhappy?" he managed to ask.

Wladyslaw looked off into the distance. "Our cousins know how sunlight causes this sickness and will use it against us. Men will too, when they hunt us."

Peredur fought against another wave of illness, keeping his attention on the Polanie. "How long was I in the sun?"

"A few moments only. No more."

"Longer would be the end of me?" he asked, not wanting to imagine it.

"And not very much longer," Wladyslaw verified. "You must act quickly or perish. Moving out of sunlight is paramount."

Peredur nodded, unable to imagine how he could have moved as he succumbed.

"I need you to sit up," the Polanie said, his voice less gentle than it had been.

Peredur looked hard into the szlachcic's face. *Unhappy task.* But sitting was impossible.

"Up," Wladyslaw commanded.

Peredur responded as he had always done on the battlefield. He gathered strength where there had been none and rose halfway.

He collapsed. If he could have done, he would have vomited, but that too seemed to be a relic of his former life. It didn't stop the debilitating queasiness from holding him in its grasp.

"If vampires or men mean to finish you, they will succeed with such feeble effort on your part." Peredur heard the same tone in his princely brother's voice as his sword master had once used. Was this something the other brethren had gone through?

They would not best him in this.

Peredur pushed himself up on his elbows with enormous effort. Panting, he rolled onto his side and pushed all the way up to a sitting position. He trembled with it, the detestable weakness, the queasiness. It took enormous effort, but he managed to look Wladyslaw in the eye.

The Polanie's arm shot forward and his hand cuffed Peredur in the head. Peredur swayed forward, then fell sideways.

Peredur rolled to keep his eye on Wladyslaw in case more blows followed. His head swam and he felt the hideous weakness swirl in his veins.

Wladyslaw rose to his feet. Peredur pushed back, trying to keep a distance between himself and the

Polanie. The sickness not only weakened him, it disoriented. Try as he might to rise and meet the szlachcic the cavern seemed to tilt and waylay him.

"Still yourself," the Polanie said, giving Peredur a stout kick that rolled him some distance.

Peredur noted with shock how little that kick had actually hurt. The force of it had punted him like a child's kicking bladder.

Still yourself. What did that mean?

Wladyslaw scooped him up and slammed him up against the cavern wall. The vampire pressed his face close to Peredur's.

"If I had so desired, you would have died the true death, my brother."

Panting, Peredur felt himself sag in Wladyslaw's grasp, unable to stop the swirling inside him. At this point, a part of him didn't care whether one of these cousins came at him. If only the swaying cavern would stop.

"Still yourself," Wladyslaw whispered near Peredur's ear. He was so close, it seemed he held up Peredur by his mere presence.

Again. *What did he mean by 'still yourself?'*

Wladyslaw seemed so solid while his own insides spun. He focused on that solidness until it seemed he could feel the other vampire's heart beating. Peredur blinked. His vision cleared.

He *could* feel the szlachcic's steady heart beating.

Just as he sought his brother's gaze, to thank him for lending him this stillness, Wladyslaw backed away a pace. Immediately the swirling resumed. Peredur went limp. Only Wladyslaw's quick grasp of Peredur's arms kept him from sliding to the cavern floor.

"Listen to your own stillness," Wladyslaw prompted.

Peredur closed his eyes and thought about his own heartbeat. He heard its erratic drumming and felt the cavern floor tip.

But Wladyslaw's hands pinned him securely. He forced himself to listen hard for the other vampire's heartbeat through those hands. There it was.

So much slower than a man's heartbeat. Beneath Wladyslaw's strong pulse was his own that skipped or disappeared entirely.

The Polanie had left off clipping him in the head. Peredur took advantage of this lull and focused as clearly as he could on his heartbeat. He listened until his flitting beats matched rhythm with Wladyslaw's. As his pulse settled down, the cavern seemed less likely to rock as though they were at sea.

Opening his eyes, he saw the szlachcic staring at him curiously. Peredur knew that the Polanie could feel Peredur's own steadily growing stillness, just as he could feel the other's heartbeat.

As if transfixed by Peredur, the szlachcic stayed as he was, holding his brother against the cave even when they both knew he was no longer in danger of falling. Peredur felt excitement radiating toward him from his brother.

At last, Wladyslaw released him and backed away. Peredur kept his feet.

An idea came to him, but he suspected that he was abnormally connected to the szlachcic just now. Even as he saw recognition dawn in his brother's eyes, Peredur's fist flew out and knocked Wladyslaw nearly flat.

The szlachcic righted himself and stood before Peredur with a disarming grin.

"Outstanding," he said simply.

10

Cavan walked through the woods beside her until they neared the rise announcing the meadow where her father grazed his cattle. Tanwen slowed and Cavan turned to face her.

"Take heart, now," he coaxed. She looked up and felt relieved that he wore no flippant grin. She nodded, feeling her heart begin to beat rapidly.

Time to face whatever awaited her. Wise woman or no, it was assured there would be a scene with Tada. She took a deep breath.

"I'll be waiting just a little ways in the trees," he reminded her, flicking his head in that direction. "If you run into any trouble, you're welcome to come home with me."

Tanwen shook her head. "I'll be alright." She peered forward as though she could see through the hill before her. *Best get it over with.* Turning toward Cavan, she started to speak but the words caught in her throat.

His gray eyes brimmed with concern for her. There was a tilt to his brow she'd never seen before. Why did he care for her so much? He knew her unwavering feelings for Peredur. What did he mean?

The expression on his face changed as he read the emotions clouding hers. He took one step away from her.

"Why did you bring me his ring?" she demanded suddenly.

Cavan's face paled. She saw the raw need for her behind his eyes. "Why keep it? I know what it means to you."

"You could have given it to his mam," she countered.

He turned away from her. In a moment he faced her again, explaining, "If I showed you his ring, you would know he was really gone."

Tears started to form in her eyes, but she refused to shed them. "It did help me to believe you," she admitted. They stood together in tense silence.

She looked up toward the hill, already picturing the confrontation to come. Her chest hollowed with dread. Cavan touched her arm briefly, saying, "Be strong." Then he dashed away to disappear into the forest.

Taking a very deep breath, Tanwen forced her feet to move. She crested the hill and saw her family bustling about their work. Heads turned at her appearance.

A cry went up and her youngest sister ran to greet her. The joy on her little face gave Tanwen courage when she needed it most. She slipped her hand into her sister's and they walked to the hut together.

Mam descended upon her with a crushing embrace. "Where have you been?"

Tanwen waited until she could breathe before describing her evening with the wise woman and her son. Mam held her at arm's length, looked her up and down, then seemed satisfied with Tanwen's condition.

Her brother appeared next to her, saying, "Tada wishes to see you."

Tanwen nodded, her mouth going dry. Her brother turned and glanced over at the cattle shelter across the yard. Tada stood at the edge, absently stroking a heifer.

Mam released her and Tanwen walked stiffly toward him, bracing herself despite Cavan's reassurances.

Cavan had no father. What did he know of it?

As she neared, Tada stepped away from the cow and gestured in the direction of the open meadow. She followed him in silence as they put a little more distance between themselves and the others.

"You stayed away last night," he said eventually. She told him what she'd told her mother.

"You went to the wise woman's son?" His voice held accusation. "That was not fitting, child."

"I didn't plan to go anywhere," she tried to explain. "I needed some time away from here."

There was a heavy silence. Their footsteps padded through the lumpy meadow.

"You're in a hurry to leave us, are you?" Tada said, looking away from her.

"Not as much as your hurry to marry me off. What if Cavan did have intentions for me?" she prodded.

"He does, daughter. Make no mistake about that."

"Why did you allow Rhodri to speak to you? I've never shown the slightest interest in him."

"You loved a man who fell in battle," her father clarified. "I don't expect you'll ever have feelings for anyone in the village."

So he understood that part, at least. She stopped walking. He slowed, turning to face her.

"Peredur was a love match," he continued. "Now we'll have to find you the best man still standing."

She almost laughed at her father's way of putting things, but tears stung too close to the surface. "I won't marry the blacksmith's son," she stated.

"We won't discuss this while you are distraught," he said.

"I won't be Rhodri's wife!" Tanwen's voice tinged with panic.

Tada grabbed her hard by both arms. "You will do as your father commands you."

Tanwen felt a rising fury she'd never known before. Perhaps she felt there was nothing left to lose, now that

Peredur was gone. Recklessly, she shoved him with all her might. Her father was more than equal to that show of force. It must have been the shock alone that made him let go of her.

"Peredur was my true husband and I won't have another," she said in a voice as hard as the huge rocks by the sea's edge.

Tada stared at her with a mixture of compassion and hurt. "Tanwen, you are grieving. You make no sense."

"You welcome Rhodri here to begin the marriage deal, and I am the one without sense?"

"Rhodri has been trained well by his father. He'll be the village blacksmith in his time. You'll be well looked after."

She felt another surge of anger burst within her. "If Peredur hadn't been so concerned about looking after me, he wouldn't have gone on that last raid."

Tada sighed as if she were three years old and impertinent. "There's more to it than that."

"He knew how you felt, Tada! He struggled to please you so you'd agree to our match."

"Daughter, watch your tongue."

Tanwen thought of Cavan and his mother, of their assurances. They were wrong. She felt like goading her father now, would welcome an explosion of pain on the outside to match the agony trapped inside her. "I will marry no other man," she challenged.

"You will obey, daughter." He barked his words as he would order men in a warband. He'd been a fierce fighter not so long ago. His face told its tale in scars from his younger days.

"If you speak to Rhodri about me again, I shall leave here. You shall never gaze upon me for the rest of your days." Her heartbeat fluttered as she waited for his blow, but somehow speaking it aloud began to calm her deep inside.

Tada's eyes flashed and his body tensed. What did he see when he looked into her eyes? Why did his expression struggle between pride and outrage? "You don't fear me, do you?" he said at last.

"What is left for me to fear?" she explained. "Peredur is gone. The worst has already happened to me."

Tada sighed and turned from her, gazing back over his lands. "I am grateful you didn't turn out to be a male child," he said. "Here you are a maiden, fierce as Boudicca."

Tanwen looked at her father as though she had never truly seen him before. Perhaps he felt the same way about her. He returned her curious stare with his own.

"Am I not my father's daughter?" she said at last.

He took her in his arms, his embrace dashing cool relief over the hurting inside her. "Ah, my girl," he said into her hair.

Even as she felt her father's strength and love, Tanwen felt the loss of all the embraces Peredur would never give her. She squeezed back, trying to drive out the loneliness that intruded, even in a moment such as this.

11

Peredur was allowed an evening's rest before the next stage of his training, but tonight he awoke to Vellocatus and a summons to join him outside.

Peredur followed, curious now and knowing he could be in for some grief. All had ended well – so far. The reaction of the brethren to his training endurance, in fact, had been somewhat reverential.

Peredur found it all so very confusing. 'This is a Brotherhood of equals,' protested Melnak at every turn. He was beginning to understand they treated Melnak as a master purely for his greater experience in the Brotherhood, nothing more.

Then why did Peredur have a growing awareness that the others now gave him looks of admiration that were surely not the usual welcome for a new brother? As now. Peredur entered their midst and Brude, Adalhard, Sigbjorn, Wladyslaw, even Melnak all stepped back.

Vellocatus turned and Peredur saw two heavy swords in his hands.

A wave of relief swept over him. Swords. He knew about those, at least. In fact, his hand fairly ached for the weight of it.

Vellocatus offered one to him, pommel upright. Peredur strode to take it, noticing out of the corner of his eye that the others spread out to encircle them. Peredur bowed slightly as he accepted the weapon.

"A little sparring," Vellocatus promised, not smiling exactly.

Peredur did smile. He hefted the weapon several times and tossed it in a swift revolution to catch it. It was a wonderful blade.

Vellocatus stalked out of Peredur's range, watching him. Peredur initiated without warning. The blades rang out as he got a truer sense of the blade's qualities.

Of course, Vellocatus got a telling indication of Peredur's fighting style – but no matter. One could only keep that sort of thing secret for mere moments.

Vellocatus kept on the move, shifting slowly to size things up. He made no advance until Peredur struck again. Then Peredur observed carefully, needing to know what his opponent was made of.

After a few parries they'd both seen all they needed. Then the strategy began in earnest.

The Brigante lunged brilliantly and Peredur blocked it with an assured move. He waited again until Vellocatus thrust. Then he feinted and swung the sword in a powerful arc. His sword bit deeply into Vellocatus' side.

Peredur almost dropped the blade in shock.

The Brigante took the wound with a growl of pain. He stepped out of the way but did not lose his weapon. As Peredur paused, Vellocatus turned and thrust again. Peredur barely managed to deflect it.

The vampire was not disarmed as any man would have been. Peredur knew he was meant to see for himself what kind of punishment his new incarnation could take. It was sobering, to say the least.

The scent of his brother's blood filled the night air. It made Peredur hungry for another blow to hit its mark. He moved in aggressively, as he never would have done before.

The blades rang out and the two warriors stepped around in a slow dance. Vellocatus' blood was very distracting. Peredur had to keep pulling his attention back to the Brigante's attacks.

But the blood glistened down Vellocatus' tunic, dripping along his leggings to the grass beneath their feet. Peredur knew he must land another blow and do it soon.

It was distracting to watch this vampire fight with such power while bearing such a wound. In fact, Peredur also had to force himself to stop thinking about the hows and whys with Vellocatus going increasingly on the attack.

It must be the smell, the blood.

Even if it was his own blood, the smell of it seemed to enflame Vellocatus. A grimace of effort revealed that the Brigante's fangs had descended.

Peredur flicked his tongue to feel for his own. Both were there, sharp and hungry.

All it took was that moment of distraction. He turned too slowly away from a parry. Vellocatus thrust and his sword bit deep along Peredur's hip.

An angry hiss escaped him. Peredur bought some space to check the wound. Blood soaked his legging.

He fell upon Vellocatus like the fiend he'd become. He found himself baring his teeth as he fought – the Brigante answered Peredur's snarls with his own. He felt the pulses of the brethren surrounding them as if they were the shouts and encouragements of men.

The bout lasted until Melnak stopped it. By then the two combatants were winded and each bore several significant wounds. Peredur bowed to Vellocatus before handing the sword to Brude. He allowed himself to be led away to sit under a tree.

Adalhard and Brude took care of the blood that had spilled from Peredur's wounds, while Sigbjorn and Wladyslaw attended to Vellocatus. Melnak cleaned the swords.

The wounds stung but not as much as they should have done. They should have throbbed with the anguish of sliced muscle. Peredur kept his eye on Vellocatus as they rested. He was far too alert and robust, considering the blood loss he'd endured. Peredur supposed he appeared the same.

Melnak crouched beside him as the Frank and the Pict finished with Peredur. "You are indeed a skilled fighter," he remarked.

Peredur nodded in acceptance.

"Once again you have shown remarkable adaptation to this life."

Peredur looked around at the other brethren. All gazed at him with approval.

Sigbjorn spoke up. "I could not bear the scent of the blood in my first bout," the Norseman said wryly. "I forgot about the swords and attacked with my fangs, needing to feed."

Brude and Vellocatus chuckled in sympathy. Peredur remembered how the smell had intoxicated him, leading to the first slice across the hip.

"Who did you fight?" Peredur asked the Norseman.

"One who has since moved on. A Celt."

Peredur saw the looks of reminiscence on several faces. Perhaps these elder vampires who had moved on...perhaps he would meet with them one day.

He looked at Melnak and saw that his mentor knew his thoughts. "You have cousins to meet next," he said.

Peredur let his gaze roam from brother to brother. He felt different things from each of them.

Vellocatus was hot for it, fresh as he was from their sparring, still savoring the heightened sensations only combat could bring.

Sigbjorn was wary for Peredur's sake, though chiding himself at the same time due to the prowess Peredur had shown.

Brude had been carefully sizing up Peredur these last days and felt confident, even eager to see their newest member do battle.

Adalhard wished for a small, easily contained encounter, while Wladyslaw hoped for a rollicking great clash, big enough to spread the news in the world of vampire that a champion had come into the Brotherhood's midst.

And Melnak – what did Melnak think?

His mentor clapped a hand solidly on Peredur's arm and said, "Time to introduce you to someone."

12

Meira swept past her, scooping up her basket of wool and sitting hard upon the bench. Tanwen waited a moment, anger bubbling up inside her. It was not her doing that Rhodri exposed his two-faced nature.

Tanwen darted forward, taking her place upon the bench. She took up the spindle and twirled, forcing her fingers to a steadier pace than they wanted.

"How can you agree to this?" Meira asked.

"I won't agree. To any of it." Tanwen focused on the strand running down from the spindle.

"Tada's making arrangements."

"If it's Tada's business, how do I figure in any of it?" Tanwen said.

Meira peeled the tangled wool free of the comb. "Because you're the eldest daughter. First to be born, first to marry. Promised to mighty Peredur. And now you take second best. But Rhodri isn't second best to me."

Tanwen held the spindle still with her fingers. "Meira, listen to yourself. When have I had a moment to cast about for a husband? Mam's had you shadowing me for weeks!"

"You spoke with him."

"When he came to speak with you," said Tanwen, "his supposed intended."

"Rhodri *is* my intended!" Meira's knuckles turned white.

"Then you'd better ask him why he spoke with Tada."

Tanwen released the spindle and set it twirling, coaxing the lengthening strand into the basket in a rhythmic movement. Rhodri's image flared up in her mind – of that youthful face that always seemed at odds with his tall and powerful form. Maybe he'd always displayed his nature, and they just hadn't recognized it. But perhaps there was something else.

"I'd speak to him, Meira, if I were you. Truly. Perhaps he'll tell you what drives him to do this."

Meira stopped untangling the knot. "There's nothing to say to him. Not after... " She picked up the comb and dragged it half-heartedly through the wool.

Tanwen looked over at Gareth. He tossed another sharpened blade into his bucket and picked up a new one. He usually had a smile for her. Not today.

"If Rhodri were my man," she said, "and he did this to me, I'd be grateful that it happened before we were wed." Tanwen waited.

Their two younger sisters left the hut and hurried past, carrying buckets and heading for the stream. They ducked their heads and avoided looking at Tanwen or Meira.

"I'd be grateful if he took me as his wife," Meira said. "As he promised."

Tanwen remembered the way Rhodri avoided looking at Meira on his way past them. He'd known what he planned to ask Tada. "If he can ask for me so easily after favoring you he's not to be trusted. Is he?"

Meira bowed her head, her features crumpling into tears. "How *could* he?"

Tanwen remembered how she'd clutched her arms about herself as she stood on the rocks overlooking the bay. She'd fled from Mam's embrace. Setting the wool and spindle aside, Tanwen slid closer to Meira, taking her hand in her own. "Who can understand any of them, Meira? Why did Peredur go on that last raid?"

"That's different!"

"It's no different. Peredur wanted to impress Tada with one more victory. One more sack of loot. I didn't need any more impressing."

But hadn't he been a sight the last time he'd returned from battle? A few more scars but with a fierce gleam in his eye. His gaze had searched the crowd until he'd seen her. Then the village and all the people in it seemed to vanish for an endless moment.

Tanwen's heart grew heavy suddenly. "I know you can't stop your feelings for Rhodri. Though he doesn't deserve you. I know you're angry with him. I'm angry with Peredur for leaving me."

"Oh, Tanwen," Meira said, "you know it wasn't like that."

"I'm furious with Tada for encouraging Peredur to battle. And now this arrangement with Rhodri..." Her throat grew thick, emotion stopping her words. She pushed them out anyway. "Did they ever want to marry us, Meira? It seems like it was really Tada they wanted."

Meira sniffed silently beside her. Then she squeezed Tanwen's hand and let go, wiping her face quickly with her fingers. "It felt so good to be near him, Tanwen. I was sure he felt the same about me."

Tanwen remembered how proud her sister had looked to stroll beside him, the sweetest blush warming Meira's cheeks when Rhodri would lean in to whisper something in her ear. "It always seemed so," she said. "I'm just as shocked as you."

"You won't marry him, will you?" Meira twisted to look at Tanwen. There was a haunted pallor to her face.

"I can't stop loving Peredur just because he's gone. He's still here, Meira." She placed her hand over her heart.

"So you won't, then?"

"No, I won't. Tada can arrange as he likes. I've got two legs, haven't I? They can carry me away from husbands I don't want and a father I've outgrown."

Tears brimmed in Meira's eyes. "Don't you leave me, too, Tanwen."

She reached for Meira's hands and clasped them. "One heartbreak at a time. Agreed?"

Meira forced a smile and nodded, tears falling as the tension in her brow refused to smooth away.

Tanwen looked past her sister's shoulder at the hut nestled into the crook of the hill. Smoke rose lazily from the cooking fire within.

Tanwen wished the thought of leaving wasn't so appealing.

13

When they had gone a little ways from the cavern, Melnak turned and dug into his tunic at the neck. He produced a little white amulet like all the rest of the brethren wore, hidden away.

Peredur gazed at it, feeling a strange tugging at his legs as if he were being forced to kneel. A strange humming rose up in his head as he knelt.

The amulet flared to an unbearable brightness. Shielding his eyes with a forearm, Peredur tried to twist free when Melnak grabbed his hair at the back of his head, forcing him to look up.

"This is a fragment of bone taken from the body of Saint Cittinus," Melnak said. "It was given to us by Grigorio, a former member of our brotherhood."

Peredur made short gasps of effort as he tried to free himself from Melnak's grip on his hair. He could not bear the brilliance of the bone.

"In order to approach the souls of men that remain trapped in the bodies of our cousins, the true vampires, our brotherhood requires weapons to turn the creatures back, to free their human souls and send them to heaven." Melnak held the amulet closer.

I cannot bear it. They weren't words exactly, yet Melnak heard him clearly.

You will bear it, Melnak warned in his head. *We all must.*

Peredur cried out. The brightness threatened to burn the eyes from his head.

If you burn, you have praying to do. Melnak shoved Peredur roughly to the ground. Peredur lay still, his head feeling as if it should smoke.

When you have made peace with All That Is, you will be given an amulet. Not sooner.

"How do I do that?" Peredur asked.

No easy way, and no easier way. Just pray.

Melnak turned and left Peredur lying on the ground, alone in the wood with his sore, burnt eyes and shame-filled heart. He didn't dare get up, remaining on his stomach in the dirt.

Why had he been chosen as a member of the Brotherhood when he was unworthy of their amulet? Peredur concentrated first on getting his breathing under control. He would not give in to the panic that bubbled just under the surface.

Though it had seared through him without mercy, the heat from the amulet was merely like the first breath-taking sword cut he'd received as a boy. Eventually he'd mastered the ability to grit his teeth against such pain, in order that the next blow did not take him by surprise.

Peredur suddenly recalled one of the first things he'd ever said to the brethren. 'Fighting monks, are you?' The brethren had chuckled.

He settled himself in the dirt, ready now to pray. Prayer was to be his new form of training. Exactly like the steps, the lunges, parries and blows of his boyhood sword training.

The only weapon of any worth in this new life was that amulet, the bone fragment of Saint Cittinus. He would not be the only one called to the Brotherhood who could not prepare himself to wield it.

Peredur lay there until close to dawn, until Melnak came just before the sun could claim them both, shepherding him to his bed deep in the cavern.

14

Tanwen recalled how dearly she'd loved the fair until this autumn.

For several days beforehand she would find it hard to sleep. Then her family would finally journey to the great field where the neighboring villages met. The crowds always thrilled her as they hummed with promise. Children skipped and friends hailed each other. It once made her feel so alive.

This year held none of that excitement. As she scuffed over the dusty cart trail, Tanwen knew Peredur would not sidle up next to her, though she caught herself watching for him. There would be no more laughing or teasing all the way to the field, no more surprise at how quickly they'd arrived.

Instead Tanwen held her youngest sister's hand and listened while she prattled on about what sort of games there might be and what sort of sweets she would eat. Morvyth held a small sack in her other hand, filled with rare flowers and herbs she'd foraged from the forest that summer. After trading them at the market stalls, there would be a coin or two for the sisters to share; they could spend it on whatever caught their fancy.

Their brother would be too busy helping their father with the livestock trading. Gareth would have his fun later with the other boys. Unlike the rest of them, Peredur had always been available to court Tanwen at the fair. Peredur had been able to provide because of his skills with the sword, like his father before him. He fought the raiders constantly at their borders, supplying his family's needs with the bounty of war. So it had been an added thrill to stroll across the great field when so many young gazes had followed them impatiently. Her life with Peredur had promised to be like no one else's life.

Tanwen realized her sister had asked her a question. "I was just trying to remember," she said, attempting to disguise her lack of interest. "Where are we to meet Mam after we've sold the herbs?"

Morvyth looked up at her, suspicion clouding her bright little face. "What do you mean? We always meet by the games."

Tanwen forced a smile. What else could she do? She was like a used-up seed husk, still shaped the same with all her insides missing. "Of course we do. I was just making sure you remembered."

"I wonder how long it will take to trade what we have?" her sister asked yet again.

"Not too long, I'm certain," Tanwen replied. "You've got a lot of things in there that are hard to find."

"Perhaps he'll take all of it, right away," Morvyth said, twisting to look at someone approaching.

Tanwen looked over to see Cavan's smooth strides closing the distance between them. A grin tugged at his mouth, his eyes bright as he made his way to her. "Good day," he said to both, favoring her young sister so that Morvyth hid shyly behind Tanwen.

"Cavan," she said. "On your way to the fair?"

"Oh, I've been and gone already," he said, slowing his pace to match Tanwen's. "Mam came into some unexpected items this morning. She didn't want them with us among so many people. I took them to a safer place."

Tanwen nodded, feeling her sister's small hand squeeze her own. "You're buying herbs today?" she asked, glancing down at Morvyth's sack.

"I am, indeed," he replied, stopping.

Tanwen and her sister halted and turned to face him. "We have some things you might need," she prompted, nudging her sister forward. Morvyth pressed herself against Tanwen's skirts. "Come now," Tanwen said, exasperated.

Cavan squatted low so his face was of a height with the girl's. "Can I have a look at them?"

Her sister slowly relented, holding out the sack while gripping Tanwen a little less tightly. Cavan received the bag with a smile that would make any maiden's heart flutter.

Tugging at the drawstring, Cavan rolled down the cloth until the contents were visible. His expression grew serious as he handled the various items. The process changed his whole demeanor.

He'd always seemed such an impish sort, charming anyone within reach and keeping an agile step ahead of trouble. For several fortnights now he had revealed a far different side. He'd been the one to find Tanwen when she'd first heard of Peredur's death. He'd brought Peredur's ring to her, faced a hostile reception from her father and took her in when she'd needed refuge.

Cavan was so much more than a mere handsome lad. Why had she never recognized what a true friend he could be? She was no better than the rest of the village, seeking out his mam when someone needed a salve or a tea and ignoring her otherwise.

He dipped his hand into the sack, crushed a petal between his fingers and tasted the residue. He raised his eyebrows as he nodded. "Very good, that," he said, still addressing Morvyth. He poked carefully through the other stems and leaves, lifting one to chew and decide upon.

Then he pressed his palms together, touching the tips of his fingers to his lips as he thought it all over. Her sister looked up into Tanwen's face, her brow drawn.

"Would two silver coins be a fair price?" Cavan asked.

Morvyth's eyes grew round. She looked up at Tanwen in disbelief.

"It must be worth four coins if you're willing to pay two," Tanwen replied. Her sister shot her a look of alarm.

Cavan stood slowly, the familiar smile returning. "You can always take them to the fair and try your luck."

"If we sell them to you here, you're closer to that 'safer place' where you stored the other herbs," Tanwen said. "It would save you both walking and worry. They're probably worth five coins." Morvyth yanked at her hand even as Cavan chuckled.

"You would do well alongside your father, trading cattle," he said. "You'd get him a very good price." His gray eyes looked Tanwen up and down, making her flush.

"I shall get a good amount for these – for myself and my sisters. That will please me well enough." Tanwen returned his gaze, aware that she shouldn't allow hers to linger so long, but she couldn't drive a hard bargain and appear modest.

"Two coins and a powder prepared for chills," he said, folding his arms in front of him.

"Three coins or no trade." Tanwen remembered Cavan's expression as he'd tasted the herbs. Even now there was an obvious desire behind that cool exterior. She watched in fascination as he let the twinkle creep back into his gaze.

"Three coins, then." He reached beneath his tunic for a small leather pouch. It was so full the coins did not jingle. Cavan took out three and handed them to Tanwen.

"It is well that no one suspects you of carrying so much silver," she said.

"One doesn't always need a sword to be well-armed against attack," he replied. His eyes flashed, revealing more secrets behind that gaze.

Tanwen nudged her sister. "We must go on our way," she said, wishing she could decipher the riddle that was Cavan.

Raising the sack in salute, he said, "I shall see you at the field," then seemed to disappear as was his habit. There one moment, gone the next. Perhaps he really did have faerie blood in him, as some said.

Morvyth looked at the coins in Tanwen's hand. "Why did he give us so many?" she asked. "They just grow in the forest."

Tanwen started them back on the trail to the fair. "I told you those were rare herbs you'd found. His mam knows what to do with them, and he'll pay a fair amount to get them for her."

"I remember where I found them. I can show you. We'll go back next year for more."

"Keep that to yourself, mind," Tanwen said. "Let's keep that a secret."

"We can play every game!" Morvyth said, already hopping with anticipation. "Maybe twice!" Tanwen allowed her sister to pull her along, wishing some of her sister's exuberance could rub off.

"Morvyth, we can't spend all this money on games. Don't be silly."

There was Rhodri as they rounded the last bend. He stood with an arm around her brother's shoulders, a laugh choking silent and his face clouding over at the sight of her.

Morvyth slipped out of her grasp to run ahead, leaving Tanwen to walk toward the man who had wanted her sister's hand in marriage. Instead, he had asked for hers, ensuring that Tanwen, Meira and himself would only drift farther and farther from any semblance of happiness.

Where did Cavan go when he spirited away into the forest? And why hadn't he taken her with him?

15

He sank down in the first dusting of snow to pray.

Her shocked brown eyes haunted him now, relentlessly, as if she saw what he'd become.

Tanwen.

He shook his head and tried to get her out of his mind, but the memory of her face as he'd said his last goodbye before the battle refused to give him any peace.

He'd been struggling with prayer ever since Melnak had exposed him to the amulet's heat. Like trying to fell a tree with a sword, barely making a dent and ruining a blade in the process, Peredur felt only a cold, stony silence when he made his appeals to God.

Whenever he tried to still himself and ascend into prayer, images burst upon him like a rain of arrows.

He carried the weight of that blond-haired boy and all those since, to whom he'd bent his head, lapping up their scarlet blood. Prayer only led him to revulsion for what he'd become.

God – forgive me. Forgive me! Forgive me...

That's all he could think of to say in his prayers. He wouldn't be allowed to remain with the brethren if he couldn't pass the final trial, and as it stood now, he was no closer to facing the amulet without burning than he'd been that first time Melnak held it before him.

He was unused to failure. As a man, Peredur had been trained to fight and had learned that well. Here with the brethren, it was said he'd passed the earlier trials more quickly than anyone else.

Sending him off alone into the forest to pray... What had that accomplished? No one had given him the words to say. No one had given any instruction at all.

At first he'd been resolute to find the right prayer. That had not lasted very long, especially when the memories began forming in his mind in the solitude of the night.

His attempts at prayer only slid into frustration, which rose like a windstorm, blowing gusts of anger where there should have been a growing sense of balance.

Now he lay on the frozen ground, tormented by images of his beloved. Pleas tumbled through his mind. *Forgive me... Forgive me...*

Until he actually mumbled the words, "Forgive me, please. God, forgive me."

He didn't care about Melnak or Sigbjorn or Brude, or whether he laid eyes on any of the brethren again. He didn't care if he shriveled away by missing any more blood feasts. He didn't care that he'd cursed God and was sent to this existence by his own folly. Peredur lay in a pathetic heap like a green youth after a first night of mead.

'You must allow yourself to grieve what is no more,' Melnak had told him. Was this what he meant? Was he grieving his old life? How could he grieve when he could no longer cry?

A groan rose up in his chest. It was only the tiniest expression of the anguish in his soul. But it was a start.

Peredur curled into a ball of grief and let the groan roll up from his belly and out through his aching throat. A long mournful cry sifted out through the trees and into the night.

He could hear it as if it weren't his own voice. As distraught as it sounded, it didn't fully express how he truly felt inside. So he sobbed a great heaving breath and let loose an unnerving howl of anguish. It rode the air currents and blanketed the chieftain's farm like a hailstorm.

God! Why? Why?

His unanswerable demand distended his mouth and twisted his body into grotesque attitudes of pleading and abasement. It was all for naught, yet he could not stop any of it.

Peredur beat his fists against the ground until all at once he saw two feet and the hem of a gown before him. He stopped the howling and looked up.

There stood a man. Tall. Stately. Gentle.

He filled Peredur with a trembling fear. It was wondrous to feel something so deeply after being empty inside only a moment ago. Scrambling to his knees, he bent deeply at the waist, touching his forehead to the earth, his entire body shaking like a leaf.

For so many nights, he'd wanted someone to let him know his prayers were being heard by someone, somewhere... anyone. Now...

"FEAR NAUGHT," the being said.

Who has sent you? Peredur asked without speaking. Just as with the brethren, this being heard him and answered in the same way.

I AM XANTROS. I AM SENT BY all that is.

What are you? Peredur gathered all the courage he possessed and looked up.

I AM YOUR ANGEL.

The being spread his hands, palms upwards, as if to welcome Peredur to an embrace. But he had no intention of trying to gain his feet before such an awesome figure.

But I am no longer a man.

I WAS YOUR ANGEL WHEN YOU WERE A MAN, AND I AM YOUR ANGEL NOW THAT YOU SERVE THE BROTHERHOOD.

Peredur's mouth dropped open in shock.

DO NOT WONDER AT ANY PLAN OF god's.

Peredur bowed his head low, his arms shielding his face. *How can a vampire have an angel to watch over him?*

ALL CREATURES HAVE THEIR OWN ANGELS.

Then God has not—

TURNED AGAINST YOU?

Why have you come to me?

I WAS SUMMONED HERE.

Peredur looked up. This being appeared as a man, yet radiated love like a mother. The angel seemed at once stern, tender, ferocious and bore the forgiveness for which Peredur had cried out.

He knew he smiled, even as his brow still creased with anguish. He kept his face turned up to the angel, though he closed his eyes. The power of this presence overwhelmed him.

A light touch of fingertips to his chin encouraged Peredur to open his eyes. The angel gazed upon him with a look that held both judgment and acceptance.

What must I do?

The angel smiled. A warmth permeated Peredur's chest, soothing the ache that was Tanwen.

YOU COME TO SEE YOUR BELOVED.

Is that wrong?

LOVE IS NEVER WRONG.

Hope grew in Peredur's heart.

WHAT DO YOU INTEND FOR TANWEN?

Peredur looked up at the angel but could not speak. The angel lowered itself to its knees before Peredur, taking both of his arms in its mighty grip. All the fear, the longing, the self-loathing – it all vanished inside of him.

I want her to know I loved her.

THEN TELL HER. IT IS A SIMPLE THING.

She thinks I'm dead.

SHE DREAMT OF YOU LAST NIGHT.

Did she?

HER PRAYERS ARE WHAT SUMMONED ME.

Peredur gasped as he felt another bolt of awe strike him.

I WILL STAY WITH YOU THROUGH THE NIGHT, PEREDUR. FEAR NOT.

The angel wrapped its arms about him and Peredur curled into its chest. He remained there until just before sunrise, when he opened his eyes and saw that the being was alone again.

In a daze he rose to his feet and made his way through the woods until he found a hollowed tree with enough room to fit inside. There he slept with no dreams of Tanwen to torment him.

But when he awoke that night, he hungered.

16

"What is it you think you're doing, daughter?" Mam asked her as they prepared the meal, The day was dripping and dreary though they had the door propped open to let in the gray light.

Halting with her knife poised, Tanwen glanced at the carrots she was chopping for the pot. Nothing seemed out of place. She looked up at her mam.

For some reason, the chip she'd been carrying on her shoulder weighed heavily under her mam's gaze. As much as her father infuriated her, seemed unable to understand that Tanwen would have nothing to do with Rhodri or anyone else, there was something in her mam's eyes that raked through the tangles in Tanwen's soul.

It was comforting and unnerving. Tanwen went back to chopping the vegetables, shrugging her shoulder in answer.

"This friendship with the wise woman's son," Mam continued, pulling expertly at the rabbit skin. "You know what they're saying about you in the village."

Tanwen shrugged again, opening her mouth to answer. She had no lies for her mam, however. Scooping up the carrots, she dropped them into the pot.

"If you think there isn't another woman in this village who's been asked to marry against her choice, well, perhaps I should take you by the hand and introduce you to them. Hmm?"

"There are two widows in the village, and no one forces them to marry."

"Yes, and strangely they both entertain the wise woman's son when they think no one is watching." Mam smiled a private smile to herself.

"What do you mean?" Tanwen asked, finding that difficult to believe.

"He may have no marriage prospects, but he is easily the most handsome man this village has ever produced. Who could resist him?" Again, Mam smiled an odd smile that made Tanwen blush.

"Well, what is that to me?" she asked, pulling more vegetables from the bin and dusting them off on her skirt.

"Cavan has always looked at you in a manner that is completely unsuitable for someone promised to another."

"Oh, Mam," Tanwen said. Cavan had been such a comfort to her when everyone else just made her want to scream. Mam's insinuation made her hurt inside – for him.

"Daughter," she said, tying the rabbit's legs together with twine, "your father is the chieftain here, and he cannot claim the wise woman's son to our family if you become the third widow of the village to fall under his spell. That is all I am saying."

"Yes, Mam." Tanwen shook her head at the ridiculous notion. When she stole a glance over at her mam, she found that private smile lurking, even in the dimness of the damp afternoon.

Mam wasn't acting like herself anymore. It made Tanwen feel even more alone than that horrible morning when she stood crying on the cliff.

Her sister entered the hut with forest herbs for the meal, and Tanwen smiled at Morvyth, needing to feel a part of her family again. But even a squeeze from her sister as she passed couldn't break through the chains of isolation that dogged her.

17

Peredur dropped the body of the woman while her life's blood ran down his chin. He spun away from the rest of the feasting, his skin crawling with the shame of what he'd done. Staggering slightly, he clambered off into the shadows, found a spot away from the rest and huddled there, shivering.

He knew Melnak would search for him. He lowered his head as the older vampire sat down beside him. The sounds of the feasting filled the night like the earlier screams of the violated. Peredur moved his head slowly back and forth, wishing he could stop himself from hearing it.

"She reminded you of *her*, didn't she?" Melnak said finally.

Peredur turned slightly away from Melnak's hateful insight.

"I know how you yearn for her," Melnak persisted.

Peredur felt anger stir but knew, without doubt that Melnak did in fact understand.

"I know, for instance, that you plan to find her. That you want her to know you are not gone."

Peredur did turn then, staring hard into the glowing eyes of his mentor. *Why did they only glow sometimes? Was it the blood feast? The intensity of speaking of their former loves?* Because make no mistake, when Melnak referred to Tanwen, the image of his own love hung close beside Peredur's.

"What do you suppose will happen to your beloved when she sees you? She thinks you are dead."

"Sometimes reports from the battlefield are untrue. I could have been taken as a slave."

"Do you suppose she would believe you were a slave? *You?*"

Peredur stared hard at the ground. Perhaps he should feel gratified that Melnak could not see him giving himself over to that fate. Perhaps he did feel it.

But he knew where this conversation was going. Melnak was going to try to convince him not to see Tanwen – and this from someone who had already reunited with his own love.

"There are reasons each new brother has one of us to look out for him at first," Melnak began gently.

If only Peredur could fly away, get up and run until the horrible knot in his gut dissolved at last.

"I know you will see her again, Peredur. I have no illusions about that."

Peredur met the other vampire's gaze. He saw only compassion and even respect lurking there.

"The problem is you could go to her too soon. All of us, at first tried to do this on our own, the whole matter being such a private one. But this solo event will be noted by our cousins, who have a series of bones to pick with us. Could use it against us."

Peredur felt a prickle of understanding fight its way through his hurt.

"I'm not saying you can't go to her. You must plan and wait. That is all I ask."

Peredur nodded, though he might as well stretch his hands out to be bound in chains as agree to this request. This demand.

Melnak reached across and laid his hand on Peredur's arm. "All of us here have things that need to be put to rest. If I told you Adalhard the Frank is the only one among us who never went back to do so, would you understand that at some point it will become essential that you go to her?"

Peredur thought of the air of sadness that permeated the Frank's every movement, the despair that lived at the edges of his eyes. He nodded.

"I need you to accompany us on one of our raids before you contemplate a reunion with Tanwen."

Peredur shivered at the mention of her name, as if it made her more substantial and less a figment of his fevered need.

"Within the coming nights, I will need your skills as a fighter. There are things you must know before facing the others. And I believe you are ready for the training now."

Annoyance and pride swirled within his breast like a whirlwind. He was ready to learn what he must. Why should he need training to fight?

The memory of Melnak picking him up to hurl him triple the length of the farthest spear-throw flooded his memory.

Peredur raised his head and gazed again into the eyes of his mentor. The memory of his own father – that towering figure who'd tenderly harnessed his power to play-box with his little son – sifted up to join with his growing regard for Melnak.

His father had expected him to excel and Peredur had not disappointed. He was born for warfare and had been unstoppable – until that spear caught him and sealed his doom.

No, Peredur corrected himself. He'd been called to the Brotherhood, hadn't he? Perhaps that spear had been sent by his own father, watching over him from the heavens.

There was so much to learn.

But so much more to let go.

18

Tanwen felt compelled to seek out another widow's company the next time she was in the village. There had to be someone besides Cavan who knew what she was going through.

After the dream she'd had the other night – the one that left her with prayers on her lips and tears soaking her face – Tanwen felt like she was back where she'd started. It was as though no time had passed since she'd first heard the news that her Peredur was lost to her.

She made a point to seek out the younger of the village's two widows, dropping by the hut that once belonged to a fierce warrior who'd died when Tanwen was a girl. As an excuse for visiting, she brought some extra herbs that Morvyth had harvested from the forest, herbs that were good for aching joints of which the widow sometimes complained.

As the widow invited her in and insisted Tanwen partake of some hot brew from the fire, she thought of her mam's words and the private smile she'd seen – and what that smile could mean. When she tried to imagine this gruff woman and Cavan together, it nearly made her burst out laughing more than once. Thankfully, the brew was there to sip instead.

"I'm very grateful for these." The widow tied the stems together to hang from the beam overhead. She grabbed a stool and climbed up with only a little difficulty.

"Morvyth has a knack for finding herbs," Tanwen said. "She's sold quite a few to Cavan for the wise woman."

Even focused on securing the herbs overhead, the widow managed a private smile at the mention of Cavan just like the one Mam had given the other afternoon. Tanwen looked away, suddenly feeling as though she'd come across something that wasn't hers to see. Her face grew hot with embarrassment...and annoyance.

Climbing down, the widow picked up the stool and carried it to the edge of the hut, where she set it down. Tanwen could have sworn she saw the widow give a lingering caress to the stool's seat, as though it held memories dear to her. Perhaps her late husband made it for her.

Or was it true what she'd been told about Cavan and the widow? Did he do other things besides deliver herbs and remedies? Perhaps Cavan had simply made the stool for her as a kindness.

Returning to the fire, the widow sat beside Tanwen, her countenance less stern than usual. "I hear your father is making arrangements with the blacksmith," she said.

Tanwen took a deep breath before answering. The widow looked at her with understanding and without pity – unlike others in the village. Was it possible that she missed her late husband the way Tanwen missed Peredur? Or had she been forced to marry him, as Mam suggested so many of the women in their village had been?

"Tada makes them, but I will not take Rhodri as my husband." She met the widow's gaze and, by doing so, invited her to see whatever she was looking for in her own eyes.

"It's hard to imagine being with another, after the joy of being with a warrior," the widow said. "I know."

"You still miss him?" Tanwen asked, feeling reckless in the widow's presence. "Your husband?"

"Always. But sometimes a gift comes my way, Tanwen."

"What do you mean?"

That private smile flitted over the widow's face once more. "Sometimes the next man to come along can bring new delights along with him."

Tanwen forced herself to return the widow's smile. Why did she suddenly feel that the women she'd grown to adulthood with, all shared previously unsuspected secrets? Because she'd never become Peredur's bride, she'd remained on the outside of this sisterhood. But there were compelling glimpses lately.

Would taking Rhodri to her bed as his wife push her over that threshold? Could that ordeal ever be worth her entrance into the village's sisterhood of wives? Tanwen glanced over at the stool, so fondly touched by the widow moments before.

Was Cavan aware of this need she had? Is that why he'd known to meet her on the path that terrible day? Did he collect widows' tears and turn them to sighs? A part of her flared up with outrage at his assumption she might want physical comfort. But another part glowed with gratitude for acknowledging her status as a widow.

Beneath it all was a burning anger at Peredur. All her memories of him carried anger lately. How she wished for a reason for that private smile she'd seen on the widow's lips. How she craved a life that was not this one – where she sat in the widow's hut sorting through ghosts and memories.

19

It was in the crispness of winter that Peredur finally discovered where he'd been taken that first night they'd carried him from the battlefield – they were in the same forests of Conwy, three days' journey from Yn Wyddfid. Three days' travel for men, at least.

If he wanted to return to Tanwen, it was a half night's steady run, for her home was not much beyond the battlefield. Peredur's mind focused on nothing else. Not even the desire to feed.

Brude had to cajole him to come on the next hunt. Peredur helped them corner the unfortunate – a shivering traveler laden with far too many packs. The Brotherhood relieved him of his burden, then of his blood.

Peredur tasted of the ruby liquid but only enough to satisfy his most basic need.

When he rose at last from a restless day's slumber he slipped quietly from the cavern, expecting to be trailed for quite some distance.

Memories of his old life loomed large with every frosty breath he took. The air was filled with the scents of his youth. His last days – when he marched toward his final battle – had been the best of days. The camaraderie, the string of fine weather nights, the sword bouts to keep one's skills honed – how sweet those had been.

Peredur turned and looked back the way he'd come. He should return to Melnak and the others.

He gazed again toward the hills, knowing she was just a sprint away. Peredur sat among the shadows and trees. Seeing her once more...seeing her would be all for him. If he loved her truly, he wouldn't cause her any more grief.

Peredur rose to his feet. As he took the first steps back toward the cavern and his brotherhood, a terrible spear of anguish shot through his chest, as piercing as the fatal wound upon the battlefield had been. He looked toward the hills, then between the trunks and branches where Melnak and the others surely stood. He shook his head.

Then he raced off to see his Tanwen. Only to see her. Nothing more.

The round hut where Tanwen slept with her family nestled among the shelters for the flock and several small outbuildings. It was a tiny kingdom unto itself. Peredur crept along the ground sprayed with wisps of snow. Sheep shied from him and bleated. The wind swallowed their protests.

Peredur stood before the door for a long moment; the wind howled about his neck, whipping his hair into his eyes. He pulled the door flap aside just slightly, peering into the gloom that revealed all to him.

Peredur's heart nearly stopped beating. *Tanwen. Oh my love. Tanwen.*

There she slept in the bosom of her family, still unwed. He would not interrupt her life. He would hope only the best for her, hope that of all the young men in the village she might choose the blacksmith's son. Rhodri had the best prospects without danger of falling to a spear as Peredur had done. Even if she chose someone laughable, someone like Cavan, Peredur must leave her to live her life.

He would go back to the Brotherhood, that for which he had been called from the brink of damnation. He would not continue to seek the flames of Hell by ruining the future days of this lovely woman whose arms he so longed to feel about his neck.

Peredur stood in the bone-chilling wind that did not freeze him, watching Tanwen sleep. Tendrils of cold reached in from the opening he'd made at the door. Some of the sleepers tugged their covers higher. Some rolled to be nearer a warm body.

Tanwen tossed and rolled so her face revealed itself. Peredur beheld his love and stood transfixed. Her lashes sprayed across her cheeks like lacy winter branches over a snowdrift. Her hair, all askew around her forehead, curled under her chin. Oh how he wished he were that curl, nestled close to her lips that parted so sweetly. Why hadn't he tried to steal a kiss from her as the other hopefuls had?

But he had been so confident that she would choose him. Why steal a kiss when he could accept a willing one upon their wedding bed? Now here he stood on the periphery of her life, from which he could never move. Not if he truly loved her.

Peredur leaned his forehead against the rough wood of the hut, the stiff animal-skin flap banging against the wall. He should have listened to Melnak. The skin rattled again and Peredur grasped it to stop anyone from waking in the hut. He peered inside to be certain all was quiet.

Tanwen.

Risen from her bed, she stood only an arm's length away, gazing at him in disbelief. Chills erupted over his skin as her mouth worked to form words.

The air surrounding Peredur lifted as though he'd been caught in a whirlwind. When her whispers grew in force, he finally understood what was happening.

Tanwen was praying. Praying for him.

Peredur tried to stay focused on her blessed face, but the energy surrounding him intensified so that he could not see past a hazy light forming like a mist around him. He could not keep his feet. Peredur swayed once and crashed to the frozen ground at the base of the hut.

For one clear moment, he wondered why he shouldn't just die there, at Tanwen's door.

20

Tanwen clapped both hands over her mouth. Her shaky breathing filled the hut as she realized Peredur truly lay at her father's front door.

"Tanwen," he whispered. He regained his feet then reached a hand to her. "Come away."

She looked back toward her sisters, at her brother curled by the fire, at her parents under the covers. So odd that none had awoken. Plucking a cloak from a peg on the wall, Tanwen wrapped it about herself, pushing aside the door flap to stride outside into the cold night.

Her Peredur swept her up in his arms, running easily for a spell until he'd brought them far into the woods and out of the numbing wind. She clung to him, marveling at his solidness.

How it hurt to be separated as he set her down on an overturned tree. He knelt before her on the thin powdering of snow. Tanwen clutched the woolen cloak tightly, her breath frosting white in the air between them.

"I was told..." she tried. Reaching forward to touch his cheek, a part of her recoiled at the whisper of death she found there.

Her beloved brought his hand up to cover hers. "Here I am," he said at last.

"But Cynfelyn," she said. "He saw you fall. To a spear."

Peredur looked away.

"How did you survive it?" she said, a tinge of fear underneath her words. She pulled her hand back, away from his face.

"I didn't," he said simply, lifting his head to look her straight in the eye.

What could he mean? He was right here, solid and in front of her.

"I did fall to a spear." He lifted his tunic but there was no scar from the wound. His flesh was white as a corpse. She covered her mouth with her hand, but the shriek of pure panic escaped her.

"I am no longer a man, Tanwen."

Tears poured down her face. Why stop them?

"I did not survive that battle. Cynfelyn was right to tell you what he did. I am no longer the Peredur who grew up here in this village."

"Why have you taken me here?" she asked, noticing, for the first time, the remoteness surrounding them.

"I wanted to tell you I love you."

What he had never actually said to her in his life as an ordinary man, he said to her now as if that would help their plight. It just made her angry.

"Why did you go off to fight, Peredur?" She no longer felt the need to hide her pain at being second best after the adventure of war.

He looked away from her. "I wanted to make a proper home. For you."

Tears dripped from her nose and chin. He held his arms out and she fell into them. It felt good to sob with Peredur caressing her hair, nuzzling her face.

"I was visited upon the battlefield as I lay dying," he said at last. "My curses brought him, Tanwen. I knew I'd never get a chance to do what we're doing right now." He could barely form the words. "So I cursed God."

She pushed back from his embrace. "What are you saying, Peredur?" An unbearable pit of dread formed in her chest.

"I cursed Him as I lay dying," he said. "I should have prayed and asked for forgiveness, but I didn't."

"What do you mean?"

"I am doomed."

"*Doomed*? What do you mean?" she asked, hearing the lunatic edge to her voice. "Tell me!" She let go of him, and the loss of him even for a moment took her breath away.

He sat down heavily, seeming faint all of a sudden. "I live by drinking the living blood of people, Tanwen." He bared his teeth, exposing two long fangs like wolf's teeth.

She couldn't stop her gasp that seemed to pierce him. "I use them to get to the blood," he said, a look of despair clouding his beautiful face. "I must feed soon. I must leave you or I will feed upon your family. And I won't be able to stop myself."

21

"Stop saying that," she said, shaking her head.

"You must hear me." He crawled to her feet and took her roughly down from the log to sit on the cold ground beside him. Her eyes grew large but she did not protest his rough treatment. "It has been too long since I last fed. Even now I can feel your heart beating. I can almost taste the blood in your veins. My new life wants to take you, to drain you."

"Are you a demon?" she asked as though already convinced he was not.

"I am called vampire. I've been brought into a brotherhood of vampires, who watch over the affairs of men. We've done such a good job of it in this part of the world, no one from Cymru has even heard of us." He laughed without any humor.

"Where must you go? Why can't I go, too?"

"There is nothing to join with anymore. Haven't you been listening to me?"

"Take me with you."

He shook his head. "I'm a member of the Brotherhood now, Tanwen, where there are no women. In any case, you'd have to die to join me. Don't make any sort of mistake about that."

"Am I just dreaming?" she said to herself. "I should get back to bed." She turned and rose.

Peredur moved with his newly acquired speed and met her along the path as she headed toward her home. She stopped in her tracks and squealed.

"You are not dreaming, Tanwen. I am as real as you are. Yet I am no longer such as you are."

"Perhaps I'm being punished for not obeying my father. He told me to take the blacksmith's son to my bed and be grateful for such a match."

Though he'd tried to be noble-minded at the beginning of this ordeal, Peredur shuddered at the image of Tanwen in the arms of that ox-like man. He grabbed her quickly, embracing her, burying his face in her black hair. "Why should you suffer, when I am fated to suffer enough for both of us?"

"Why did you wait until now to tell me that you love me?" she said.

"What...?" He released her, gazing deeply into her face.

"I never knew for certain whether you felt the same way I did."

"But I was courting you."

"And so were others."

She was so angry. Had she always been like this? He didn't recall such fire from his Tanwen. "Well...if I was courting you along with them, you had to know how I felt."

"I was waiting for you to tell me."

He didn't hear the words in her head, not like he did with the brethren. But they were there, all the same.

That you love me.

"You have lost me either way, Tanwen," he whispered, finally.

"You're certain there are no women vampires in this new life?"

He shook his head. "We are a brotherhood of warriors. There are but seven of us. There are more in the world I am told. But my brotherhood here is small, and we are, all of us, warriors."

She said nothing, only gazed at him as if she might never see him again.

"My brothers died as I did, with curses upon their lips," he said. "When I first awoke to a demon biting into my neck, I thought I was in Hell. But it was only Melnak, the one who made me into a vampire."

"Make me into one. Let me come with you."

Peredur shook his head. "You don't understand. Even I don't. I was chosen somehow. The seven of us were all chosen. God still has need of us. He has not cast us down with the devil as we deserve."

"Hush, now," she admonished, tenderly brushing the hair from his brow.

He coaxed her back to the fallen tree and settled her upon his lap. A part of him warned that she must not discover that there were other vampires. Not when she wanted to join him. But he had to make her understand.

"I have yet to see a true vampire with my own eyes," he said. "But I know that they prey upon men and women. They eat as I do – they dine on living blood. They truly are fiends, these cousins of mine."

She only listened, did not turn away. How he loved her.

"Vampires create other vampires with their bites if they don't kill their victims at the feeding," he said, hoping to repel her with the gruesome facts of it. "And these new vampires would have to feed and so on, until the world would be full of them instead of men. It is the task of my brotherhood to stop that from happening."

She gazed up at him without fear. "I have prayed for you, my love," she said simply. Her brown eyes gazed into his, beckoning him to kiss her.

He bent his head to hers, pressed his lips to hers. So sweet. He clutched her roughly, tasting her blood through the membranes of her mouth. Tanwen did not protest his treatment, but he knew he was being too harsh with her.

As his passions rose, one crucial part of him did not. Tanwen clutched her to him, swept up as she was in her own desires. How could he even think of keeping Tanwen as a secret bride when he could never love her as a wife must be loved?

He pushed her away suddenly.

She shifted her disheveled curls from her face to stare at him.

"I can't," he apologized. "I can't."

She pressed herself against him, cupping his face in her hands. She forced him to look at her, to see the desire in her eyes. Peredur shook his head.

"You don't understand, Tanwen."

"What is there to understand?"

"I'm not a man any longer. I cannot love you that way."

"You plucked me out of my father's house in the middle of the night, confessed your feelings for me, and then say you cannot love me? What do you take me for?"

"Tanwen," he said, taking her hand and placing it upon his genitals. All remained unready – as though they had not kissed and explored each other's curves and hidden spaces. Tanwen looked up at him, taking his meaning but refusing to pull her hand away.

"I am no longer fit to be the lover of a woman who deserves to be loved. And loved well."

"No one shall ever touch me but you, Peredur."

"Don't say that."

"I am yours and yours only. I didn't wait for you so I could be married off to anyone else."

"Tanwen, my life with you died on the field. I have come here to say goodbye."

The forest seemed to swirl around him. He needed to feed. He needed to get away from her.

"You can go, Peredur, but you have no say in what my heart will feel for you, or for anyone else. I made my choice before you left the village with your sword and your comrades. I vowed to wait for you because I loved you. I waited. You died. I still love you. It doesn't change anything."

He shook his head at her obstinacy. "I should not have come to you. I should have left things as they were."

She shoved at him with all her strength. "Stop it. Stop it!"

He grabbed her wrists. "You must promise me you will forget about me."

She scrambled to her feet, gathering her cloak about her and standing with her back to Peredur. He crouched behind her, fighting to ignore the heightened smell of blood in her flushed cheeks. Had he known before of her immovable determination?

"Please, Tanwen," he begged. "I cannot return to my brothers if you refuse a proper life for yourself."

"Since you are not my husband, you have no say in how I live my life."

Peredur shot to his feet to stand at her shoulder. "I would have asked for you, Tanwen. I would have called upon your father and asked for your hand."

"But you did not, and so now here we are."

He whipped her around to face him. She did not cringe.

"A spear took me here!" He grabbed her hand and placed it at the spot where it had entered him. She recoiled at first, then held it firm. "It pinned me down, stuck me into the earth, and I could do nothing but lay there and feel the life I had fought for – the life I was to have with you – slip away from us both. I should have been praying to God, but all I could think of was you."

Fresh tears filled her eyes.

"You've got to promise me, Tanwen. *I died.* I am no longer a man. I cannot be your husband. You must say goodbye to me. To tell you this, to free you from... This is why I came tonight."

Tanwen grasped his face in both hands. "I prayed for you, Peredur. God must have heard my prayers, for he gave you a new life. I wanted you so much. I needed you to come back to me. And you have."

Peredur stilled for a moment. His hunger was making him more confused. "I love you, Tanwen," he said simply.

Her face glowed as he had never seen anyone glow before.

A great lightness spread through his chest. How could he feel so alive if he were dead?

22

"I must feed," he warned, holding her an arm's length from his teeth.

"On blood," she said. Pulling him down to sit upon the log with her, she took his face in her hands and gazed deeply into his unfocused eyes until he could see her. If he thought she was going to let him slip away from her again, he was mistaken.

"I have blood," she said. She knocked a hand solidly against her breast. "In here."

Peredur laughed wryly. "I would have to kill you, once I had fed. I cannot make you into a vampire."

Tanwen pulled her small dagger from a pocket in her cloak. His body tensed as if he fought against what she offered.

"You can have some of mine without biting me," she said. "Can't you?"

Peredur's breathing shallowed. He shook his head. "I don't know."

"Please, Peredur... my love. If God sent that ancient one to fetch you to your new life, he must not want you to perish here when I have blood to give."

"No," he forced out, shoving her away.

Tanwen knew she'd have to act before he gave her leave to do so. Drawing the dagger against her arm, she watched the blood well up with a steady pulse. It was so cold here, she barely felt the sting of the cut.

He looked once into her eyes.

Then he dragged her roughly forward as he dropped to his knees. He pulled her wrist to his mouth and began to drink.

She watched her beloved as he tipped his head up and made a sound that mirrored his pleasure. He pressed his mouth with more force, now that he'd tasted some of her blood. This time she couldn't stop her cries of pain from joining his moans of pleasure.

Peredur stopped as Tanwen sagged forward onto the log. "My God," she heard him whisper. He scooped her up, only to lay her down carefully upon the ground. Her arm now throbbed where the blood oozed free.

She heard him scrambling on the ground for the dagger, then heard the slice and tear of cloth ripping. He braced her arm in his lap and wrapped something tightly about her wound, securing it with a fighter's practiced precision.

He took her into his arms, cradling her against his chest. She heard him say, "No! Please, no!" before she slipped from consciousness.

Finally Tanwen's lids fluttered open. When she realized he was rubbing a slice of apple along her lips, she licked at it. A wave of relief left Peredur shaken inside.

"I know what you're going to say to me," she whispered.

Peredur smiled. "I was going to say how lovely you are when you're not half-dead from blood loss."

She giggled weakly. "You must admit it was a good thing you listened to me," she said.

"Listened?"

"Well, you weren't in any sort of shape to make a good decision anyway."

"Would this be like the shape you were in, after I 'listened' to you?"

They both laughed. What a delicious feeling it was to hear their shared laughter snagging in the branches overhead.

"Is this the sort of wife you would have made me?" he asked.

"I'm afraid so."

"Not very obedient."

"Not really, no."

"You're not a good daughter to your father?"

"I am an exemplary daughter. And a thorough study of my mam."

"I see."

"Why do you look at me like that?" she asked.

Peredur shrugged.

"You want me to say it's alright for you to leave me."

Guilt washed over his face before he looked away from her.

"I know God sent the ancient one to take you off that field," she said.

Peredur nodded, relieved that she understood.

"I just don't understand why I can't join you."

"Tanwen," he sighed.

"I don't mean, why can't I become a vampire like you are now," she said patiently. "Can't I simply live near you? You could visit me."

"I want you to have a normal life, Tanwen."

"I don't choose to have a life in another man's arms, if that's what you mean."

"I do mean it."

"You would want to think of me, pleasuring another man in the marriage bed?"

Peredur sighed deeply. "I don't wish to think of that, specifically."

"You'd best think of it. Exactly that. A normal life means becoming the blacksmith's wife or marrying the son of the wise woman."

"You weren't sweet on him? Cavan?"

"A charming man and a handsome one, but not one to match you."

"What will you do, then? Never marry?"

"I have chosen you, Peredur. I shall think of myself as your widow, whether we were joined by holy ceremony or not."

Peredur scooped her into his arms and held her close. "If we had indeed married, if I had asked you to promise to marry again if I did not make it back from battle, would you have obeyed me then?"

"Does this mean you intend to forget me when you leave? Is that why the insistence on a husband for me? So you can go back to your brotherhood with a clear conscience?"

He held her away from him so he could look into her face. "Do you know, within the brotherhood, we can hear each other's thoughts in our heads, as clearly as if we were speaking," he said. "Sometimes I swear you can hear the thoughts in my head too, Tanwen."

"I shall never take another into my heart, Peredur. I am your widow." She would not let him off the hook.

"Come," he said. He raised them both to their feet, starting them on their painful walk back to the edge of the wood.She shook, not caring if he could feel her weakness and distress.

The meadow stretched before them. In the distance lay her father's farm. She turned and burrowed into him.

But the dawn approached. Peredur had to fly before the sun's rays could find him. He took a very deep breath.

Turning her to face the farm, he kissed the top of her head. They did not speak. She started walking, then her steps turned into running and she did not look back.

23

Peredur watched her until she entered the hut and the door closed behind her. Then he turned and ran as fast as he could, to race against the sunrise.

He thought he could make his way back to the cavern in time, but the gray sky warned otherwise. Stopping to take a quick survey of options available, Peredur began a panic-driven search for a day's resting place. The horizon pinked along the edge, reaching him through the spaces between the trees.

He felt the sun sickness start up in his veins, heating his brain. For one moment he considered simply lying there, letting the sun take him.

But his weakness was only for a single moment. If Tanwen could face this sentence, so could he.

There seemed to be nothing remotely appropriate for his needs. In desperation, Peredur wrenched up a heavy branch from the forest floor and started to dig. He broke up the loamy soil easily, dropping to his knees and digging furiously with his hands.

The sun rose and he fought the dizzying sickness. Grunting with effort, he squirmed as deeply as he could into the shallow grave he'd dug for himself. Peredur pulled the earth back over his legs, pounding it into place. He could barely think anymore. He lay down but there was something burning him...

His arms seemed to move of their own accord. They scooped more earth over his chest and shoulders.

Before losing consciousness, Peredur thought he saw a figure looming over him. But it had to be the sickness. Tanwen had run back to the hut. He was alone.

As soon as the sun went down, Peredur opened his eyes.

They filled with dirt. He inhaled. More dirt.

Peredur coughed and lurched upright. Dirt, leaves and pine needles slid off him. He shook his hair like a wet dog.

More coughs dislodged the remaining debris from his lungs. He knelt on all fours, spitting and gagging. Then he sat back on his heels, gazing about him, trying to remember how he'd arrived in this place.

The hunger rose inside Peredur like a scream. His gaze darted about, his senses searching for a whiff of blood. There was still too much dirt in his nose.

He staggered to his feet and nearly stumbled into the grave he'd occupied over the day. Is this what had become of him?

Before he could dwell on that the blood lust took him hard. There was only his hunger. He must have blood.

He walked but without direction. He stepped around obstacles but barely saw them. He'd not understood what true need was when he'd lived as a man. Now he did. Nothing compared to this.

He wandered until he heard the first faint tapping of the heartbeat he'd been listening for. Not the tiny tapping of the little forest animals. He was done with that.

The blood of men was what he craved. A strong rhythm and a healthy whooshing sound as it forced its way through the veins – he could hear it, and it wasn't too far.

Peredur gathered what shreds of sense were left to him and crouched for a moment, honing in on the direction of the heartbeat. The smell of a man came to him on a faint breeze.

Dashing off through the shadows like a hunting hound, Peredur felt the saliva rise in his mouth. The fangs pressed down on his lips. *Not long now.*

He stopped just short of bursting upon the fellow who lay curled around a sputtering fire, tucked into a crook in the base of a large rock. All the same, the man heard something in the woods beyond the firelight and turned with a start.

Peredur barely registered the face. The heartbeat had quickened. It was like a roaring waterfall. It pumped the blood...the blood Peredur needed.

"Who's there?" rang out just before Peredur leaped.

A scream matched the pitch of the hunger inside him as he pinned the man, stretched the neck and sank his fangs deep, so deep. Blood spurted into his mouth, slid over his tongue and down his grateful throat.

Peredur moaned his pleasure as the man flailed his protest. The passion this man exerted in the attempt to push Peredur off him actually filled the blood with a powerful energy. Peredur brought his head up to breathe a contented sigh, baring his blood-mottled teeth. Then he dipped his head again to drain every last drop.

He let the man slip to the ground and stood, waiting for his breathing to calm, feeling the strength ease back into his body. He saw, for the first time, that a mist clung to the evening air. He felt for the first time a thawing beneath the chill of this winter – a whispering of spring.

He closed his eyes and thought of Tanwen. Was she crying now? Was she done with crying?

If she could see what he'd just done, she would not be so eager to join him. Peredur looked behind him at the crumpled form.

Who was this man? Why was it necessary for him to die so that Peredur might live?

He forced himself to return to the man's side. Peredur knelt beside him and laid him out properly, as for a wake. The man looked like a pleasant enough sort. Not a peddler – there was no pack to speak of. There was just a small sack of a few essentials.

Peredur opened it and looked through it. A wooden cup. A tin whistle. A roll of twine. A whetstone.

He looked again for a blade that would need sharpening. Attached to a belt around the man's waist, and near the small of his back, was a sturdy little knife. Peredur had need of a knife.

Detaching it from the deceased man's belt, Peredur held the knife in his palm and acquainted himself with the weight of it. He hefted it a few times, then tucked it into his own tunic.

He hated to leave the man out in the open like this. He would become food for carrion.

Peredur decided to bury him. He dug another grave, this time for a more permanent occupant. He placed the man in the trench, filled the grave back in and placed the sack upon the earth mound. If anyone came looking for him, this would leave a clue, at least.

Then he knelt beside the grave, bowed his head and prayed.

God, he prayed. *I am Your servant and must obey Your will. You have made of me a vampire. I now seek blood as my means of living, as my means of serving Your will.*

How can I face this new life if I must take the lives of men? Please God, I pray for the strength to do as You command me.

He lay upon the ground, the strength of the soil seeping into his body. It was a type of comfort.

Peredur lost track of time as he lay there praying. He didn't know how much time remained until he must race the daylight once more. But he would have the strength for it this time, at least.

He didn't feel up to rejoining the brethren just yet. Once he re-entered the cavern, this interlude with Tanwen would truly be over. He had to hold onto the memory of those precious moments he'd held her in his arms. Remembering what she had offered him...what he took.

Peredur reached the cavern as day broke, just a step or two ahead of the pink glow of dawn. The roiling turmoil in his veins had just come upon him. Peredur stumbled forward but kept his feet until he reached Melnak.

His mentor took him by the arms and held Peredur up before he could collapse. Without a word, Melnak walked Peredur to a quiet spot in a bend within the cave. He guided Peredur gently to lie down on reviving soil.

Peredur said nothing. Melnak said nothing. Not even words inside his head. He simply sat beside Peredur, who lay staring darkly into the gloom...glad of Melnak's company.

For some time they remained like that. Then Peredur rolled onto his side and propped his head on his hand. He couldn't quite look Melnak in the eye.

"Has anyone failed to return from a similar...journey?" Peredur asked finally.

"No. All have returned."

Peredur shrugged. "So I'll feel differently about this, one day?"

"At some point."

"She asked if I could make her into a vampire." He looked at Melnak this time. His mentor gazed back without surprise.

"I refused her." Peredur sat up. "You said we must stop our cousins from creating too many vampires. I assumed that prevented us from creating any ourselves."

"It's not impossible for us to do. Just inadvisable."

Peredur was dismayed by the rush of hope that ignited in his chest.

"You resisted her request, Peredur. I know what that must have taken from you."

Peredur knew his face revealed his complete need for Tanwen. He knew by the way Melnak looked at him. The only thing that made such raw exposure bearable was the memory of Melnak in the vision with his beloved they'd shared during the ceremony of Peredur's Becoming.

For now at least he'd returned to the brethren. His Tanwen would have to face her coming days knowing he would never come for her again. And he would have to face the coming nights with the taste of her blood forever seared in his memory.

24

Tanwen sat at her place near the fire, acutely aware of her father's gaze boring into her from the opposite side of the hut. There was usually talk between him and her brother, but this evening there was none.

She was in such a mood that she was glad everyone in the hut was as miserable as her. Slopping the peas back and forth in her bowl, Tanwen knew she couldn't eat them.

The wind howled outside, pushing underneath the woven seams of the walls. Her family huddled closer to the fire, but Tanwen edged further away from all of them. She'd thought Tada had understood her out in the meadow that day when they spoke about her feelings for Peredur.

But the plans with Rhodri progressed nonetheless. Not with Meira, as they should be. No.

These were all strangers to her, these people who sat in this hut, who claimed her as family and yet schemed to be rid of her. Meira, who had begged her not to think of leaving when they'd scrubbed the clothes at the river, now rarely spoke to her. Meira, who had been her friend her whole life.

Her sister began collecting everyone's bowls. When she came to Tanwen, she saw the food still plentiful there and looked at Tada.

"Bring her bowl to me," he said.

Meira glanced quickly at Tanwen, fear sparking in her eyes. But she did as she was asked.

Tada took the bowl, peered at the peas for a long moment, then handed the bowl over to Gareth. Tanwen didn't want this scene to play out before her mother. It was not Mam's fault if her daughter became reckless in her grief. Mam had taught her to be dutiful, respectful and to honor the food set before them.

Tanwen rose to her feet, heading for the door. Tada jumped to stop her.

Mam dragged at Tada's arm, saying, "No, Husband!"

Tada shook her off, gaining the doorway almost at Tanwen's heels. She ran then, heading into the night with sobs in her chest. But she didn't get far.

Tada's hard grip bit into her arm as he yanked her to face him. Tanwen pulled and whimpered like a terrified child.

"Tanwen!" he barked, slapping her hard.

"Please, Tada, please!" She crumpled to her knees before him, not knowing what else to do. If he did not relent, what other options did she have but to flee or simply die?

"What has possessed you, daughter?"

"Don't do this!"

"The arrangement has been made. You will marry the blacksmith's son. You will obey your father, and once you are wed you will obey your husband."

Tanwen shook her head back and forth, grasping at his hand though he tried to shake it off.

"Must I teach you to behave?" he asked, raising his other hand. "I thought this was long past!"

"My tada would not hurt me so," she said, dropping his hand as if his touch burned.

"My daughter would not question what her father has done for her."

"You know my heart." Her chest squeezed, clutching at her voice so that words barely formed on her lips. "I cannot marry another man."

"Don't start with this again!" he said, grabbing her to shake her hard.

Tanwen grabbed at his hands, crying out. "Please, Tada!"

He flung her away from him, and before she could see whether he meant to carry out his threat, she scrambled to her feet and ran.

"Tanwen!" he shouted.

She didn't look back. She listened hard for his running steps behind her, but there was only her own ragged breathing, the crunching and crashing as she tore through bracken. No more calls rang out for her in the darkness.

Her father, her family, the hut and all the days of her life receded into the night. She ran for the wise woman's hut, towards Cavan.

His gaze never made her feel alone.

Her feet flew over the path she'd trodden so many nights before in need of his mam's assistance. She was almost on top of it before she realized no one followed. She was well and truly abandoned by a father who not only had schemed to yoke her to misery, but had just stood there and watched her disappear into the forest.

25

Peredur settled down to rest, noticing Melnak and Vellocatus bending their heads together, staring at him just as he fell asleep.

Upon awakening, Peredur no longer lay comfortably and there was an audience of the brethren, all attention directed at him.

Peredur hung forward, his arms stretched awkwardly behind him, bound behind a large tree. His feet were bound at the base. His tunic had been removed, though his leggings remained. Now fully awake, he tried to stand upright and surge forward, but the bonds held.

His brethren gathered all around the tree. Melnak, who stood farthest away in the shadows, pulled his amulet from where it hid in his robes then lifted it over his head. As he approached, Peredur's insides turned to jelly.

Before he'd been altered by God to perform His work upon the earth, Peredur had been fearless – almost to the point of recklessness. Now he truly dreaded what Melnak might do.

All he could focus on was the amulet nearing his side. He felt the heat of it and shrank from it. He didn't care if the brethren saw him cringe. He was beyond that now.

"God our Father, our brother now descends into the trial you have given him," Melnak said.

The brethren intoned, "Our Father, hear us," just as Peredur's body began to jerk away from the amulet as though compelled to do so. Moans started in his chest, but he fought them.

Melnak held the amulet aloft. He continued speaking, but Peredur couldn't hear him past the music that had started up in his head. Peredur looked in awe at the amulet's small form, which now seemed to be giving off light waves, rippling like water after a stone's disturbance. How could that be?

Peredur suddenly felt an intense connection with all brethren present. He knew without anyone telling him that each member of the brethren carried a scar from his own amulet. It seemed that each of their amulet scars reached back toward the amulet and then toward Peredur, just as Melnak brought the shining polished bone to rest against the bottom rib of Peredur's left side.

For a moment Peredur couldn't see. All before him was blinding white light. The singing in his head stopped immediately. There was silence, pure blissful silence.

Then he heard a voice, a gentle male voice. Somehow Peredur knew it was the voice of the saint who belonged to the bone that was fashioned into the amulet.

Peredur, it said.

Most Holy, Peredur replied.

Are you ready to receive that which I give freely?

I am ready if you will have me.

That's when the searing began. Peredur heard it even as he felt the incredible heat reach into his flesh.

Peredur arched back into the tree, pulling hard against his bonds, head thrown back, mouth open, but no sound escaped through the force of his torment.

Every part of his flesh seemed about to separate from his bones. Every bone threatened to fly loose, his skin to flay off from the inside out. His mouth worked to give voice to the agony, but still no sound escaped.

The image of a man floated into Peredur's consciousness. He knew it was the saint himself.

Peredur, tell me what you have discovered about your desires and your curse.

Words could not form themselves through Peredur's torment. The best he could do was to think of Tanwen's face. He could see her now and knew the saint could too.

That was his desire. But that wasn't all – an image of himself leading his men back from a successful engagement followed that image of Tanwen, then an image of his mam laughing, of his baby sister running toward him, arms outstretched. These were all his desires.

He remembered his own words after the spear struck, when he was still gurgling with the blood then trapped in his lungs: 'God, I curse you! I curse you for this day!'

How his insides quailed at those words. Peredur tried to fall to his knees, but was restrained by the bonds that held him in place. Though he'd revived to full consciousness, the amulet still pressed into his rib and Peredur's body still thrashed against the tree with the energy emanating from the saint's bone.

Why did you curse Him? the saint asked.

Peredur grasped onto the question as though it could pull him out of the torment. Why *had* he cursed God?

'I offer you another life,' Melnak had whispered to him. With men dying around him and his old life in ruins, a promised new life had seduced him.

There are few souls with such an attachment to life as the ones who are called to the Brotherhood, the saint explained.

Now he understood that what he'd truly wanted was the future he would never have with Tanwen. A thousand lifetimes would never give that back to him. That is why he'd cursed God.

Peredur still felt split apart by the intensity of the amulet, but the relief he felt from an answer finally given was a powerful soothing balm.

26

Cavan met her on the doorstep.

She didn't know if that frightened her, or soothed her. Though her cheeks were wet with tears, Tanwen gazed at Cavan as though from a far distance when he stepped aside and gestured her inside the hut.

She entered, the warmth of the wise woman's fire choking her instead of bringing comfort. Cavan's mam sat staring into the flames, her back to Tanwen. She didn't turn or greet her. Tanwen stood by the door until Cavan joined her.

He took her hands in his, his gray eyes large and perceptive as they looked into hers. "He wouldn't believe you," he said, shaking his head at the injustice of it.

More tears pooled in her eyes, blurring everything. Bless Cavan. The one person remaining in her life who knew her. Tanwen shook her head.

"You must stay with us," he said, tugging her gently until she followed. He pulled a stool from under a shelf and settled her down upon it. Joining his mam at the fire, he whispered something to her, and she poured him a cup of soup from the pot hanging at the edges of the heat.

Cavan knelt before Tanwen and pressed the cup into her hands. She hadn't realized how cold she was. She shivered. Cavan nodded at her, taking her hands once more, pushing the cup until it neared her lips. She bent her head, sipping slowly at the hot broth, the warmth spreading into her chest.

Cavan knew best. She was right to come here.

It took awhile, but she managed to get all of the soup down. It did the trick, stopping her shivering, somehow untwisting the knot that her last moments with Tada had coiled inside her. Cavan slipped the cup from her fingers and handed it back to his mam.

The wise woman likely knew why Tanwen was here. That's why she didn't turn to greet her. She must sense Tanwen's dismay, in her manner of knowing things that others didn't.

Tanwen looked into Cavan's eyes as he once again knelt before her. He took her by the arms, but Tanwen flinched when he touched the bruises her father had made. Cavan relaxed his grip but didn't let her go. She felt compelled to look into his eyes.

"You've been sent to me. Do you know that?" he said.

Tanwen shook her head, remembering her father's warning that Cavan meant to claim her for his own. Tada had recognized Cavan's intention when he'd returned Peredur's ring to her, yet she had pushed Tada's concern aside.

"All I know is that you have opened your home to me," she said, "and I'm grateful, Cavan. So grateful."

"I know that he's come to you in the night," Cavan said without warning.

Tanwen gasped and looked up into his eyes. Their normal twinkle was gone, replaced by a cold, calculating gaze that seemed to slice right through her.

"Don't try to deny it, Tanwen. Not to me."

"You've been spying..."

He laughed an impatient laugh. Cavan stood abruptly. "If you can call what my mam and I do spying."

"So you do know," she said, an odd mixture of fear and relief flooding her body.

"I know you want him. No matter that he's dead, you still want what's become of him."

Trying to get Tada to see reason had used up every bit of strength she'd had. She couldn't make her way past this vulnerability which Cavan's knowledge exposed.

The memory of Peredur's face appearing in the night when she had risen from her pallet crowded into this hut.

"I still want him," she whispered. "I want him so much."

"Even when he told you what he was."

"Even so. I begged him to make me one."

"And he left you to mourn him."

Tanwen looked up. What had gotten into Cavan? He was jabbing at her wounds when normally his presence offered salve.

"Did he offer any reason as to why he refused you?" Cavan's gaze turned cruel.

She bowed her head, Peredur's words still echoing in her ears.

'Vampires create other vampires with their bites if they don't kill their victims at the feeding,' he'd said. 'These new vampires would have to feed and so on, until the world would be full of them instead of men. It is the task of my brotherhood to stop that from happening.'

"He is bound to protect us from what he himself has become," she said. How her heart weighed heavily at her own words.

"Peredur is naïve. He is new to that life. He doesn't know what he's talking about."

"And *you* do?" she snapped.

"I know anything I want to know. I rather thought you knew that."

She watched in fascination as his harsh mask softened into the Cavan who could charm a smile out of a dying man on the rack.

"I thought I knew you. That's why I came here." She looked over at the wise woman, who still hadn't moved from her seat before the fire.

He crouched before her, taking her hands in his. She couldn't prevent herself from looking deeply into his eyes. She lost herself there, feeling like she'd come home.

At the back of her mind, she questioned why he'd been so perverse with her just now. As his gaze held hers that question began to fade. Tanwen shook her head to clear it. She must be overwrought. Mixing him up with Tada's anger, his rejection.

"You've been through so much," Cavan said, his voice silky with tenderness.

She closed her eyes and bowed her head forward so it touched his.

"It's not enough to hear that your intended perished on the battlefield, covered in grime and mud. If it's true that he has become something else, why would Peredur allow you to see him when it's clear he never meant for you to have him?"

She shook her head in confusion. "I don't know."

"Well I do. He could see you were set to continue your life without him. And if he couldn't have you for himself, he made sure you would never give yourself to another, not if you held the wild hope of being with him again."

Cavan's words sliced into her with butcher-like efficiency. Tears rolled down her cheeks as she shook her head. "It's not like that."

"Isn't it?" There was pain in his eyes. "You think I don't know what it feels like to love someone who won't accept the heart I offer?"

"Cavan, please."

He released her, only to reach up and tenderly take her face in his hands. "You think I don't know that I was never in the running for your hand? The son of the wise woman?"

"Must every man hurt me?" she asked.

His hands gripped her face tighter. "Not this man. Never this man. I want only to love you." His eyes filled with ferocious need.

Tanwen went ice cold with dread. Cavan dipped his mouth toward hers. She sat on the stool, trapped against the shelf by Cavan's kneeling form before her. His lips covered hers. Cavan kissed her tenderly at first, then deeply. Hungrily.

She sat still as a frightened fawn as his tongue traced the lines of her mouth. She felt the same starved need in his kiss as her own frustrated desire for Peredur. Because of that recognition, she didn't try to pull away, but her jagged longing for Peredur kept her from returning Cavan's desperate reach inside of her.

27

He seemed to be somewhere else entirely.

No longer bound to the tree, Peredur brought his hands before him and rubbed them absently, expecting them to be numb. As he looked around for the brethren, he realized his wrists and ankles were fine.

Yet the heat within part of him still burned.

In the distance, a figure waited for him, a miserable bent man barely clothed in rags. Peredur tried to join him, but at the hint of motion his legs shot through with fiery tendrils and he gasped. The figure turned his face to see who approached.

Such a man. His face held the expression of one who had endured a torturous vigil, rather like the one from which Peredur could not free himself. But the face also held a beauty that hurt to see. Peredur wanted to turn his face away, but the gaze of those tormented eyes held him and, despite the pain, he forced a step or two forward.

This was Saint Cittinus. Peredur wasn't sure how he knew. He just knew. Peredur wondered why he couldn't hear the saint's voice in his head when it was clear that he needed Peredur's help.

I'm coming, Peredur tried to tell him, but the bent figure lowered his head as if overcome by agony after all. Peredur grit his teeth and pushed forward with all his might.

His feet finally moved, but suddenly it seemed the saint was miles from where Peredur could reach him. Peredur's heart sank.

He remembered, in his boyhood, how heavy the sword had been at first, when the sword master made him swing it again and again. His legs just now were the same. They rebelled against his commands.

Move! he shouted at them. *Move!* Peredur tucked his head down and concentrated on the ground in front of him. One step. Another step.

Time was meaningless. Had he not been here forever, inching forward? And the saint no closer.

To Peredur's horror the saint toppled to the side and fell. He'd not been able to reach him. What Peredur could have done for him, he had no idea. But now it was too late.

Anger at the injustice of it coursed through him. As the anger rose, the binding stiffness released his legs and his steps grew easier.

Peredur wanted to race to the saint's side, but what use would there be in that? Now that he could move, he walked with dread toward the fallen bundle of rags and limbs. Kneeling there, he took the saint in his arms and brushed the matted hair from the bruised face.

Saint Cittinus' eyes fluttered open.

Peredur's heart soared. He smiled with relief.

28

Tanwen glanced over at the wise woman, humiliated that Cavan should kiss her like this in her presence. But his mam continued to sit, unmoving, in the identical spot. Something wasn't right. No one sat like a stone for that long, and certainly not Cavan's mam, who always bustled about the fire brewing her herbs.

Cavan broke the kiss, his love-drunk gaze large before her. He quickly snapped to attention when he saw where she'd been looking.

"She can't hear us, the poor dear."

Can't hear us? His mam had no trouble with her hearing. Tanwen looked at Cavan. She recognized the cool tone he'd used with her earlier. This stranger kept intruding, shoving aside the man to whom she'd fled for friendship. Now the merest hint of his smile gave her chills.

When he put his arms around Tanwen, pulling her close to him again, she reared back. He rested his head upon her breast anyway.

"I had to block her," he said. "Her visions would have told her you were coming. She would have known what I was going to tell you."

Tanwen felt the strength of Cavan's desperation in his embrace. Something coaxed her to stop fighting it. She slowly curled toward him, placing one hand upon his head. He sighed.

"There's no real way to stop the visions from coming," he said. "I can only block her from receiving them." After a long moment, he gazed up at Tanwen with a naked vulnerability she'd never seen in anyone.

Had Peredur seen this same expression on her face when she'd begged to be taken with him to his new life?

"What if I told you I could give you what your precious beloved would not?" Cavan said.

Tanwen's heart jumped around in her chest like a lamb bucking to escape the killing stroke. "How do you know what he gave me or didn't give me? That is *my* affair."

Cavan's face clouded over with an unfamiliar look of dread. He gripped her tighter. "You must understand about my mam and me. We can't help ourselves. The images...they just come."

"Why have you never told anyone that you have the same sight as the wise woman?"

Cavan looked off in the direction of the village. "What is barely tolerated in a woman is feared and loathed and hunted down in a man." He glanced back at his mam for a long moment, then gazed back up at Tanwen. She'd thought he already appeared as emotionally naked as a man could get, but the expression he wore now was heartrending.

"Do you know she foresaw everything that would happen to me, including this night, Tanwen? And she was urged by her spirit guide to put an end to me, there and then....with the blood of her womb still upon me."

Tanwen shook her head at the horror of such a thought, even though his words 'including this night' set her trembling.

"Mam has been everything to me, Tanwen. Everything a man could ask for. Everything except a lover. And she had no idea what her little darling was up to all these years. I made certain of that."

Tanwen chilled inside at his words, at his tone. She brought her hands up to clutch his face and force him to look into her eyes. "What have you done with her, Cavan? This woman who spared your life, who *gave* you life. What is wrong with her? Why does she not hear me? She doesn't even know I'm here, does she?"

The shock of her gesture played over his features, only to be replaced by a wily, malevolent smirk. "I have indeed made certain that she neither hears nor sees you, Tanwen."

She tried to rise, to go to the wise woman's aid, but Cavan forced her back onto the stool.

"Don't mistake my mam for a weak vessel simply because I have stayed her considerable power. I am merely her better. I'm so much stronger than she ever realized, for I've been distorting her perception of me since I was a small boy."

Tanwen shrank from Cavan's touch.

"Her spirit guide is doing its best to break through to her right now. It knows what this night is for. It cries out for my mam to rise and take action." He smiled proudly and shook his head at such folly.

"What is it trying to warn her about?" she asked, glancing over at the wise woman, who sat as still and untroubled as could be. Tanwen listened for signs of a struggle. She heard only her own wild pulse in her ears.

"You are about to witness something for which our village would put me to death, if only they knew." Cavan rose to his feet.

Crackling energy splashed from him like rivulets of water.

29

The saint seemed too feeble to form words, even in his mind, but he looked up into Peredur's eyes and seemed comforted by his presence.

God, Peredur prayed, *if there is anything you can take from me to ease this man's suffering, I freely give it.*

He repeated the prayer over and over until he heard the rasping whisper of the saint.

"I thirst."

Peredur knew immediately the only liquid he could give this battered being was his own vampiric blood. But in so doing, would he create a new vampire – a thing forbidden by God Himself?

The saint's lips were cracked and white. Peredur's heart ached to know what to do.

He gazed upwards, wishing with all his heart for Melnak's aid, though his mentor hardly ever answered questions the way he needed an answer right now.

God – please help me. Please.

Peredur curled his body around the saint. He would have wept if tears were still allowed him.

Peredur felt a hand upon his shoulder. A presence stood behind him. He knew at once that it was his angel, Xantros.

YOU ARE VERY NEAR THE ANSWER YOU SEEK.

Peredur looked down at Saint Cittinus, so frail as he lay in Peredur's arms. How did he even linger?

He thirsts, Peredur explained.
YOU THINK TO SHARE YOUR BLOOD.
Would that be wrong?
WHAT DID MELNAK SAY REGARDING BLOOD?
Peredur shook his head in frustration. Under no circumstances were they to create a new vampire. They were called to the brotherhood to stop that very thing.
YOU KNEW THE ANSWER. YOU KNEW IT BEFORE YOU CALLED FOR ME.
Peredur looked at the youthful saint in his arms, made old before his time by the captivity and mistreatment he'd endured. As if for the first time, Peredur saw the clear white line of a scar across the saint's neck, as if a rope had choked him there.
Saint Cittinus looked into Peredur's eyes. Those cracked lips moved. Instead of 'I thirst,' the saint spoke clearly, if softly. "We have no one else to fear," he said, "but our Lord God. Who is in Heaven."
Peredur nodded. He stayed as he was and watched the saint expire before his eyes. All the while his angel never took his hand from Peredur's shoulder.
Saint Cittinus faded from Peredur's grip, though he still felt the weight of him in his arms. Peredur was not surprised to find his own amulet dangling from his right hand.
No sooner than he'd seen it, but Peredur came to.
He found himself still straining in his bonds against the tree. With breathtaking intensity, the pain in his rib returned. Melnak held the amulet to him still, with unyielding grimness.
It was hard to get his breath. But Peredur inhaled deeply, needing to speak.
"I accept this," Peredur said through gritted teeth. "I accept it. Freely and of my own will."
He thought of the scar upon the saint's neck. Instead of struggling and cursing as Peredur had done on the battlefield against the spear, Cittinus had accepted the

wound that had given him the scar. In fact, the saint's acceptance had been so profound, it had somehow melded holy fire into Cittinus' very being. That was the fire that had burned Peredur all along.

It was time to stop fighting.

"As God wills it," Peredur said, "so do I."

The pain came to a screeching halt. Peredur sagged forward in his bonds. He felt his brethren exhale collectively.

Then hands loosened the bonds, lowered him gently to the ground. His skin no longer burned, his bones felt whole. But the touch of the solid earth upon his skin was like a balm on an angry wound.

He panted as he lay still. Melnak knelt beside him. He cradled Peredur's head in his lap as he held his arm above Peredur's mouth. The *szlachcic* reached over and sliced Melnak's wrist with a tiny jewelled dagger.

Then blood, glorious blood, dripped onto Peredur's waiting lips.

'I thirst,' Saint Cittinus had whispered.

Drink, then, Peredur thought, knowing a part of that beautiful, abused and holy youth now resided in him.

30

The hair all over Tanwen's body stood on end. Her scalp tingled. She could almost hear a snapping in the air. Cavan strode to another shelf on the opposite side of the hut to retrieve a clay bowl, along with several small packets and a vial.

He knelt before a sturdy bench, which he covered in a silken cloth before laying his bowl and ingredients there in a ritualized manner. Quickly and expertly he poured a dash of this and a measure of that into the bowl. As she watched, Tanwen desperately wanted to tell him to stop, but her tongue seemed so heavy in her mouth.

Cavan pulled a short, slender rod from inside his tunic to stir the mixture, speaking foreign words in a monotone.

'What if I told you I could give you what your precious beloved would not?' he'd said. The wild possibility that Cavan could somehow reunite her with Peredur lit her up inside like a flame to a haystack.

Before tonight, had she imagined what lurked beneath Cavan's irresistible smile and comforting presence? Before that cold and disorienting night when Peredur took her deep into the forest, could she have imagined a world where her beloved now resided?

She could hear her own pleas for Peredur to take her to that world with him. Had Cavan heard those words through his mysterious gift? No wonder he always seemed to guess her feelings, to know her better than she knew herself.

The air in the hut grew even thicker with expectation, just like a storm's pause before a thunderclap. Cavan poured a thin stream of something milky into the bowl. Tanwen's heart leaped into her throat when the contents sputtered and foamed.

Cavan picked up a knife, nicked his hand and counted exactly three drops of blood as they joined the roiling mixture. At the moment the third drop hit the bowl, the ground beneath her rumbled, sending her sideways.

The wise woman twisted as she now wrestled with an unseen entity. Inhuman shrieks split the air. Unseen beings buffeted Tanwen as a scream rose inside her. She was too frozen in terror to let it out.

Cavan stared at her through the maelstrom, his eyes filled with greedy ferocity and pride.

What have you done? What have you done? The wise woman lurched sideways as though pinned down at last. The door of the hut crashed open and closed. A hundred tongues seemed to lick and taunt her skin. Masses of disgusting worms seemed to thrust and squirm through her hair. If the scream couldn't find its way out, she would surely lose her mind.

With enormous effort Cavan picked up the bowl with both hands, as though the bowl weighed hundreds of pounds. He raised it above his head, turning toward the directions of the four winds. Then he tipped his head up, pouring the contents into his mouth.

The wriggling and pressing and prickling all over her body ceased. Tanwen's knees buckled and she dropped to the floor of the hut. Cavan's throaty laugh filled the air as the door flew open once more.

This time, however, it wasn't an unseen figure. A towering man stood in the firelight, his eyes glowing as orange as the flames. Yet the temperature in the hut chilled. His gaze swept the hut until it rested upon Cavan. Then the man's mouth opened, and Tanwen realized he was not a man at all.

"Enter," Cavan commanded, gazing upon the creature with the same wary desire a hunter would give a cornered boar.

She barely saw the glinting flash of white fang as the dark being rushed through the hut, quicker than a blink, to stand before Cavan. "Who *dares* to summon me?" it hissed.

Cavan returned the creature's wilting stare with a blood-chilling gaze of his own. "Someone you'd best learn to obey, wouldn't you say?"

"Vampires are not summoned," it said, voice filled with menace.

"I see," Cavan said, grinning his best charmer's grin.

The vampire's gaze swept the room, taking in Tanwen and the wise woman. "Spit it out," it said.

"This woman wishes to join your number."

"Does she?" the vampire said, almost to itself. It appeared before her without seeming to move. It inhaled her scent deeply.

Cavan joined them. "And she's got a little something special about her."

"She'd better have. Hadn't she?" The vampire's threatening manner paralyzed Tanwen, yet Cavan gazed upon it as though he were in the first flush of infatuation.

"I'm surprised you can't smell it on her," Cavan said.

The vampire gazed over abruptly, fixing her with its eyes – dark now. It leaned in closely, inhaling deeply around her neck, her hair, her breath. When it caught the scent it had been searching for, it recoiled momentarily.

"That's right," Cavan said. "She fed the new vampire allied to the Brotherhood, the one that's caused such a stir in your circles."

"Lord Muiredach can watch over his own affairs." It flashed a monstrous grin, filled with gleaming white fangs and teeth.

"Yes," Cavan said. "But this woman needs your assistance in a rather delicate manner."

The vampire growled its lack of concern for her desires.

"She wishes to be turned," Cavan said simply. Throwing its head back, the vampire laughed uproariously.

"She is the former intended of the newest vampire," Cavan explained.

"Ah," the vampire purred.

All of Peredur's attempts to explain why she could not be turned taunted her like children pointing fingers, knocking playmates into the mud.

This vampire exuded power and masculine grace, just as her beloved did. Yet he had no qualms about turning her. He demanded her full attention, making her feel as though she were inexplicably in love with him.

"I agree that a vampire is not to be summoned," Cavan said. "I'm not quite sure it's ever been successfully attempted."

"I have never heard of it."

"Yet I summoned you, and you arrived at my door."

"What manner of man are you?" the vampire asked, looking intently at Tanwen before Cavan could answer. She tried to resist the incredible pull he exuded as he held her gaze. She could not stop her pulse from racing.

"I am Cavan, the son of a powerful witch," he said. "That is her, there."

The vampire nodded his head in begrudging greeting. "I am Osfrid." He glanced over to where the wise woman lay on her side on the floor, still saying nothing. "A son, you say?"

Tanwen felt the loss of the vampire's attention keenly. If she had been weeks without food or water, she could not desire anything more.

"There are barely any of us that survive infancy," Cavan said. "I won't fault you for your confusion."

"You wish me to turn her?" the vampire said.

"It is her wish, and that is all that concerns me," Cavan said.

The vampire looked very closely at Tanwen. Her heart froze, then seemed to break into hundreds of pieces. Peredur had forbidden it. He worked to maintain a balance, he'd said.

She should honor his wishes. She should trust her love – that he knew what was best, especially in this sinister and dangerous new world.

But all Tanwen could think of was the sensation of Peredur's arms enclosing her in an embrace. All she could see was Peredur's piercing gaze taking her in, drinking up the sight of her like a man dying of thirst.

Well, she thirsted. She hungered. She wanted Peredur, and Cavan had turned the world upside down to give him to her.

For an instant – a long, suspended instant – she could clearly see the look of joy that would wash over Peredur's face when he realized what she went through to find him again. Tanwen faced the vampire, forcing her feet to move the few steps 'till he was a breath away from her.

"Please," she said simply.

It took only a heartbeat before fangs punctured her neck. Tanwen gasped raggedly at the blinding pain, toppling back into the arms of the vampire. The force of the blood leaving her made the hut swirl around her.

She'd spent more hours than she could count, imagining Peredur taking her this way. Sometimes she'd been too terrified of her own madness. Didn't she need to die for it all to come to pass?

Tanwen heard more shrieking. It was closer than the other cries she'd heard before, almost as though the wise woman had finally found her voice. There was something so heartbroken about it.

Peredur...he'd been very clear. In order to live as a vampire, the woman she knew as Tanwen must die. And death never came easily – it was either drawn out and excruciating, or shocking and short. As her blood poured forth in waves matching the lusty sucking of the vampire, Tanwen reeled between the sense of protracted agony and the breathtaking speed with which he drained her.

She fought to keep her eyes open, unable to bear surrendering to the fading image of the wise woman's hut. She could still discern the crumpled form of Cavan's mam. She could still see Cavan's predatory leer as he lunged for the vampire.

The vampire stiffened under the attack, releasing her. Tanwen slid slowly to the floor. As she landed upon the packed earth, she sensed once more the odd, squirming feel of the air itself. More of Cavan's magic.

Angry voices clashed like rams. Two male bodies shoved and flailed, struck and recoiled. Tanwen watched the vampire straighten, dumping Cavan on the floor. All went dark for her as Cavan's pale, drained face fell into view.

31

CAVAN

The deep forest surrounding Yn Wyddfid, beyond the wise woman's hut, eighteen years earlier. 559

My cries filled our hut. Mam roused long enough to soothe me. I was too distraught to fight off her quick charm. I slipped back into sleep, slipped back for more torments.

I jerked awake. Mam stirred as I moaned, forcing myself past Mam's whispered charm. She was too strong for me. An eerie comfort, her strength.

Sweating with effort, I fought her, fought the invisible bonds. I lay as though deep in sweet slumber. I sensed Mam rising, sensed her creeping over to look. Felt her soft fingers brush my forehead.

Mam bent down. She kissed me. Mam whispered a soothing charm, thinking to keep her son safe from dream demons. Couldn't she hear that my moans were really screams? Her charm only muffled them, like thick cloths stuffed hard in my mouth.

I fell into dreams, down and down to places no one should be made to go. 'Hush, now,' Mam had said, forcing her breast in my mouth. I shook my head from side to side, protesting this outrage. She guided my face with unyielding hands. I was made to suck.

In a while it comforted me. But I had sharp little teeth. I watched as Mam's face lined with the pain of feeding me.

32

Clan coastal territory, 577

She stretched, clumps of soil loosening around her like warm bedding, the rejuvenating grains washing over her skin like bathing water.

She sensed the murmuring, the low growling coming from somewhere above. *Must rise.* She pushed herself up.

Her eyes opened, but everything was black.

She inhaled sharply. All she could smell was the sweet mineral scent of earth. *Mmm. So sweet.*

The growls and muffled words grew stronger. She must find out who made those sounds. The sense that she must join them rose higher. She tried to sit up, but the embrace of earth held on tightly.

A voice sharpened over top of her. She sensed activity, then someone reached for her through the veil between the dream time and this waking.

Hands swept the soil from her face. A set of eyes gazed down upon her − black eyes glinting in the torchlight. A roar of expectation started from many throats.

More movement, more sweeping aside the earth that cradled her like swaddling clothes. An elegant hand reached down and found hers still under wraps. A compelling tug she absolutely must obey gave her the surge of power she needed.

She burst from the earth like a geyser. Torchlight, black night, white fangs, hunger pangs. Sensations threatened to overwhelm her. She landed soft and catlike, poised for battle, surrounded by a throng of creatures just like her.

A howl of celebration filled the starry night.

The one who'd plucked her from her sleep took several steps forward. With both hands outstretched, he welcomed her.

Standing tall, taller than she'd ever felt before, she placed her hands in his.

An undercurrent of dismay snaked through her. She couldn't quite remember. That was it. There was something important she couldn't remember.

But the feeling of homecoming was seductive. Why should she trouble herself with memories when this assembly of beings was so overjoyed to see her?

The creature gazed deeply into her eyes. He seemed like a god. A king or a god. He smiled a dazzling smile filled with great sharp teeth. A thrill ran through her, ran through every part of her – she knew she'd never felt the like before. Her own smile spread over her face, her lips stretching over teeth just as sharp and exquisite as his.

He cupped the back of her head with a strong hand, pulling her close. He laid his lips on her forehead, kissing her there, then tipping her head back for a deep kiss upon her mouth.

She opened her mouth for it hungrily. She had never wanted anything like she wanted this kiss. Nothing and no one mattered to her. Only this creature, his lips covering hers, his tongue possessing her mouth, her need growing, growing.

33

The deep forest surrounding Yn Wyddfid, beyond the
wise woman's hut, fifteen years earlier. 562

My mouth was stuffed full of cloth. Strong swaddling
clothes kept me immobile in the sling Mam carried me
in. I was too old to be in swaddling clothes.

She carried me deep into the forest, dark with night. I
felt kidnapped by a different mother, for my adored
mother would never do this to me.

She finally arrived at her destination, lowering me
onto the ground behind a screen of bushes. Then she left
me there, ignoring me, watching anxiously, staring into
the shadows until finally he arrived.

My eyes widened at the strange man sporting antlers
like a great stag. He walked up to Mam and grabbed her
to him. Mam did not protest, but meekly allowed him to
plunder her mouth with ghastly sucking kisses. His
rough hands grabbed her bottom and lifted her almost
off the ground.

"Take it off," he ordered her, and she undressed at
once, as though he were her god. My beautiful mama
knelt before him, and he shed his own clothes before
pressing his belly into Mam's face.

His actions became frantic while Mam's sounds grew
anxious. With both hands he grabbed her face and held
her as his body went rigid.

Mam! I wanted to cry. *Mam, is he hurting you?* But the cloth she'd pressed between my tender lips silenced any sound I could have made.

This great horned beast-man knelt and laid my mam out on the ground before him. With large hands he spread her wide, revealing her dark, glistening heat. The horned beast lowered his great head, so low that his mouth chewed at Mam's belly.

My eyes widened as I watched him crush her with his powerful body. Mam cried out as if he were striking her. I was scared.

With a bellow, he froze. Mam made a sound of intense pleasure and collapsed, reaching up to caress the stag-man's face.

This went on for many years, as I grew older. Several times a year, at the changes of the solstice, Mam brought me to these secret scenes of savage mating with the horned man. As far as I knew, he never saw me there. Mam always made sure I was tied up and tightly gagged, so as not to betray my presence. She never told me why she brought me along for these frightening displays, never told me who the man was or why they met.

We never discussed it, either. Without warning, she would bring out the special swaddling clothes she kept for this purpose, which she waited to put on me after we'd walked together to their meeting place. She would wrap me in her cocoon, stuff a thick cloth in my mouth, tie me to a tree and walk forward to meet the beast-man.

As I got to be an older boy, I came to learn that this was an old magic ritual, and that she and the stag-man were standing in for primal forces in our world. Why she needed me to be a silent witness to it, I never worked up the courage to ask.

But one day my boyish curiosity made me remark on her beautiful sex. Mam turned around and slapped my face before I could take a breath.

"Don't ever say such a thing to your mam," she said, angrier than I'd ever seen her.

"Why not?" I asked, suddenly angry myself, for being made to watch something I was never supposed to mention.

"What has got into you, child?" she said, her voice shaking.

"Nothing's got into me. Not like what gets into you sometimes."

Mam's face paled with shock. Then she grabbed my arm, half lifting me off my feet as she dragged me to her pallet and threw me down hard.

"No Mam! Please!" I cried, sorry too late for goading her. I'd found an ordeal for myself and now had to suffer it, just as I'd always witnessed the mating sessions.

She was so consumed with rage, with terror that perhaps I'd mentioned the rituals to anyone else, words failed her. Unseen hands grabbed me and held me down, though I squirmed and protested. I well knew to whom those unseen hands belonged. Like all wise women, Mam had a familiar, a spirit that now came to its mistress' aid.

Mam probed inside my mind with her thoughts, like hot needle points demanding answers in my head. I gasped with the shock of it. I stared up into the face of my beloved mam, but she was too busy watching and listening to the secrets I kept.

I couldn't let her know about my own sorcerer's powers, or her familiar would make sure I never rose from this pallet. I had to simply lie there and let her rummage through my mind while I used my rough skills to shield my true abilities from both Mam and the spirit. It was more than I could handle. I screamed finally.

But our hut was far from the rest of the village. No one came to my aid. Even if they'd heard me, who would have dared to enter?

34

Clan coastal territory, 577

She sat on a wide, rounded boulder overlooking the sea, its rhythmic pulse reminding her of something.
Something...
The god-king appeared beside her, lowering himself to sit on the great rock which hummed with generous bounty. They sat awhile in this way.
"Such a night," he said.
She turned to him, eager for his lips on hers again. He gazed at her with the same hunger. He bent his head and they kissed deeply. But better even than the taste of him and the feel of him were the traces of blood she sensed on his tongue.
When the kiss broke, she stared into his eyes, her questions too unformed to give them voice. He reached forward and stroked her hair out of her eyes.
"You must feed," he said.
Feed. *Yes.*
"Come." He rose to his feet and helped her up. Before she realized it, he'd scooped her into his arms and sped over the coast in their manner of near-flight. In a blink they entered a secluded cove, where they stood in the inkiest part of the night to watch two fishermen pull their boat onto the shore.

The god-king looked at her with doting assurance. Then he sped across the sand in the way they all had, overtaking the man before he had to chance to cry out in fear.

The other man shrieked, dropped the bundle in his arms and stumbled away to the cliff path. She watched him go, not caring if he fled, while her eyes feasted upon the sight of the other man dangling in the grip of the creature beside her. The fisherman's blood scented the air, making her tremble with the need for it.

Her teacher held the man in his grasp. Two eyes, huge with terror, gazed at her as she approached. Her mouth salivated with desire. But the god-king smiled, encouraging her as she closed in on the man who shook violently and whimpered.

Why did that sound make it all the more delicious as she lowered her mouth to his neck? She placed her lips along the throbbing artery, lowering her fangs to his goosebumped skin. It was there, so close she nearly swooned with need.

Her teacher nodded silently. So she sunk the sharp points into his flesh.

Intense energy filled her mouth, thick and red. The pulsing strength of it was magnificent. She got a jumbled sense of this fisherman as she swallowed his blood – impressions of his loves, of who would mourn him once she was through with him. The blood flowed so strongly it smeared her face and neck. It seeped into her hair and onto her tunic.

The god-king held the slackening fisherman securely. The man's moans slowed as she drank and drank. Soon he was nothing more than a shell. When she straightened, wiping her mouth, her teacher dropped the carcass with a wet thud.

The sensation of supercharged energy flowing through her brought with it jagged memories and impressions.

A whisper of a name – *Tan* something – chased images of a family, of a handsome warrior, of a spot by a stream where a basket of washing waited. All of it crowded through her brain. She looked down at the used-up fisherman but didn't recognize him.

Her teacher closed the distance between them, taking her face in his hands. "All of that is behind you now," he said.

She nodded, the high of feasting on the blood overruling anything else.

"This is your life," he said. "Here with us. In a few hours your name will likely return to you, but here you may chose an entirely different name if that is what you desire."

She nodded again, licking the blood from her fingers. He gripped her face and lowered his mouth in order to trail his tongue over the smears of blood on her face. She laughed.

Tanwen, she heard from her memories. That was it – Tanwen. Yes, she had once been called by that name.

Fancy that. Yes, she supposed those people revealed to her were once her family. But she was quite certain that no one had ever taken care of her the way this magnificent being had done.

"Did you keep your name?" she asked him. "Or did you take a new one?"

"I took a new name." He kissed her. "Why hold onto the scraps of my life as a man, now that I am vampire?'

Vampire.

She liked the sound of that word.

"Do many of us take new names?"

"Many keep their old names. It is entirely up to you."

She rolled the sound of that name back and forth over her tongue. *Tanwen. Tanwen.*

Something about keeping it burrowed under her skin. "Must I make up my mind right away?"

He took her hand, and they walked across the moonlit beach. "Take all the time you need. We should get back to the group, though. There is another brand new vampire due to emerge at the waning of the moon."

Another one? Did they come through in pairs, usually? He must have sensed her question, because he answered, "You were collected at the same time as this one, but he required more rest in the earth before joining us."

She tried to recall anyone she would have known that might be this new arrival. Something told her there was someone she should be missing very much.

It was difficult to think of anyone else as she walked hand in hand with her teacher. "What name did you chose for yourself?" she asked.

"Muiredach. Lord Muiredach"

She couldn't imagine anyone who could command her attention like this vampire lord.

35

PEREDUR

Yn Wyddfrid village, fifteen years ago. 562

I watched the men from our village return from the latest raid, their solemn procession all too obvious, even from here. A still form lay upon the sledge they'd made. They dragged it behind them with heavy steps.

Even before I could form the thought in my mind, Mam rushed up behind me, where I stood in the door of the hut. Her whispered *'No'* behind me made the hair rise on the back of my neck. My little sister cried as Mam knocked me down in her haste to get to the sledge.

I felt my sister's chubby little hands wrap around my legs as she toddled to keep Mam in her sights. I reached down and hoisted her into my arms, but I was only a boy myself and not very comforting. She continued to cry, my stomach continued to churn and Mam ran, ran toward the sledge with its immobile burden.

When she stopped and looked down at him, I hoped for one wild moment that she and I and the entire village were mistaken. This couldn't be my own father upon that sledge. The body must belong to some other unfortunate family whom I could pity, from whom I could then turn gratefully away.

That was not my tada there.

Mam sank to her knees beside the sledge, falling over the body in her grief. Her cries filled the damp night. I clutched tight to my little sister, rocking her as she matched Mam's cries.

I couldn't shed tears because I refused to believe. My heart seemed frozen, my sobs not yet formed even though my eyes saw and my ears heard.

After a very long time, some women from the village arrived to join their cries with Mam's. One young girl walked up the hill to our hut, gazing down at me with sorrow, her face wet with tears. She reached for my little sister, who mutely stretched her arms out for the village girl and her more practiced way of holding a wee sister.

I walked down the hill, wet with dew. The nearer I got, the easier it became to see my proud father's face, eyes closed, hair brushed back yet still caked in dried blood. My chest felt heavy yet still frozen. It was hard to breathe.

One of Tada's closest friends stood near, his face lined with the sorrow I should have been feeling. He looked at me, then reached down and slipped a ring from Tada's hand.

I held out mine and he placed the ring in my palm, covering my small hand in both of his warm, strong ones. It was the feeling of a man's hands more than anything else that made me miss my Tada, that made my chest unthaw.

The tears came, then.

36

Clan coastal territory, 577

The other vampires stood in a circle around the grave that already moved with the stirrings of its occupant. Tanwen gazed with fascination at the soil that had so recently held her in its embrace.

She did notice that some of the largest males were placed at even distances around the circle. She hadn't noticed anything of the sort when she'd emerged. "Is this a common welcome?" she asked, gesturing at the show of strength.

Lord Muiredach returned her hard stare, barely acknowledging her criticism. "With this one, I can't afford taking chances."

"This is the one collected along with me?" she asked, as the earth heaved and split.

"Yes." Lord Muiredach focused his attention on the emergence. A murmur of expectation raced through the crowd. Then the grave opened up.

A figure shot high into the clear night, howling with triumph. He landed like a fabled warrior poised for battle in the center of the circle, his attention on the lord and Tanwen. The guard closed in but he ignored them, his gaze resting on Tanwen and the lord exclusively. He smiled a dazzling smile.

Something about it tugged at her memories.

He walked a few paces toward them, then bowed gracefully at the lord's feet. He looked up and performed a reverence. His manner was sophisticated and ferocious all at once. *He had never been so nakedly masculine before.* She didn't know why that leaped into her mind, but it did.

Nameless longing raged inside her. Perhaps it was for *him.* Her vampire lord had done a fine job of distracting her, but mourning for something lost still ran through every moment, even when her lord pinned her down with kisses.

Her past was a stranger to her since arising from the earth. In place of the spine-sturdiness of memories, all she had was nameless longing.

He closed the distance between them in a heartbeat. "Tanwen," he whispered, his lips only a breath away from her own.

Lord Muiredach raised his powerful hand and swung, flattening the newest vampire to lie at his feet. "This is the sorcerer who summoned one of the clan."

The new one dared look up, but did not attempt to rise. Blood from the lord's blow smeared his brow. Tanwen felt the ripple of desire for a taste of that blood that desire ran through every vampire in the gathering.

Lord Muiredach tipped the new one's face higher with his foot. "Vampires are not summoned by mortals."

The new one struggled to calm his breathing. "I am no longer a mortal, My Lord."

"Indeed you are not. How did you manage to be turned by one of us, when that vampire was the most outraged of us all?"

"Expectation quite often creates its own reality," the newest one said. "However, expecting something doesn't match the more focused power of intention. A subtle difference, but your vampire unwisely assumed that he could not be commanded, whereas it was my clear intention to be turned."

"Why was I not aware of your powers while you lived? You are a full-grown male."

"I armored myself against detection, even from my mother's spirit guide, who cautioned her to kill me at the hour of my birth."

Lord Muiredach eased his foot from the new one's chin. Not caring perhaps that it might provoke the vampire lord further, the new one's gaze reached up to Tanwen's.

She knew she should feel something just as powerful in return, and there was something there, something to do with her heart. She wanted to smile encouragement at him, but she merely stared back.

"Who turned this one?" Lord Muiredach called out to the assembled vampires.

A stir in the crowd created an opening, and a vampire emerged at the edge of the inner circle. After gazing down at the new one, the vampire bowed elegantly to Lord Muiredach. Yes, it was the one who'd come for them, she realized. Another memory. Perhaps it would all come back to her eventually.

"Osfrid," the vampire lord said. "Had you ever encountered such an affront before?"

"Never, my lord."

"And you could not resist it?"

"There was no fighting it. Once I arrived at the source of the summons, I confess I expected to see a witch. A female."

"And instead you found this. Him."

"She was also there," Osfrid said, gesturing toward Tanwen. "Once I'd managed to regain my wits, I realized this new arrival was warning me about the future value of her – a thing he had foreseen many times before."

Lord Muiredach turned Tanwen to face him. Suddenly he didn't seem pleased by what he saw. Tanwen pulled herself up as tall as she could go.

Something told her this was just the sort of reaction she'd always had to accusations.

"When you went to his hut that night, had you any intention to be made a vampire?"

She remembered fleeing from someone. "None, My Lord." At least, that's how it felt inside.

He gave a signal to the guards, who closed in on the new one, grabbed hold of him and dragged him to his feet. The new one fought to retain his dignity, but they held him fast.

"She did not know of my powers until that night," the new one said.

"Not a soul in your entire village seems to have suspected what you are."

"I had to keep up the masking spells to prevent my mother from taking action against me. She is a powerful wise woman."

"But not as powerful as you," Lord Muiredach said.

"You summoned me," the vampire said, "and told me she was a particular prize because of her former connection to the newest member of the Brotherhood."

"I have foreseen it," the new one replied. "My whole life up until this moment has led to this. Only this."

Lord Muiredach made his way to where the new one stood. "How is it that you remember any part of your former existence? Memories return, but not at this pace."

The new one didn't bother answering. He simply braced himself for what he must sense would come. Lord Muiredach withdrew a scarf from a fold in his tunic and wrapped his hand in the cloth. Then he withdrew a silver pendant from a pouch hidden in his tunic.

The arrival of the silver in their midst set a frightened hum through the vampires. Lord Muiredach rushed the new one, giving him no time to withdraw. The vampire lord slipped his hand behind the new one's neck, pressing the silver pendant onto the younger one's skin.

The new one shrieked and writhed.

"There are those you have a power over. And there are those you don't."

The new one nodded, growing faint in the lord's grasp.

"I can only assume your sorcery has rendered you able to bear this much at least," Lord Muiredach said.

The new one tried in vain to pull free of the guard. A sizzling sound accompanied a nauseating smell. The new one stiffened and bit back more cries of pain.

"Men dance to vampires' tune." Lord Muiredach's tone chilled her.

"Sorcerer," Lord Muiredach taunted.

The new one nodded frantically. Tanwen's heart broke for him.

"It would have been so much better for you if you'd not been so awfully clever."

"Forgive me, Lord!"

"Why should this fine assembly of vampire accept you as one of us when you so clearly serve your own needs before those who would be your family? Are you a coward?"

"No, Lord."

"I think you are." Lord Muiredach removed the medallion from the new one's neck. At a nod from Lord Muiredach, the guard dropped him. The new one scrambled on his knees to the vampire lord's feet and bowed low. She saw clearly the burnt brand upon the back of his neck.

"Please. You know I am not the same man who dared this grievous offence against you. I am turned now. I am one of you."

Lord Muiredach placed his foot firmly atop the new one's back. "You knew to look for her, the moment you broke free from your rest. None of us have done that before."

"I was not like other men. I never have been. I was an
outcast. I have never learned to live among my own
kind."

"That is painfully evident." Lord Muiredach removed
his foot from the new one's back. Tanwen saw the burn
mark heal rapidly before her eyes.

"I beg your indulgence," the new one said.

"Begging. I do enjoy begging when it's done right."
The vampire lord chuckled. Tanwen's heart chilled at the
cruelty so easily displayed by one who had been tender
with her these past days.

The new one looked up into the face of Lord
Muiredach. "I *am* a sorcerer. A clear reason for my
superior memory level."

Tanwen's heart flipped inside her chest. This new
vampire was his own worst enemy.

"Did you say you have foreseen this?" Lord
Muiredach said, his gesture encompassing the clan
gathered around them.

"Yes, Lord."

"Had you ever attempted to summon one of our kind
before?"

"Of course," the new one said. "Practice, learning
from past errors – what other way brings mastery?"

"I was never aware of your practice. If it was for
summoning, I should have sensed that."

Bowing deeply, the new one said, "Your pardon,
Lord. But I was adept from a young age at pulling a
cloak of secrecy over my powers."

"I suspect you have never had to explain yourself
before. You don't know the first thing about even
appearing to be sorry."

The new one finally bowed his head. Relief swept
through Tanwen.

"You know what you have become," Lord
Muiredach asked the new one.

"Vampire."

The assembly growled its approval.

"You know what sustains us."

"Blood."

Cries of allegiance rang out from vampire throats. Tanwen's pulse quickened. Her body thrummed with arousal.

"The night world is our kingdom, and I am its lord."

Lusty cheers filled the gathering. A female made her way to the front of the crowd. She made eye contact with Lord Muiredach, then gazed hungrily upon the new one.

Tanwen realized this female staked her claim upon the newest arrival. She should be outraged, jealous. *Was he not the source of her longing?*

She made her own move toward the new one. He was more than agreeable to look upon. He was far more handsome than the vampire lord. It must be the charged scent in the air. Everyone seemed to be just as aroused as she.

Lord Muiredach raised his hand once more, but not to strike. He held the back of his ringed hand to the new one, who gazed up at it, and then into the vampire lord's eyes.

After a long moment, the new one leaned forward and touched his lips to Lord Muiredach's ring. A crafty smile crept over the lord's features, chilling Tanwen deeply.

The gathering of vampires cried out as one.

The female knelt before the new one, taking his face in her hands, bringing her mouth to his. Tanwen enjoyed the sight of their kisses. It stirred her so that she dropped to her own knees, reaching for them both. Not to part them – to feel their passion through the palms of her hands.

The new one glanced over at her, his gaze troubled, as if the touch of another was foreign to him, no matter which life he was in. Tanwen leaned into him, her hands roaming over his lean muscles. She didn't mind one bit that the other female continued to caress him as well.

The gathering of vampires hummed their approval. Tanwen turned his face to hers and kissed him. So many emotions played out over his face. The one that moved her the most was an angry expression. But a delirium of joy overwhelmed the anger.

He reached for her. Tanwen opened her mouth to feel his tongue possess her, the way the vampire lord had possessed her. But this man – no, this vampire – held an obvious desire for her that Lord Muiredach could never hope to duplicate.

His tongue ran tenderly inside her cheeks, over her teeth, her gums. He cupped her head in his hands, his fingers spreading so she felt encased by his need for her. Lighter hands ran down her sides. Tanwen opened her eyes to gaze at the other female, whose cheek pressed tightly to the new one. The desire in her expression excited Tanwen beyond anything she had known before. Even in her former unremembered life, she couldn't have felt this way before.

She looked for confirmation of this feeling from the new one. He stared with burning intensity into Tanwen's eyes, unaware of the female who stroked her fingers over his shoulders and up through his hair.

Tanwen wanted to feel the same pull toward him as he had for her. He'd flown up from the earth intent only upon seeing her again. He must be the source of the longing, the mourning that swept through her like a lonely wind.

She wrapped her arms around his neck and fell into his embrace, though still glad for the presence of the other female. Tanwen could turn her face away if his scramble for intimacy cut too deep.

37

PEREDUR

Yn Wyddfrid village, fifteen years ago. 562

My mam grew so cold and distant afterwards, as though she wished the ground had swallowed her up when Tada died.

But my sister and I were still there. We needed her to take care of us, but it was as though she couldn't see or hear us. I never felt so frightened or alone.

I was just a young lad, then. What did I know about caring for a little sister or a grieving woman? She didn't even want to eat, while the both of us had rumbling stomachs.

One day I saw the son of the wise woman staring at me while I fished along the riverbank. He did not wave or speak to me, but merely stood among the trees staring at me. After awhile I just continued to fish and forgot about him.

By the time I leaned down to the grassy bank and collected the few fish I'd caught, I'd forgotten he was there. But when I arrived back at our hut, a basket of bread and fruit sat outside the doorway.

I breathed in all the scents from the wise woman's hut that still clung to the basket. My stomach growled hungrily even as it dropped with embarrassment that we should receive charity.

It didn't take long before hunger won out over pride...without so much as a scuffle.

CAVAN

The forest beyond Yn Wyddfrid village, 562

I watched Peredur struggle to catch fish for himself, for his hungry sister and his mam who had no appetite anyway. He seemed preoccupied for one so young. Yes, my own age, really, but I looked upon him as a boy and upon myself as something else entirely. On this particular day it was as though I could see the man he would become, already emerging in his features.

But of course that ability to see things no one else could see always happened with me.

What troubled me was the blue haze that glowed around him, like an aura – but not quite. Auras I saw all the time, but this glow was different.

It was shaped like the adult warrior of a future Peredur, mirroring his every action, but several sizes larger. My experience was that auras were simply glowing ripples reaching out from the person into the air surrounding him, not a giant, perfectly formed version of that person's future self.

I didn't know what to make of it.

I stood watching him until he eventually felt my probing stare. Everyone did that, found my gaze disturbing, because I hadn't perfected the ability to get the information I wanted without revealing my mental probes. Sometimes I got so near to asking Mam how I might try this or do that. I yearned for the simple joy of learning from her store of experience, but that was simply out of the question.

I had to keep up my cloaking spell in her presence, and that took everything I had.

CAVAN

The wise woman's hut, ten years ago. 567

The second time things escalated with Mam, I had asked whether the stag-man had died, since we had skipped two solstices without a trip into the night woods.

I'm not sure why I felt compelled to ask that question, but the words slipped out into the quiet evening before I realized it wasn't me simply thinking – I'd actually spoken the words.

"What did you say?" she asked in that terrible voice she'd used on that other horrible night.

I whirled to face her. "I'm sorry, Mam. I didn't mean to say it."

She took two steps and slapped me hard, nearly knocking me over. "Don't you dare say you didn't mean it. Don't be a coward, Cavan. If you say something, then stand by your words."

I stood in shock, holding a palm to my burning cheek. I didn't say anything else, afraid to make it worse.

"Tell me what you said," she demanded.

I shook my head.

"You know I can find it all out for myself," she said.

It was a strange elation to be this scared of something. My knowledge of my own powers left me with a sense of being untouchable. The idea that I was suddenly at my mam's mercy made my blood rush joyously, and with breathtaking alarm.

I didn't attempt to cast a protective charm because she was in such a heightened state, she would have seen through me. I was not yet powerful enough to take on my beautiful, destructive mam.

So I planted my feet, lifted my chin and looked her in the eye.

38

Clan coastal territory, 577

Tanwen stretched in the embrace of the new one, clawing for his clothes to be off. Another smiling male obliged her, slipping the new one's trewes down. The female pulled his tunic over his head. He ignored them all – ignored everyone but Tanwen.

Still a feeling dogged her, the feeling that this lover was not the one she wanted. His face lined with the exquisite pain of being so near to his desired one. Tanwen looked into his eyes.

Large and gray, rimmed by violet blue, they looked at her – looked through her. They told of desolation, of triumph, of deception as they revealed naked emotion. He looked for some sign from her, something that would tell him to carry through and take her at last.

Tanwen closed her eyes, grabbed him and pulled him to her, crushing her lips against his. She couldn't return his emotions, but she needed him to stop this building hunger.

She opened her lips in a grin that he was welcome to interpret any way he chose. Someone lowered her to the ground. Languidly, she turned her head and opened her eyes.

The crowd closed in around them, growling encouragement. Her mind withdrew, away from the new one's breathing in her ear, away from the weight of him, away from his touch upon her, away from the madness and heat he stirred up inside her.

She heard her own moans of pleasure. And there was pleasure. It rolled through her, forced her to meet it when she writhed and discovered the new one's weight stretched along her body, trapping her. She gasped from it, ached to call *his* name. She didn't know this new one's name, but even if she had, his wasn't the name she wanted to call.

Tanwen opened her eyes. He gazed down at her with those accusing, sad gray eyes. She wanted. She craved. She demanded. It almost didn't matter that this new one was not the one she sought to remember.

The vampires surrounding them filled the air with sounds of lusty encouragement. Some of them already followed into their own carnal celebration. She'd never felt so alive.

Impatient, Tanwen grabbed the new one down to her again, shutting her eyes and dissolving into a deep kiss. Suddenly she saw in her mind's eye a precious face – his glistening green eyes gazing upon her with sorrow. Hair dark and thick, tousled by a wintry gust. Gathering her into his arms, wading deep into the night, into the frozen forest.

Her eyes opened to gaze upon the new one, who looked at her as if he knew what she'd seen. Drawing quickly back from her as if she'd spewed poison into his face, he allowed himself to be pulled away and down into the mass of writhing arms and thrusting hips.

Another female entwined her body around the new one, who kissed her as though he'd never burst through the veil between lives, intent to claim Tanwen for his own. The sight of them twisted together should make her violent with jealousy, but he had not been the one to carry her into that forest.

Her memories would return to her in time. Lord Muiredach said they would. This first glimpse was only the beginning. Her dark lover would appear to her again. It was for him alone she'd done this. For him alone.

39

CAVAN

Along the road just outside Yn Wyddfrid village, ten years ago. 567

I am not crying. I will not cry.
The boys from the village push my face into the mud. If I wanted to, I could hurt every one of them. I could make them cry and it would be easy. But the fear of Mam burning on a mound of brush, tied to a stake while the village looked on—

Well, it's just easier to spit the mud out of my mouth, whip my head back and forth and push with all my might.

"Stop!" I hear dimly. "What is going on there?"

The pressure on my shoulders lets up immediately. Squelching footsteps splash muddy water over me, but I'm grateful that it's over.

A frantic chase ensues as I wipe my face with a soggy sleeve. Four boys and only two adults, but two are caught and that's better than none. The men haul the squirming boys back over to me, where I stand, trying to salvage some dignity, at least.

"Were they ganging up on you?" the old warrior snarled.

I merely nodded, still trying to catch my breath.

"How many of you were there?" he asked the unfortunate boy in his grasp. "Eh?" He shook the lad hard.

"Two more, Sir!"

"And how many were you against?" he asked.

The boy hung his head. "One, Sir." I knew he was only contrite because he knew he was about to catch it. It was only a matter of time before another group of village boys got after me again. But I had to admit, this was a moment to savor. Few and far between they were, so I would take my pleasure where I might.

The old warrior swung his arm, thick as a tree limb, clipping the boy on the head, knocking him nearly off his feet. He swung several times till my tormentor was red-faced and sniffling.

The second boy held out slightly longer than the first one, but this warrior was warming to the task. All I had to do was remember the feeling of their hands pushing me down to stop the cries for mercy that rose to my lips.

Once he'd let up on the second boy, the old warrior forced them to look at me. "This boy has no father, and will never be trained to fight alongside you."

My heart dropped into my stomach. Did he suppose this made me feel any better? It made me feel closer to crying than I ever had, even down in the mud.

"He will need your protection when you are all grown to manhood. He is a part of our village, and as one of us he deserves better than what I saw here today. Is that understood?"

The boys nodded glumly, their eyes filled with blame directed at me for their humiliation. I had to do something, or I would be looking over my shoulder until the next time they caught me, and more stealthily next time, for that would be the only lesson they learned from this – to avoid being caught.

"It's my fault, Sir," I said.

The boys looked confused, and the two men looked bemused.

"Is it?" the other man asked.

"I called the one who ran off a mam's boy, and he sucks his thumb, and this one." I pointed to the blonde one. "He's thick as an ox."

The men laughed. "Is that true?" the old warrior asked the blond simpleton.

The boy nodded, eyes filled with confusion at my words. I had obviously been victorious over them for the first time in my lonely life.

"Come here," the old warrior motioned. This was a risky attempt to gain a sense of fraternity with boys I honestly despised. The blond one *was* thick as an ox.

But I was giddy with the hope that this might work in some warped, painful way. I took the few steps forward until I stood before the unnerving man. He stared down at me as though I was something stuck on the bottom of his shoe.

"You don't like what I said about you just then."

I stared straight into his eyes. He seemed completely stunned by my lack of fear, but what was there to fear, really? From any of them.

"No, Sir."

"You wish you were being trained to fight alongside these boys?"

I simply nodded.

"And you wish you were treated the same as they are?"

"Yes, Sir."

He and the other man laughed then. Resentment burned in my chest, until he grabbed for me and hauled me forward. Then my heart surged with anxious dread, because this was a man accustomed to separating heads from bodies.

My breath caught in my chest at the blinding pain as his heavy paw swiped and connected. I tried to dodge out of the way of the next blow, but he made sure that I was unsuccessful. It was almost too much to hold my cries back, but I had to best those boys. I just had to.

It seemed that he went on a little too long, that he dished it out to me a bit harder than to the other two. But of course that was from my new perspective. When he finally let off swinging, I'm sure I appeared as red-faced and teary as they.

"If you call one of these boys thick, they're liable to make you regret it," the old warrior chuckled.

I looked the blond one in the eye, then. "Sorry I called you that," I said.

He seemed stunned, and glanced over at the other boy to be certain he wasn't hearing things.

"I'm sorry," I said to the other boy, too, wiping my tears with the back of my hand, though I hadn't called him anything. He'd been the one to hold me down in the mud.

The other boy shrugged and said, "Sorry about the mud."

"Yeah," the blond one said. "Me, too."

The men seemed very satisfied with how it had all worked out. They headed down the road to the village along with the boys, neither of whom belonged to either man, other than the fact that they all belonged to the village.

I stood in the road and watched them walk away from me, starting to shiver from the cold muddy water plastering my clothes to my skin. A chill wind blew rattling leaves around my feet.

Turning in the opposite direction, my head and neck protesting the movement, I walked through the forest to my mother's hut. Tears welled free when there was no one to see or hear. Best get them out of the way before Mam sorted me out from my tumble into the stream bank, which is what I would tell her.

40

Clan coastal territory, 577

Tanwen sat up from her day's slumber, turning to look around the cavern at the prone forms strewn about like the aftermath of a drunken revelry. *Boom, boom...* In the distance surf crashed against the farthest reaches of their subterranean home.

She hungered. Images of porridge and bread, thick stew, apples baked at the hearth crowded into her mind, but these brought a surge of queasy distaste. She couldn't remember what it was she had to have. All she knew was that she must have it soon.

Rising to her feet, she nearly collided with the new one, who looked as though he'd kept a vigil for her. She hid her unease with a kiss. It had the desired effect. Now he was just as unbalanced as she.

"Have you been awake long?" she asked.

He looked away, at the cavern. Then he turned back to her. "I doubt I've ever been awake, before this."

"You know my name."

He smiled warmly. "Tanwen," he said, as though speaking her name made everything right. And hearing someone else say it did make her feel better.

"I thought so." When she put an arm around him a little warning call began inside her. She felt she was being rash with the new one, as though another form of her would not proceed as she now meant to. "Do you know, I've tried very hard since you arrived, but your name never comes to my lips."

The clue she craved shot through his eyes. It hurt him to realize she couldn't remember him. And he suspected something, perhaps the very thing that bubbled up inside of her. "That is the way it is here," he said. "You'll remember more things. Just give it time."

He smiled, a rueful smile that tugged at her.

"I had a short memory flit through my head," she said. "Just a short one. A blink, really."

He glanced warily at her, even as he slipped an arm around her. "Mmm?" he encouraged.

"Do you recall being in the forest with me?" she asked, fixing him with a direct stare.

He did not flinch. "Of course."

He seemed so confident. What if her memory was the thing that was suspect? It was merely the first thing to break through. Perhaps it wasn't fully formed. "What were we doing there?" she asked.

"In the forest?" he asked, a smile tipping up one side of his mouth. "We did many things in the forest."

Tanwen recalled the face that had gazed at her in her memory. The dark hair, not this vampire's golden hair. The green eyes, not these gray ones concealing truths like mist. "Well, in my memory we were doing something you'd likely remember."

"Did you say you can't remember my name yet?" he asked.

"Yes. I did say that." She pushed back from him a little, but his grip tightened.

"Maybe if I help you out with another memory, my name will come to you," he said.

Tanwen nodded, sighing at the way he avoided her question.

"One afternoon," he said, "you and your sister came upon me on the road to the fair."

She closed her eyes, images flooding her. Morvyth's hand in hers. This man kneeling in front of her sister, making her feel special. Herbs. Pouches. Coins.

This vampire saw inside of Tanwen mind, somehow. Suddenly she wasn't certain of her original plan. If he could peer into her mind, he might take her memory and rework it, make it reflect him instead of the true man she recalled. He wasn't a normal vampire. She'd learned he was a vampire who had once been a sorcerer, the first to come through with his memories intact.

Another scene opened in her mind. A ring fell into her outstretched palm. His gray eyes looked solemnly into hers as he helped her to hold onto it, so she wouldn't drop it.

Cavan.

She saw that he knew, somehow. He heard her mind whisper his name. His eyes crinkled into a triumphant smile.

"Yes. You have it."

"Cavan," she said aloud, refusing to let her mind do the talking for her.

He tugged her closer. She crushed the urge to resist, relaxing into his embrace.

"Oh, my love," he whispered, nuzzling her neck.

He appeared distracted now by his feelings for her. She must try to coax the name of her true love from him while he was off guard.

"I don't know why it took me so long to remember," she said, pressing her cheek into his hair.

"I knew you would reach for me one day. One night, I guess we should say now." He laughed.

"Nights have always been my favorite time, anyway, ever since..."

He stilled. "Since you ran to my mam and me? You remember that night?"

"No," she said. "Not that one. I mentioned earlier...the forest."

He pulled back from her, holding her out so he could see her face. "Go on," he said.

"You came to me while my family slept. We went far into the forest so we could be alone. No chance for discovery."

He said nothing. Forcing a smile, his eyes grew hard.

"You see how special that night was for me," she said. "It's the first memory to break through."

"Ah," he said, his eyes revealing emotions battling with his mask of calm.

This was harder than she'd hoped. He wasn't giving an inch, and the other man's name refused to surface. "I'm hungry," she said. "Aren't you?"

He remained silent for a moment, his gaze probing hers. "Very hungry," he said, releasing her.

She forced herself to maintain an even pace as they made their way to the cavern entrance. How she wanted to bolt – away from Cavan or nearer to a meal, it made no difference.

41

CAVAN

The wise woman's hut, ten years ago. 567

Dashing inside our hut, I looked everywhere for Mam. She was nowhere to be found. I felt abandoned. Tears welled up in my heart and my eyes burned with crying that wanted to come out, but wouldn't.

Then she was behind me. I don't know how I'd missed her in my frantic search, but there she was. I turned.

She glared at me, as if I'd betrayed her to the village elders. As though at my say so, she was to be burned as a witch.

"It's your doing," she said.

"No, Mam!" I cried, dropping to my knees and clutching her hands.

"Let go!" she said, trying to shake me off.

"No, Mam! Please listen – I didn't do anything wrong!"

She pulled my hands off hers with superior strength. I was shrinking, shrinking, until my words were no longer words, only the impotent cries of a baby.

"Hush, now," Mam said, forcing her breast into my mouth. I shook my head from side to side, protesting this outrage, but she guided my face back to her breast with

unyielding hands, and I was made to suck on her nipple. In a little while it comforted me. But I had sharp little teeth, and I watched as Mam's face lined with the pain of feeding me.

I thrashed about with all my might – in my mind. In reality I lay there as though deep in sweet slumber. I sensed Mam rising and creeping over to look at me, felt her soft fingers brush a sweaty tendril of hair from my forehead as she'd so often done.

I moaned. Mam bent down and kissed me, then whispered again, a soothing charm that she thought would keep me safe.

I heard Mam return to bed. I lay fighting her sleep charm with every ounce of fight I had in me. I prayed not to be taken where these dreams were leading me. But the darkness blotted it all out again.

PEREDUR

Yn Wyddfrid village, 567

It made me itch to go with the war band – I'd seen the spoils with which the fighters returned. How much easier we would have it, if we didn't need to rely on extras brought in stealth to Mam's door.

Naturally, I was grateful. I would be an unbearable little prat if I wasn't. I already had a reputation for knocking the more idiotic boys down a peg or two when trouble brewed in our village.

This morning I nearly tripped over a parcel laid directly in the path before the doorway. I unwrapped the worn cloth that held it together, and found an old wineskin filled with excellent wine, a round of cheese and a wholesome loaf of bread. As always, my stomach rumbled at the delicious aroma that rose up from the food.

If I could start going on those raids, I could find enough loot to keep us eating like kings and queens, and no one from the village would have to take food from their family's stores to leave for us like this.

I looked out over the village rooftops and watched the smoke rising lazily into the morning. It was time I approached the sword master. I had no father to approach him on my behalf. I must do it for myself.

I re-entered the hut and handed the food to Mam, who had at long last begun to take some interest in herself and us for the past few weeks. It was several years since Tada's body had been carried back to us, several years since we'd all gathered around the pyre that scorched his earthly remains into cinders. I looked at her smiling at my sister, as Mam went through the supplies in the cloth bundle before beginning to make a meal out of it.

Yes, the first thing after we ate and after my chores were done, I meant to pay the sword master a visit, and ask humbly to be taken on for training.

Of course, that's not how it played out at all.

First of all, Mam had picked this morning, of all mornings, to want to clear out some old wattle at the north side of the hut. That meant my entire morning and part of the afternoon was gone, and with it my uplifted mood. I was surly by the time we were finished—was bad-tempered enough to make Mam reach for me, grabbing hold wherever she could make contact to lay reminders on me.

That did nothing at all for my mood, for why would the sword master take on a whelp, young as me, still being treated like a boy when I wanted desperately to be a man? I took her blows as bravely as I could, but I was also angry and humiliated.

When she left off hitting me, I turned on her, accusing Mam of treating me like a baby. Then I did something completely unconscionable. I shoved Mam and said, "Don't ever strike me again, Woman!"

The look on her face shredded my heart, but I couldn't go back on what I'd just said, or I really would be a child unworthy of beginning my training with the sword master. Instead, I stormed out of the hut and ignored the sound of tears in her voice as Mam called after me.

42

Clan coastal territory, 577

Lord Muiredach sauntered toward them. Cavan placed himself slightly in front of her – a protective gesture Tanwen would have found endearing if it hadn't been Cavan who did it. He bowed stylishly before the leader, who inclined his head ever so slightly.

"We've sent a hunting party to bring our meal to us tonight," he said. "More celebrations for our new arrivals." He raised his hand to take Tanwen's. She stepped past Cavan and took it, resting her hand upon their lord's. He led her toward the cavern entrance.

Tanwen felt Cavan fuming as he fell into step behind them. She was in a mood to let him stew. If he meant to make her believe that she'd always been his, when her real beloved's memory had burst through, then he could fret like a fussy brat.

The sound of the ocean and the moist air rolled over her as they stepped out into the night. The water's energy made her dizzy. Lord Muiredach put a steadying hand over hers.

"The water is not our friend, Dear One," he said. "We use it to our advantage. Our cavern entrance is far enough away to keep us from sickening under its power, but our enemies wouldn't think to find our home so near it."

As they walked farther from the sea, her strength rose. She wasn't quite as famished as when she awoke.

"Who would our enemies be, my lord?" she asked.

Lord Muiredach glanced back at Cavan. "He can tell us," Lord Muirdach said, glancing back at Cavan. "Can't you?"

"My Lord," Cavan said. "Vampires have many enemies. Humans, of course. Werewolves. The elves can be problematic at times. The ones who seek us most stubbornly are the brethren."

Tanwen's heart surged with recognition. She knew about them. She turned and looked back at Cavan, her pulse surging with excitement. He met her expression with brooding disapproval.

Looking back at Lord Muiredach, she asked, "Who are the brethren, my lord?"

"They are foes not to be taken lightly." The three of them rounded a large outcropping of jagged rock that helped to conceal their cavern from the curious. This shield blocked the sea energy even further. Tanwen felt incredibly alive once she'd passed it. If she had to go for a week without feeding, she felt quite able, now.

But the promise of more blood like she'd tasted a few nights before set her into a state of high arousal. Before her a throng of vampires already gathered at the protected clearing, turning at the entrance of Lord Muiredach and parting to allow him into their midst. Males bowed slightly and females curtsied.

"Don't you worry your pretty head about them." He gazed at her with assurance. "I shan't let any of them near you. And of course the sorcerer will look out for you." He smirked.

Tanwen glanced again at Cavan. He wasn't close enough to hear them, but his gaze met hers like daggers. His continued possessiveness angered her. Perhaps she ought to be flattered by someone who'd cross the veil of death solely to claim her as his own.

But she wasn't.

In the center of this gathering, a small group of people knelt upon the springy bracken. A young man sheltered a maiden in his embrace. A sturdy farmer pushed a younger man behind him, while a villager in fine clothes held himself like the leader of this group of prisoners, even in this hour of despair.

"You see, the brethren aren't happy with how we feed. How we live," Lord Muiredach said as they neared the frightened knot. "They're not happy with anything we do, when it comes down to it."

The people craned their necks this way and that, keeping the encroaching ring of vampires in their sights. The maiden whimpered. Instead of feeling pity for her, Tanwen's blood stirred as she sensed the girl's fear.

"I find it tiresome and hypocritical in the extreme. The brethren drink blood as we do."

Tanwen looked up into the vampire lord's eyes. "The brethren are vampires?"

He nodded. "Vampires. They hunt down their own."

She looked behind her once more at Cavan. This time he gazed at her with smug satisfaction. He shouldn't know what they said. It really was insufferable.

Two of the hulking vampires stepped forward and grabbed up the maiden, who set up a howling. Her would-be-protector got several kicks for his efforts. Even the well-dressed villager spoke up for her.

But it was clearly in vain. Dumped at Lord Muiredach's feet, the girl saw Tanwen and flung herself upon her feet, crying piteously. Shivers of delight ran up Tanwen's spine – clearly not the effect the maiden intended.

The vampire lord gestured toward the girl and smiled. "You and Cavan are the guests of honor at this feast. You may take first bite."

The girl looked up in hopeless dismay. She shook her head and tried to back away, but Tanwen gazed down at her, a sense of power overtaking her as she looked into the maiden's wide eyes. The longer she stared into the girl's eyes, the more still the girl became. Tanwen's sense of mastery grew.

It was as though Tanwen herself were commanding the fear to dampen. The maiden looked up at Tanwen with complete trust, without any of the terror that still made the girl's blood sing in those veins.

"Go on," Lord Muiredach said.

Tanwen leaned forward, took the girl by the shoulders and pulled her to her feet. The girl smiled through tears that glistened in the firelight.

The protests of the men grew in volume as Tanwen's mouth opened, her teeth bared. She couldn't remember when her fangs grew to be so prominent, but right now it seemed her entire being was stored in those two sharp teeth.

Her mouth neared the white neck, the skin fluttering with the force of the girl's pulse. Lunging forward, Tanwen sunk her fangs deeply into the sweet flesh. Dimly she heard the girl's cry of pain.

Blood gushed into her mouth. Every part of her rose up in celebration of the flood of energy, power and life itself. She swallowed greedily as it trickled down the sides of her mouth.

Tanwen crushed the girl close. She struggled at first, but to Tanwen it was of no more consequence than the scrambling of a kitten. A part of her marveled at such new found strength.

Just like the fisherman, this maiden's thoughts and memories flowed along with her blood into Tanwen's consciousness. The brave young man who tried to protect her screamed out his agony as the images of their love played for Tanwen to see. She drank up the memories and pulsing blood. Both.

Impressions. Passions. Sensations. All jumbled together in a disorienting cascade. Tanwen could no longer hold onto thoughts – not this girl's, not her own.

The blood was sweet and light, light as the girl's hair when it hung down, as she kissed her darling.

Bubbling energy rose as blood coursed into Tanwen, spreading outward like euphoria. Her own triumphant laughter started a cacophony of roars, cheers and growls.

A male scream filtered its way through her feeding frenzy. Tanwen shrugged it off, sinking her mouth deeply over the girl's opened throat. As the girl's pulse grew weaker, the few fragmented memories dimmed. Yet the scream grew louder, punching its way through to Tanwen at last.

Raising her head from the girl's neck, Tanwen focused hard on the form that crawled on hands and knees to her feet. Looking down, she saw the brave young man clutching at his beloved's legs, ignoring Tanwen altogether.

Tanwen gazed at him with fascination. His screams became wails. His wails became sobs. His loss touched her deeply, stirring up memories of her own.

More of her own memories returned to her, images of the beloved face framed with dark hair. Of eyes huge with longing for her, longing like this man's for the maiden whose essence now tripped and flitted through Tanwen.

More details of that night – when her own lover's arms scooped her into an embrace, carrying her deep, deep into the winter forest – rose up inside of her with every sob the man uttered. She knew what he felt. Knew his hopeless confusion in the darkest part of herself.

Tanwen let the maiden's body slump to the ground. The young man crept forward in horrified disbelief, touching the girl's face. He shook his head – *no, no, no.*

Breaking out of this bubble, she looked up, searching for Cavan. He hadn't yet taken a drink from the nobleman stretched and held before him. His attention was fixed upon her, and her alone. He looked ill, as though he sensed the memories breaking through. Her memories of the one she truly loved were so close to the surface.

She looked down at the weeping man. By that strange wordless compulsion which had calmed the girl moments before, the young man tore his teary gaze from the maiden and looked up at Tanwen.

She must taste his life force. If she could suck his memories into herself, she was certain the name of her own beloved would finally surface.

43

PEREDUR

Sword master's hut, Yn Wyddfrid, ten years ago. 567

I approached the sword master with my heart beating so fast I thought I might faint. Yet more blows to my smarting pride. What more must I be forced to swallow today?

No matter – if I meant to begin training, this would be the least of the problems I faced. The sword master looked up from where he sat, carefully cleaning a blade. The expression on his face was impossible to read – to hide one's emotions from an opponent was probably a good thing.

I resolved to keep my own swirling emotions in check as I closed the gap between us. He set down the sword and rose to his feet, which gave me hope. It was a sign of respect, and my self-regard badly needed some of that.

I bowed before clearing my throat. "I have come to ask you to take me on as a student."

"Have you?"

"Yes, sir. I realize that, normally my...my father would approach you." I dared to look up at him. He gazed at me kindly, so I took heart and continued. "But, as my father is now gone, I've taken it upon myself to ask for permission to train with you."

I tipped my chin up, praying I seemed confident, while my hopes collided with dread inside my chest. The sword master strolled slowly around me, looking me over. I stood before him, skin prickling at the state of being on display.

Without warning, he set upon me, grasping me by the arms and twisting. I knew he meant for me to tumble backwards. One part of me warred against striking back at the sword master, but another part recognized this for what it was. So I grabbed his hands, yanked and slithered and did everything I could to avoid being slammed to the ground. Somehow I slipped from his grasp and landed a kick at his leg.

My mouth gaped open in shock. What was wrong with me today? Shouting at my mother, who'd had every right to correct her rude son. Kicking the sword master after asking to become his student?

But the sword master merely inclined his head toward me, in recognition of my success in giving his surprise attack the slip. "Do you own a sword?" he asked.

"No, sir," I replied, only too aware that my father's sword had been lost on the battlefield where he'd lost his life. I glanced down at my hand, turning it so I could see the ring that my father's friend had given to me in my father's memory.

"Well, we will see what we can do to get you a blade." He motioned for me to follow him. As I passed him, he placed a hand on my shoulder, and I liked that male contact. To be honest, Mam had been so lost in her grief that she'd kept all the caresses that she could have given me freely, locked up inside her broken heart. The only bodily contact had come from my little sister pestering me.

Once again I felt like crying – with relief and joy this time, not from frustration and wounded pride. I managed to keep my swirling emotions in check, but just barely.

The sword master brought me into the shed he used behind his hut. The back wall of the shed was hung with swords of varying lengths, and many different states of integrity. He walked me over to them and gestured with an elegant sweep of his hand.

"You may choose one of these to be your sword," he said.

I couldn't trust my ears. "Sir?"

"You heard right, Peredur. Look them over carefully. And you must heft them," which he did with one. "See which one feels natural in your grip."

I nodded and took a steadying breath. I forced myself to move along the display of swords and took the time to regard and assess each of them.

I passed the one I wanted, but immediately felt remorse and backtracked. The sword that called to me was a beautiful blade which was frankly too large for my size – but no matter. The pommel was solid and simple in design. I removed it from the pegs that held it in place.

What a beauty. It felt good in my hand, though its heaviness was somewhat troubling. As though he could read my thoughts, the sword master said, "Don't worry about that. You'll develop the muscles you'll need to wield it properly."

I nodded, enamored of my new blade as if it were a love affair I had embarked upon.

And that's exactly what I had done.

CAVAN

A few weeks later – Sword master's hut

It was not easy to watch Peredur embark upon his sword training without being consumed by jealousy. After that day in the forest, when I'd risked a harsh beating to be considered as one of the village boys by the two who'd tormented me, I held out a strange hope that maybe one day I might be considered for training by the sword master.

When Peredur broke with tradition and approached the sword master himself to ask for training, and was granted it, I felt sure that a similar request from me might also be granted. When I walked up to the sword master one morning, resisting the very strong urge to simply charm him into agreeing to whatever I desired, I knew I'd miscalculated.

"Young Cavan," he said in greeting.

"Sir," I bowed slightly with the perfect amount of respect.

He inclined his head slightly as if to question my presence there.

I took a deep breath. "I am of an age..." I began. This was intolerable. I hated the way he looked at me, as though he could see through my nervous attempt at an adult chat with him. He was very intimidating, just sitting there – even to a young sorcerer like me.

"I am of an age when most boys begin their sword training," I said.

"Yes," he said. He didn't smirk, didn't belittle, and yet something about him emanated disdain for my request. I admit, I had no muscles to speak of, and was a social fringe-dweller of the village. Still, this sword master could turn anyone into a hardened warrior by the time he was finished training them.

"I have no father to make this request of you, Sir," I said, not realizing until I said it how sad those words made me. "But this has been a cherished wish of mine, all the same. I beg of you to consider my request, made on my own behalf."

There – it was out. I'd done it.

Before a single word left his lips, I regretted not having used a charm to influence him toward a favorable reply. I knew the opportunity had already slipped through my fingers.

He explained how everyone in the village is needed for their various strengths, and that my service to ours would be much better demonstrated in some other way.

"I know I am not much to look at now, sir," I said, using my most self-effacing tone. "But I am certain with your superior ability to train practically anyone, even some dullards—" Here I snickered. "Surely I can be no worse a student than they?"

I looked up at him then, pleased with my show of humility. He returned my gaze with a troubled one of his own.

"I appreciate your passion for it." Thankfully he did not use a patronizing tone at all. "Perhaps your knowledge of my training skills will help you to understand that I only train those born to a warrior's path. It's something I sense in a person, and I never train someone who doesn't have that."

My heart sank. Truly.

I lowered my gaze and fought the urge to cry. I took a moment to compose myself. Then I raised my head and walked away from him.

44

Clan coastal territory, 577

With the speed of their new vampire bodies, Cavan closed the distance between them. Before Tanwen could cast her eyes back down to the grieving man, Cavan stood before her. It was Cavan's gray eyes she saw before her, not the young man's sorrow-laden ones that seemed to trigger her memories.

He meant to deprive her of this chance to discover the identity of her beloved.

Tanwen moved then, diving fast and hard between the young man and Cavan's bared fangs. A growl she didn't recognize as her own, burst from her chest. Two outstretched arms rammed into Cavan, toppling the vampire from his intent to bite.

She whirled and rolled, leaping to the young man's side and lifting him to her chest. Tanwen needed this chance to feed and gather power, her own memories so very close now. Cavan rebounded, already a hair's breadth from her face. They bared their fangs at each other, hissing and growling their warnings.

With her connection to the young man broken, Tanwen couldn't keep him calm. He scrambled to his feet and ran.

The assembly of vampires cheered at the prospect of sport. They stepped back and formed a large circle, hemming in the young man, who ran anyway, looking for an opening for escape.

Tanwen leaped to cut him off, but was in turn cut off by Cavan. Did she look as fearsome as he did? Cavan's face twisted into a mask of malicious delight as he recognized her despair.

Growling and baring her fangs, Tanwen looked for her own opening to slip past her rival. He was fast, too fast to dodge. The young man evaded them both while Cavan's show of force distracted their quarry. That gave Tanwen the opening she needed.

Leaping high and across the clearing, Tanwen grabbed fast to the young man, mid-stride. Before he could cry out, she sank her fangs into his throat.

She fell forward with the force of the collision, pulling the man down with her. A grunt of pain burst from him as they landed hard. An immediate rush of energy from his bid to survive surged forth into her eager mouth.

Tanwen knew she'd have to act quickly or lose her chance to get as much of the precious blood as she could gather up. She swallowed and sucked again, only to feel the young man's body lurch with the force of Cavan landing on top of them both.

The man screeched in horror and pain as Cavan ripped into his legs like a maddened dog. Tanwen hissed and growled in outrage. The young man trembled violently with the shock of the assault and his profound loss of blood.

There was nothing else to do. Tanwen opened her mouth and ripped into the young man's throat. A gush of blood – and images – flooded her mouth and senses.

But Cavan sucked just as hard at the finite supply within this man. Warped memories half-rose in her mind and retreated before she could absorb a true impression of them. It was like grabbing for outstretched hands before being swept over a waterfall.

The body convulsed and went still.

Tanwen sat back, catching her breath, stilling her temper. As she watched Cavan empty the last drops from the young man, she saw Lord Muiredach approach from the corner of her eye.

He reached out for her. Tanwen took a steadying breath, placed her hand in his and rose to her feet. With tender care, the vampire lord leaned in as for a kiss...only to lick the blood from her lips and chin.

45

CAVAN

Yn Wyddfrid village, seven years ago. 570

I laced Peredur's porridge with a spell to put him on edge – a quick-acting one whose effects wouldn't last much longer than an hour or so. Just long enough to set his day on the wrong course.

I watched from my vantage point, patient in the knowledge that he would come to grief this day.

The sword master's 'darling' would feel some of what I'd felt every moment I had to watch him mature into the warrior I would never become.

The boys – nearly men, now – practiced their close fighting skills with sloppy moves. I'd only placed the spell on Peredur's breakfast, but his sour mood spilled over onto the others. I couldn't have asked for anything better.

PEREDUR

In the sword master's training yard.

It was the boy I liked the least who taught me something valuable after a rather frightening close call. Owen lashed out at Bledros when the latter kept dodging out of reach during the practice for close fighting skills with daggers.

For a reason that now escapes me, I couldn't bear their constant nattering at one another. Owen taunted Bledros as a mam's boy, for not standing and fighting.

"Stop joking about," I snapped with uncharacteristic belligerence.

"Who died and put *you* in charge?" Owen said, shoving me.

God knows why I shoved him back. That was all it took for us to charge at one another, kicking, punching, falling and rolling in the dust. We really gave it to each other, until we tired and stopped for breath.

Out of the corner of my eye, I saw Cynfelyn held around the neck by the sword master, who had disarmed him, of course. I scrambled to my feet, Owen already upright. Silence hung over our group like a disapproving spirit.

When he figured he'd impressed upon us the ease with which he'd 'dispatched' one of our number while our attention was diverted elsewhere, the sword master released Cynfelyn, who took a few steps and turned to face him, his head bowed in disgrace.

But the sword master shook his head. "It is not you who should bear the disgrace, but these two, whose personal affairs took their attention away from the safety of their war band."

Cynfelyn stepped aside, that Owen and myself could approach the sword master. My stomach was in knots.

"Which of you started the fight?" he asked.

After a slight pause, only long enough to gather my courage, I said, "I did, Sir." I felt everyone gazing upon me, especially Owen who'd goaded me into my rash behavior.

"You?" he asked, unconvinced.

"Yes, Sir." No one contradicted me. I was the one who tried to stop Owen from picking a fight with Bledros. Look what a success I'd made of it.

"You see how vulnerable that made your fellow members of this war band?"

I nodded, unable to speak. In the field, we needed to be able to rely on one another. But my frustration had gotten the better of me, and in turn had put my friends in danger. I actually felt sick at the vision that swam before me – of Cynfelyn dead on the ground, his neck slit, blood pooling around him.

"Cynfelyn," the sword master said. The boy stepped forward. "Hand me your knife."

CAVAN

At the edge of the village

I noticed that some of the villagers stopped what they were doing and found a spot where they could see what was unfolding. Even better, Peredur would have a crowd to witness his humiliation.

Could I even begin to hope that Tanwen was among them to see it? She'd been making eyes at Peredur lately, and nothing cast its gloom over my already dismal existence in this village as did his preening for Tanwen.

When Cynfelyn slipped his knife from its sheath and passed it to the sword master, my heart leaped in my chest. This promised to be wonderfully memorable.

Then Peredur stepped forward, knelt before a wooden bench and held his arm steady upon it. I held my breath in anticipation, wishing my rival looked a little less stoic, but I would enjoy this gift nonetheless.

PEREDUR

In the sword master's training yard

My stomach curdled, my skin crawling with shame. I tried to convince myself it would be alright, that I would not disgrace myself, but I trembled and the sword master could surely see it.

I shut my eyes and took a shaky breath that had been meant to calm me. It only reminded me of how petrified I was. How did I ever think I could face down a yelling, sword-swinging enemy if I couldn't face this?

Yet no faceless, future enemy held a candle to our sword master, who had broken every one of us to the point of tears during our training.

He knelt on the opposite side of the bench and took a firm hold of my forearm.

You can take it. I repeated this to myself in my mind. *You can take it.*

CAVAN

At the edge of the village

Peredur's body hunched forward as the sword master carved into his arm, while a wonderfully embarrassing yelp rang out in the clear morning. Ah, this was perfect.

Villagers began to gather round, craning their necks to see. It was too good to be true. Tanwen's brother was one of them, hurrying to get a closer look.

Peredur groaned, just as the sword master turned the point of the blade and continued to press it into his flesh.

A perfect screech wrenched free from his throat. Tanwen's brother raced off to spread the news.

It was too bad that I'd chosen this spot to watch. A view of his tearful face would have been so gratifying.

The sword master took his time and methodically drew a bloody pattern in his young student's skin. When Tanwen finally arrived with her brother, dismay marred her features. I don't know why that angered me, but it did.

It almost distracted me from the show Peredur performed so beautifully – twisting and trying to jerk away. His fellow students seemed to feel these agonies in sympathy. They all flinched in unison with every turn of the knife blade.

Finally it was over, and Peredur knelt there for a moment, breathless and shaking as the sword master rose and turned away.

Eventually Peredur pushed himself up, turned and quickly wiped his face.

Then, what a shock. Owen walked toward Peredur. This I hadn't predicted at all.

PEREDUR

In the sword master's training yard

I looked around at the other boys. They were grim-faced but returned my gaze with solidarity. The sword master seemed as surprised as me, but flicked his head to motion me out of the way.

I took several pain-filled steps back, till I stood with the other boys. They put comforting hands on my shoulders as Owen's ordeal began.

He got the same as me – the sword master's personal mark, used on all his blades and now a part of us forever, once our wounds turned into scars. Owen was in tears by the second turn of the blade. Soon he pushed back from the bench, but the sword master took hold of him and yanked him back into position, and so he remained until it was done. Owen sobbed and shrieked, but did not rise from the bench until he wore the same mark as me.

CAVAN

At the edge of the village

I glanced over at Tanwen, who wiped tears from her face. The sight of that nearly ruined this whole glorious moment for me. What did she need to get all teary-eyed for – on his behalf?

I turned back to the spectacle unfolding below. This wasn't what I had foreseen at all. To be honest, I hadn't exactly focused on the future outcome of my spell. I had been so certain of its success.

Sullenly, I watched as the mood among the boys rose to a solid sense of fraternity. Recalling my own attempt to create a sense of brotherhood when I'd taken those cuffs that day in the forest, the shift in mood among the boys really soured my own.

PEREDUR

In the sword master's training yard

When Owen got to his feet, Cynfelyn took his place before the bench. The anger and frustration I felt toward those boys, just before the fight, cleared along with the blood that pooled on my arm and then wiped away. We clapped Owen on the shoulders when he returned to stand among us, as the sword master took up his grim task once again.

Cynfelyn took his mark as we had, but when it was done, he proudly returned to his place among us.

The decision of the two boys to share my fate gave me a sense of brotherhood I'd never known until this moment. I'm certain the sword master would not have called them up to the bench, as we had established my responsibility in starting the fight.

However, I could tell the sword master was pleased. For myself, I'd never been so sore, so humbled, so proud and so filled with camaraderie. That was the only time our sword master ever had to carve his mark on any of us.

46

Clan coastal territory, 577

"What was all that?" Lord Muiredach asked.

He led Tanwen away from the gathering and onto a windswept meadow high above the sea. She walked without looking back, though she wanted so very badly to see whether Cavan watched their departure.

The moon glinted off every blade of grass. Everything was clear, except for the memory she so desired. "He knew I was close to remembering," she said.

"What is he trying to keep from you?" Lord Muiredach turned, demanding she return his gaze. She glanced up but couldn't meet it.

"I lost someone. There is a face," she said. "Not his."

Lord Muiredach tipped her chin with one finger. She felt so vulnerable that she couldn't bear to look at him. Yet she couldn't resist the strength of his gaze. "What was Cavan to you before?" he asked.

She trembled. Her mind felt shredded, as though he raked through her memories before they were ready.

"You know this, Tanwen. Who was this man to you, before you were brought to us?" His eyes took on the soulless white glint of moonlight. She was unable to do anything but rummage through her fractured mind as he commanded.

"I thought he must be the one I longed for. He looked for me the moment he was on his feet."

Lord Muiredach let go of her chin. "You have doubts that he is who he says he is?"

"I'm only starting to remember, Lord."

"Tell me what you know." His voice rumbled through her, prickling across her nerve endings. The memories flared up again.

"I remembered meeting him on the road to the fair, and that he brought me a ring."

"A ring to adorn his love?"

She shook her head. "He returned a ring from the man I lost. He was killed. In battle."

"Was he, now?"

"I've seen his face in my mind. My love's face. He had dark hair, not golden. Green eyes, not gray."

Lord Muirdach probed deeper with his gaze.

The wind blew her hair in her eyes, in her mouth, but the cold did not make her tremble. Instead, the force of Lord Muiredach's demand shook her. She swayed, and he grasped her arms to steady her. She wanted this. Let him scratch through her memories. Let him gouge and bruise her.

"It is close," he said.

Yes, she nodded.

"You can see his face."

"He took me into the forest," she said. "He wasn't dead." The truth of this memory hit her hard. She gasped.

"Go on," he said quietly.

"They told my father he was killed. Cavan showed me the ring." She wanted to cry so very badly. Why wouldn't the tears come?

"How did Cavan get the ring?"

"His mam." The words came so easily. Why hadn't they come before? She could see the wise woman. See her lying on the floor of her own hut, unable to move.

"Who was his mam?"

"The village wise woman."

Lord Muiredach nodded somberly.

"He always seemed so harmless," she said, wondering how the vampire lord dragged this up from the uncooperative depths of her mind. "Why didn't you do this before?"

"You're barely ready for it now," he said, smiling ruefully. "If you've ever witnessed a mad vampire, you would know why that's inadvisable."

"Go farther," she begged, gripping his arms.

"It's already coming to you," he said, reminding her of someone else, someone who made her infuriated.

She looked inward, turning away from Lord Muiredach. Walls remained, so thick she couldn't hope to gain entry. Nothing new presented itself. There was only the urge to cry and the inability to do so.

"Why do you suppose Cavan followed you here – to this life?"

She whirled to face Lord Muirdach. Once he had her in his gaze, she felt once again that raking sensation inside her mind. Images rushed at her like stampeding animals.

Cavan dropped the ring into her outstretched palm.

He offered a coin to her sister for the rare herbs.

He stood waiting for her in the doorway of his mam's hut, knowing she'd be coming to them for shelter.

He whispered something into his mam's ear so she wouldn't be able to warn Tanwen to run.

She opened her mouth to tell Lord Muiredach that Cavan was dangerous, but the images wouldn't stop. Cavan had somehow known that she'd been alone with her beloved in the forest, had known she'd begged to be made a vampire. Had known Peredur had refused to take her with him to his new vampire life.

Lord Muiredach nodded. "Let it come," he said in a soothing voice.

"The brethren," she whispered.

His fingers dug into her arms as he grabbed her. "What about them?"

"*He* wouldn't make me into a vampire. The brethren won't allow it." Her voice was laden with the crying that would not come, could not give her relief.

"Your lost love. He's one of the brethren?"

She nodded slowly. "They have no females. They are forbidden from creating more of their kind. That's what he said."

"He," Lord Muiredach said.

And then it spilled from her lips. "Peredur." *Oh. At last.*

"Who was this Peredur?" Lord Muiredach asked.

Tanwen released her grip on him, but he did not do likewise. "He was a warrior," she said proudly, the images falling into her consciousness like a hailstorm. "He died in battle."

"Yes, you mentioned. And what of Cavan?"

"He was..." She returned to the scene inside the hut. To the herbs he'd purchased from her sister. To her father saying to watch out for Cavan, for he had designs on her. "He was the son of the wise woman. He did not go with the other young men when they learned to use their swords. He was not a part of them."

"You had feelings for him, though?"

"For Peredur," she said.

"But Cavan had feelings for you."

"No." She shook her head.

"Think, Tanwen. Cavan summoned the vampire to you, so you could be turned to this life. That has never been done before. It is not a simple thing."

She remembered the way Cavan had looked at her in his mam's hut that night, his need for her painfully raw. "I see it now. He must have long held strong feelings for me."

"The warrior. He visited you after he was turned, but said you could not follow him."

She nodded miserably.

"Did you notice whether or not you were followed into the forest that night?"

"We were alone," she insisted. "If there had been anyone there, Peredur would have sensed it."

"Yet, somehow Cavan was aware of this interlude you had with your warrior."

"But he wasn't there with us. He couldn't have been." Lord Muiredach released his grip and she backed away, clutching her arms around herself.

"If he is an adept – a sorcerer, as he claims – he would have had many means of seeing what you were doing there."

She nodded. "He is very powerful."

"He summoned a vampire. No one summons a vampire."

"Just as no one remembers so soon after bursting up through the earth?"

"Exactly so," Lord Muiredach said. "I have great concerns about Cavan."

"He could sense I was close to remembering about Peredur. He tried to make it seem that he was the one I longed for, but I just knew...I knew it wasn't him."

"Tanwen," Lord Muirdach said, his serious tone making her uneasy, "I face a significant quandary."

She stood breathless. The sensation of recalling so much, so fast making her dizzy.

"I have never encountered a sorcerer vampire," said Lord Muiredach. "Something warns me that he is to be feared."

"He was cruel to his mam," she whispered, recalling the invisible fight on the floor between the wise woman and an unseen spirit, while Cavan forced Osfrid to bite him, so he could follow her to this vampire clan.

He took her face in his hands. "You must think, now. Would this Peredur have cursed God at the point of death?"

Tanwen recoiled, breaking free of his grasp.

"Think!" he said.

"I *have* been thinking! I can't make sense of anything, anymore. Please! I need some rest."

"Our future depends upon you remembering."

"Our future?" Her voice shook. "I've only just remembered his name."

"Why did Cavan summon my vampire to you?"

"I don't...I don't know..."

"You needed something."

"I wanted him. I wanted him back."

"And you went to Cavan for help," he said.

"I went to Cavan because he was the only friend I had left."

"Tell me."

She stumbled her way through the story of her last night with her family, ending with her flight to the wise woman's hut. "I hadn't known about him. I hadn't known."

"That he was a sorcerer?"

"His mam, the wise woman – she didn't know what he was."

He pulled away from her, glancing around uneasily. "It is as I feared."

Tanwen slumped to the ground, too woozy to stand any longer. Now that her memories were unlocked, they flooded her with overpowering momentum.

Standing. Overlooking the sea on a gray drizzly day. Overcome with sorrow. No one to help her. No one but Cavan.

Her father insisting that she marry her sister's intended. No one to speak up for her. No one to comfort her but Cavan.

Peredur leaving for one last raid against the Irish. The warrior from his war band speaking with Tada, coming to tell him Peredur would never come to claim her hand. Cavan hadn't left her, had he? He'd stayed in the village. He'd been there when Peredur had not been.

Why did these thoughts plague her? Peredur had come back to her, even though he'd been told to leave her be. Was it his fault he'd fallen to a spear?

"It troubles me, this situation between the three of you," said Lord Muiredach.

"What do you mean?"

"There are tales making their way to me about this Peredur. That he is not like any other brethren before him."

She smiled, proud that her beloved should be so.

"This is nothing to celebrate. The brethren are our worst enemies. Their only aim is to deliver us to God through the true death."

"Why should it be so?" she asked.

"No one knows when this began. Vampires have long memories and long pasts. Still, no one recalls when the brethren became our cruelest hunters."

"What does Peredur have to do with any of this?"

"He has mastered the others of his group," said Lord Muiredach, "who imagined that they were a collection of equals, with no leader, only brethren of equal stature. Now you and Cavan come to us, you who were once the intended of this anomaly. The third person in this triangle is the first sorcerer vampire I've ever encountered. Whether you are aware of it or not, he has a passion for you which has burned inside him for years."

"He certainly acts upon the assumption that I return his feelings, and that is just not true."

"Did you ever feel anything for him? Try to remember."

She shook her head.

"His feelings for you unbalance him, and that is dangerous for us. I can feel the undercurrent of his power, and I know he's blocking me from accessing everything there is to see about him. If he can do that, I truly fear his future intentions."

"I can barely keep my own thoughts sorted out," she said.

"More memories will come. And when they do, I will need you to share them with me. Even if they don't make any sense."

Tanwen nodded, unable to feel anything at the moment. Her mind was numb from all the remembering she'd longed for.

47

The forests of Conwy, near Tan y Gopa, 577

This time, assured Adalhard, Peredur's instructions were very clear. No breaking away from the role of observer. Under no circumstances was he to take any action upon himself.

Tonight he and Adalhard held back slightly as Melnak and Wladyslaw ran over the countryside toward Bekelert. They kept the others in their sight and trailed them easily, slipping through the trees in the moonless night. Peredur would see his cousins, the true vampires at last, as his brethren fought to free a man on the verge of being turned into one of their kind.

Before long they came to a modest hut where a light glowed in the seams around the shuttered opening. Melnak and Wladyslaw disappeared behind the hut.

Adalhard touched Peredur's arm to slow him, then jerked his head to indicate a change of direction. After following the Frank, they settled in a dense thicket of bushes a short distance from where they'd been.

They remained silent, waiting for what seemed a very long time. The arrival of the cousin, for there was only one, was announced by the subtle change in Melnak's and Wladyslaw's heartbeats. Peredur was surprised that he could sense the rhythms from here.

A movement from the woods caught his eye – a slow, deliberate approach without fear of any eyes watching. Did this cousin not sense their presence, as they sensed his?

Without warning, the figure turned from a tangible being into a wisp of vapor. Peredur almost gasped.

Adalhard placed gentle fingers upon Peredur's lips.

Tanwen slipped her hand into Cavan's outstretched one and disappeared into the night, knowing that Lord Muiredach watched her every movement.

It was challenge to follow one of their clan, the one called Dengel, who went to collect his latest acquisition. He shot forward in the manner shared by all of them, and if it had not been for Cavan she never would have managed it. Before too long, they reached a hut where hearth light burned along the edges of the door. Cavan had informed Lord Muiredach he was certain that members of the brethren would be here, which is why Tanwen had been sent along.

Dengel slowed to enter the clearing surrounding the hut. Cavan crouched with Tanwen behind a screen of young trees. She knew they were merely there to watch. She must not show herself, not make a sound...do nothing to betray their presence.

She could do it, as long as her Peredur didn't appear with his brethren.

Despite her intention, when their clan-fellow disappeared into a trail of mist in order to enter the hut, Tanwen gasped at the unexpected transformation. Cavan clamped a cruel hand over her mouth.

Melnak and the *szlachcic* slipped from the shadows behind the hut and entered calmly through the front door, behind their cousin who had entered as vapor. A scream rang out from a woman's throat.

Instantly Peredur's heart leaped. He felt the Frank clamp his hand, with an irrefutable warning, over Peredur's mouth.

"We will wait," Adalhard cautioned. He released his hand so Peredur could catch his breath. They both heard the sounds of a scuffle coming from the hut. Then the door burst open and an imposing figure stalked into the open, carrying a man slung over his shoulder like a grain sack.

Melnak and Wladyslaw shot past the figure, passing to either side of him, turning to block the vampire's passage with practiced assurance and phenomenal speed. Turning to face both adversaries, the vampire hissed with rage, two long fangs gleaming in the faint light from within the hut.

48

Cavan kept his hand over Tanwen's mouth. She put up resistance, but he whispered hotly in her ear, "If they find us here, we will fall to them."

Dengel snarled and hissed at the two figures, who cautiously dogged his every step. She anxiously sought out their faces in the night, but Tanwen already knew that neither of them was Peredur.

Still, there was such a strong sense of him, close by. So very close.

A woman stood in the doorway, mouth moving in prayer. Tanwen felt an extreme desire to crush the words from her lips – they irritated her as nothing had ever irritated her before. The more the woman prayed, the more Tanwen's wished she could leap up to slice the woman's throat. The words made the very air an impossibility to breathe.

Cavan simply held her in place. The solid form of his body wrapped around hers – the strength of his arms encasing her, gave Tanwen a measure of calm.

She needed it when one of the brethren began speaking in a deep, resonant voice.

The two brethren appeared to ignore the woman standing in the doorway, focusing instead on the precious cargo being spirited away from this rude little home, by another. This vampyric cousin – for that is surely who this was – kept Melnak and Wladyslaw in its range of vision while pressing his way ever further toward the darkness of the forest.

Peredur heard the woman's whispered prayers through the gloom of the night. Almost as though he could sense the heartbeats of the brethren, Peredur felt the air around him change as the woman sent her pleas heavenward.

The night became lighter, somehow. Peredur felt a familiar prickle move up the back of his neck – the same sort he'd feel if Tanwen had suddenly appeared before him. He glanced over at the Frank. He'd bowed his head slightly, as though in the presence of greatness.

"You will not take this man," Melnak's voice said with irresistible persuasion. It was such a powerful command Peredur felt his mouth drop open in disbelief that this dark cousin did not yield outright. But in fact the vampire clutched its parcel even tighter, whirled and bared all of its teeth. It let out a growling hiss that made Peredur's muscles tense.

"Drop him," Wladyslaw insisted with all the princely expectation of being obeyed. Melnak circled with nearly imperceptible sidesteps while the creature roared its disdain at the *szlachcic*.

"You have been well warned," one of the brethren said. Dengel didn't drop the man, whirling back and forth instead. The two hunters closed in without mercy.

One figure leaped up to grab the man to freedom. The other fell upon the vampire. The double attack was too much. Dengel crashed down but gave no ground – instead he demanded an intense struggle with the figure who had come to divert him while the other took his newly-turned vampire from him.

From the corner of her eye, Tanwen saw the other figure pull the man to safety some distance away in the forest. The pitch of prayers in the night increased. There had to be more people praying than just that one woman. Tanwen's torment was excruciating.

She was proud of Dengel's crazed resistance to the focused might of the two determined brethren. Shrieks, howls and roars filled the air. She felt an answering tumult in her breast. She longed to join in the fray, to drive these brethren back, but Cavan's hold upon her was like rock.

The vampire tried to turn but Wladyslaw shot like a loosened arrow to where Peredur crouched alongside Adalhard.

The Frank gathered their human prize to his breast like a mam with a sick child. Wladyslaw set a piercing glance into Peredur's face before disappearing again, quicker than a hummingbird.

Peredur looked down at the man, whose pale clammy skin did not speak well for his health. *But what of the cousin?* Looking up, Peredur saw Melnak locked in a strained embrace with the vampire.

Adalhard cooed to the man and dabbed some of the dampness from his brow even as Wladyslaw set upon the vampire alongside Melnak. Peredur did not know where he should look. His head bobbed back and forth between the Frank attempting to revive the corpse-like man and the battle raging off to his right.

Horrible cries and howls filled the night as the three fought. Peredur had never heard the like. The vampire shrieked and moaned, high-pitched and low together in an unnerving chorus. Melnak and Wladyslaw answered with roars that made Peredur shiver, even as he rejoiced to see them display their full powers.

In the same way he'd noticed the lightened feeling in the air as the woman prayed only moments earlier, Peredur now felt a subtle weighing down of the night around them, heard the ghastly sighs of unseen beings that Peredur knew without doubt surrounded them.

49

Something shifted in the air for Tanwen, as if an answering blow splintered the anguished prickling in the air that encircled her.

Cavan's lips moved as he whispered. The air loosened, allowing Tanwen to hear the words Cavan launched into the night. They were in a strange tongue. Sorcery.

Soothing coolness spread through the forest. The sounds of little unseen beings moving across the forest floor surrounded them. She tried to see what they were, but they were quick. Cavan withdrew the pressure over her mouth, so she wiggled free of him.

He glanced at her briefly, his eyes lit with delight. Lord Muiredach was right to fear a vampire who remembered his sorcerer past. Energy flowed outward from him, wafting past her like a breeze.

She saw Dengel sink beneath the weight of two brethren and Tanwen rose to her feet. Yet Cavan held her back, this time with only a touch. "Watch," he whispered.

The unseen beings which Cavan had sent to the vampire reached Dengel at last. Somehow they delivered a boost of energy, giving him the power to stand.

Dengel threw both brethren off him like dolls.

Their cousin, the true vampire, looked directly through the bushes and straight into Peredur's eyes. What an unearthly glow burned in that gaze.

It leapt forward, right at him it seemed, though Peredur knew the being wanted only to reclaim its prize.

The brethren were just as fast. Again, they tackled their cousin neatly and pinned the creature to the dew-slick ground.

The vampire writhed like a mad thing...Then suddenly it wasn't there.

Melnak and Wladyslaw barely had time to fall forward when a mouse-eared bat flew into Peredur's face and flapped wildly in his hair. His arms flailed, trying to dislodge it. In a blink, it too was gone and the mad vampire reappeared – almost in Peredur's lap.

There was barely time to register this cousin's deranged grin when Peredur was flattened by Melnak's scramble to grab hold of the vampire. Peredur saw Adalhard wrap his whole body protectively around the man, huddling close to the ground. The Polanie crashed through the chaos to sink his fangs into the vampire's calf.

Then all was kicking, blows and teeth.

All Peredur could think to do was to settle close to Adalhard, who held protectively tight to his charge. He knew the Frank would not give up this man. Peredur readied himself for the possibility that he might have to help – regardless of Melnak's directive to stay out of it.

Tanwen crept forward, as much as she dared. It was impossible to see what was happening. Everyone moved with such speed, and Dengel kept changing form to attack in disorienting ways.

As suddenly as he'd pounced, the vampire disappeared again. A silver wolf sank a full set of slavering, pointed teeth into the third brethren's shoulder. The protecting brethren cried out. Yet he did not move nor loosen his hold upon the man.

The one who'd bitten Dengel in the leg now fell upon the wolf and rolled with the whimpering beast. The previous tussle was nothing compared to this. The wolf fought with the intensity only a cornered animal can muster. Tanwen smelled the blood right away. It made her desperate to join in, to fight and to feed.

Once again Cavan took hold of her, preventing her from betraying their presence, leaning in close, as he surely felt the same intense degree of arousal as did she.

But then one of the brethren dropped to his knees as close to the rolling ball of fur as was possible. Fumbling with something held around his neck, the brethren freed a white object from the folds of his tunic.

At sight of it, Tanwen and Cavan both cringed – then recoiled from its brilliance, its overpowering might.

Peredur felt something hum inside him, something glorious and filled with longing. He forgot all about the freshly turned man he was to protect, his brethren, the thrashing wolf. For a moment *All That Was* dangled in Melnak's grip.

A cry split the night, so hideous Peredur had never imagined it in his most fevered dreams.

The wolf stopped its writhing and changed before Peredur's eyes back into the vampire it truly was. Melnak stooped over it, pressing the object deeply into the creature's forehead. An unnerving sigh escaped its bloodied lips.

"You shall not have this soul, cousin," Melnak whispered hotly.

Tanwen looked over at Cavan as one of the brethren whispered something to Dengel. Cavan countered by whispering something into the night. The vampire's eyes widened and it swung a backhand blow, unseating his tormentor.

Rolling to his feet, Dengel gave one demented cry of frustration and disappeared into the inky darkness.

Tanwen was consumed by the desire to follow their retreating clan fellow, or exact revenge upon these brethren. When she looked to Cavan for support, the expression in his eyes stopped her cold.

Jerking his head in the direction of the hut, Cavan led her through the trees, reaching a spot where they had an unrestricted view of the door to the hut. He motioned for her to turn and watch.

There were four brethren now, returning the man to the hut. The woman gestured them all inside. The last of the brethren turned once to scan the forest before entering along with the others.

Tanwen's heart splintered inside her. It was *him*.

It was Peredur.

She opened her mouth to speak. Unseen fingers tightened around her throat. Cavan stood facing her, his arm outstretched, his hand clutching the air as if it were her throat. Tanwen struggled to see Peredur once more before he disappeared through the doorway to the hut.

Cavan closed the distance between them, choking her harder with his sorcerer's grip before flinging her to the ground. Her hands flew to her throat.

"He is lost to you," Cavan said in a low whisper, kneeling over her. "He was telling you the truth that night. You just wouldn't believe him."

Moans and weeping rose from the hut. Cavan released his grip on her throat, then held out his hand for her. She gazed up at him, still shaken from his attack, unwilling to leave her beloved so soon after finding him again.

"That's not the real reason you brought me here." She rose and left him standing there, his hand still reaching for her.

50

Peredur stood like a fly on the wall, watching and trying to understand.

They were inside the tiny hut – the woman, the sick and shivering man, Melnak and Adalhard besides Peredur – with the *szlachcic* standing guard outside the door. Peredur pressed himself into a corner beside a broom as frantic work was done on the man to salvage his life and his soul.

The woman brought water and cloths and whatever Melnak whispered to her to fetch him. 'Garlic?' Yes, she had some. Trembling fingers lifted the lid of a crockery jar. The smell of it made Peredur's insides roll.

A quick look at the faces of the other brethren told him they experienced the same.

"Place it in the water," Melnak instructed her calmly, though Peredur sensed he wished she'd hurry. "Take this off," he bid Adalhard, who removed the man's sodden nightshirt.

Peredur saw two festering tooth marks in the man's neck, close to the collarbone. It was a spot to which he'd been drawn himself, when feeding.

He sensed a strange anger building inside him. Why was this man's soul at risk? Did that mean every time brethren and vampire fed, they sent the poor unfortunate's soul out of God's reaches? And why were they so concerned over this man when it was also men and even women they dined upon?

"Dip the cloth in the water," Melnak urged the woman. "Rub him down with it. Give special care to the wounds on his neck." Melnak gestured with his hand to his own neck. The woman set about her task. As she did so, the room filled with the noxious odor until Peredur wondered if he could bear it any longer.

The others seemed able, so Peredur would not be the first to leave. He swallowed hard against the nausea, though he already knew he was no longer capable of vomiting.

The man began twitching at the feel of the garlic water on his skin. Peredur's attention to the man's reaction helped keep his mind off his own torment. How he wanted to burst from there and have nothing to do with this life any longer.

The more water was applied to the man's skin, the more animated he became. Yet his eyes never opened. Pitiful moans escaped him, drawing tears from the woman who washed him.

When it was done, Melnak motioned the woman to stand aside. Adalhard stepped forward, Melnak flanking the man's other side. As one, both of the brethren knelt and bowed their heads. Peredur saw the woman's eyes widen in awe.

"Oh God, almighty and everlasting, hear the prayers of your humble servants," Melnak beseeched in a voice brimming with emotion. Peredur felt his own chest squeeze and his skin prickle. He knelt also.

"This, your child, awaits your healing touch. In his hour of need we have come at your command."

Peredur risked a glance at the man. The woman stood as if frozen, looking upon these brethren kneeling in her hut and praying over her lover. Peredur could see her nightgown trembling.

Truth be told, he felt the same as she.

The air inside lightened again as he'd felt it did when the woman had prayed. Should he pray, also? Or did his mere presence here add to the power of Melnak's prayer?

"Send him your touch through us, Lord."

With that, Melnak placed a hand upon the puncture marks on the man's neck. Peredur saw the man's body jerk at the same time as he felt a deep tremor in the hut. Melnak gasped and raised his face skyward.

Peredur couldn't tell if he imagined it or if his mentor's face really shimmered. Peredur felt a strong sense that he must not look. He lowered his head quickly.

A strange sighing breath rose from the man's lips. Then a soft groan of effort from Melnak. Wladyslaw whispered a stream of something in a language Peredur took for the Polanie's native tongue. Peredur's chest heaved as if he'd been running.

The woman fell to her knees at Melnak's feet, kissing him and weeping.

Peredur dared to look. The man's eyes were open. They were clear and shining.

Melnak swayed and this time Peredur moved. He caught his master in his arms.

"I brought you his ring once," Cavan said. "I wanted to prove to you he was gone. So you could believe. And now I've brought you here. So you can believe."

His hand still reached out for her.

A strange sighing breath rose from the hut, as the man was cleansed of his newly born vampire state. It drove Tanwen to take Cavan's hand and rise to her feet. The sound of that sigh echoed in her mind as they returned to their cavern, playing out in her mind alongside the memory of Peredur's face gazing backward toward the forest as if he sensed she were there.

Cavan stopped and turned just as they were about to leave the shelter of the trees. In the darkness his blond hair almost gleamed. "You thought I brought you there just to hurt you."

"It did hurt me."

"I brought you to see what your betrothed has become."

"What happened to the man back there?" she asked.

"He wasn't fully turned. They've removed any trace of vampire from his body."

"Why do they do it?"

"They don't understand, Tanwen," he said. "They think we're an abomination."

"But what are *they*? They have fangs, and they move as fast as we do."

"They're not men anymore, but neither are they real vampires."

"I don't understand. I don't understand any of it."

"You see why I brought you, then." Cavan tried to close the gap between them, but Tanwen kept her distance.

"Why did Lord Muiredach ask *you* to take me here? You're just as new as me."

Cavan smiled before he could wrestle it from his face. "He knew I'd be able to guard you from harm."

"What did you do to me?" she asked, touching her throat where she could yet feel the impression of his hands.

"You were going to call for him. Weren't you?" His eyes couldn't hide the hurt.

She couldn't say it. She only nodded.

"The only way we could watch was to remain undetected. If they'd discovered us, they would have put us to death. Even *he* would have done that. To you."

Part of her knew that everything he said was right. Yet, Lord Muiredach had asked *her* to watch *Cavan*, hadn't he? "When you were saying those words back there. What was that?"

He smiled again. "Just a quick incantation. Dengel needed the help, as you could see for yourself."

"Those things...the things that ran past us?"

"They helped tip the balance. Two against one. Not very honorable."

"No, it wasn't."

"Imagine. Before we turned, when we were a man and a woman, the brethren were all that stood between us and...*us*." He laughed.

"Cavan – did you know about then before we turned?"

He faced away from her and toward the distant sea. She moved to stand beside him, to look up at his profile. He really was the most handsome man she'd ever seen. Truly. Even more handsome than her Peredur. She felt able to say that to herself now. Just a simple truth.

He didn't look at her. "I knew so many things, Tanwen. So many things. I could never tell anyone. Not even Mam. Especially not her."

"I'd always thought the Irish were our worst problems," she said. They both laughed.

51

The vampire tested his bonds, fearsome but apparently well restrained. Peredur stood near, fascinated by the sight of such force and the ability of the bonds to remain intact. They were mere leather, but the brethren had a special process to cure them and that made them unbreakable to a vampire.

Melnak had assured Peredur he would be instructed in their technique when next they were made. 'Patience with that, as in all things here' he'd said.

Brude strolled up beside him. "Terrible sight, is he not?" the Pict remarked, taking care not to get any closer to the creature. He'd carried a few marks of the struggle they'd had to place the bonds upon their cousin, but they faded away as he challenged them with his gaze.

"It seems impossible that I'd never heard of these beings in my other life, and there they were, right under our noses," Peredur said, gesturing toward the snarling, flailing thing. He shook his head.

"You've visited Tanwen," Brude reminded him. "Not one of them in her family knew you even stood in their midst, did they?"

Again, Peredur shook his head.

"When you don't wish to be seen, you won't be."

Peredur looked at the bonds and remembered the different forms that their cousin had assumed. "Why does he not float out of these bonds, become a mist like the last one did?"

"You'll understand better when you see the bonds being made," Brude said, then laughed. "I'm beginning to sound like Melnak."

"I get the idea," Peredur said, laughing with him.

Brude looked behind him at where the Polanie waved Peredur over. "Can you keep your eye on our captive? I'll be back shortly."

Peredur agreed, but only as Brude strode off. Taking a deep breath, Peredur tried to make eye contact with the snapping captive. Oddly, once he achieved that contact, the creature calmed immediately. In fact, in the blink of an eye he went from an incensed fiend to the image of a docile man.

Turning to see if any of the others had noticed, Peredur found them engaged in rapt conversation. Of course, they would all be used to this sort of thing.

He faced the cousin again, shocked to see how unlike the snarling creature he'd become. Instead of seeming almost too enormous to be held securely, he now hung as if in pain, his arms stretched, his feet dangling just off the ground.

The being stared mournfully at Peredur, as if wary of what Peredur might do to him. Peredur knew he should be very much on his guard, despite the evidence the bonds would hold. Nevertheless, he took a few steps closer to this cousin of theirs.

"They are distracted, brother," the vampire said in a low silky voice. Peredur was shocked at how warm it sounded. He felt compelled to move closer to the cousin. What could it hurt?

"You are new to the brotherhood," the creature observed. "Not long to this life?"

"No," Peredur acknowledged, feeling unsure, as he would feel if Tanwen had poured her feelings out to him when he was still trying to figure out his own. It was a very disturbing sensation.

"I have been hearing of you amongst my kind," he said.

"Have you?" Peredur asked, feeling wary all over again.

"You learn quickly, we hear."

"I do learn," Peredur warned, feeling he had to. Suddenly the few steps closer felt like a grave error, but he would not retreat.

"There are many things which that old one withholds from you," the vampire said.

"He tells me what I need to know," Peredur said.

"But why does he withhold?" the vampire persisted. "Does he not trust you?"

Peredur hated to admit the tug that remark made on his gut. "What difference would that make to you?" he countered. "What if I care not a whit if he trusts me or not?"

"But you do care," the vampire said, holding Peredur's gaze with two piercing black eyes.

A shiver ran up Peredur's spine.

"Perhaps Melnak sees how fast you learn," the vampire continued. "You may be seen as a threat to his leadership."

A wash of relief broke the hold this cousin had gained on Peredur. "We have no leaders in this group."

"All groups have leaders," the vampire said confidently. "And you are clearly a leader."

Peredur felt both buoyed by that remark, and annoyed at so obvious a thing as this creature's flattery. He glanced back toward Wladyslaw, Adalhard and Brude. What were they about? Why did they leave him here with this honey-tongued viper?

"Why do you waste your breath trying to win my confidence, cousin?" he asked.

Peredur felt an irresistible attraction to this vampire, as if he wanted nothing more than to hear him speak more of his smooth words. Fighting this notion, he focused sharply on the leather pressing with raw insult into the creature's flesh. If it weren't for these bonds, the vampire would have become some other form, as he'd done just short hours before.

"It is never a waste to have sympathetic friends in one's corner," his cousin said.

"It is, if you are fated to receive the brotherhood's justice."

With relief, Peredur noticed the vampire's gaze shift to a space over Peredur's shoulder. His brethren approached at last. The vampire's brow curled down, his teeth bared and the flailing resumed with all its original force. Peredur took one step back in surprise just as the three brethren passed by him and fanned out before the vampire.

Hideous noises emanated from the creature's throat. He tensed, twisted, thrashed in the throes of some horrible torment. Peredur sincerely hoped he would never be subjected to a similar experience to what this cousin endured.

All three of the brethren reached into their tunics at the neck, producing white amulets held on leather cords. Each held it before them, their arms stretching toward the vampire. Truly hair-raising shrieks pierced the night, all from the creature whose eyes bulged red and whose fangs slavered in futility.

"*Ut nos exaudire digneris, te rogamus audi nos,*" intoned the *szlachcic.*

"*Quaesumus omnipotens Deus,*" the brethren answered. They all made signs with the white ornaments, all in the same rhythmic actions. Peredur stood beside them but knew not how to help with this ceremony. He observed as he knew he was meant to do.

The vampire looked decidedly sick. He hung slack in the bonds, eyes downcast, skin even more pale than anyone here.

"*Et fidelium animae per misericordiam Dei requiescant in pace,*" Wladyslaw said majestically, his authority unquestionable. "*Omnipotens sempiterne Deus, da servis tuis illam, quam mundus dare non potest, pacem.*" The brethren performed the synchronized actions again. This time the vampire shot forward, rigid and moaning, a giggling shriek cackling beneath the morbid sighs.

Peredur felt a true stab of fear in his gut. Would he one day perform such a ritual on another unrepentant vampire? And were they sending the vampire into the arms of God or into the fires of Hell?

The vampire laughed a truly demonic, deep-throated laugh, not bothering to look at any of his tormentors— but as the prayers were intoned for a third time, the vampire rapidly changed back into the semblance of the man he'd once been. His shadowed eyes and melancholy face turned to look directly into Peredur's own. A chill ran through Peredur's gut.

Then the imposing body twisted and bucked once more like a fish on a forked stick. The brethren once more performed their ritual and placed the ornaments against their cousin's flesh. Peredur heard a sizzling sound this time, smelled burning flesh and heard the piteous scream of a man held to the flames. Then a brilliant flash of white enveloped the vampire's form. The body shook as Peredur felt a heat uplift the air all around him.

All at once the atmosphere changed so dramatically Peredur was knocked to the ground by the force of it. He was sure he heard singing somewhere in his head. The night grew brilliant so that he rolled onto his stomach and buried his head in his arms. The singing grew stronger.

Then all was quiet, all was dark.

Peredur waited a moment before he got to his knees. The brethren were in various stages of righting themselves from where they'd been thrown. He hadn't known what to expect when he looked to the bonds and saw the body of the vampire still dangling there. But he sensed that was all that was left of their cousin. Just a body.

The face was slack and seemed to be free of the sneering expression the vampire had worn. The face did seem more human than vampire now, but there were burn marks on the flesh wherever the amulets had pressed into the skin.

Wladyslaw, Adalhard and Brude got to their knees, bowed their heads and silently prayed. Peredur didn't know what they prayed for, exactly, but he elected to do the same. He gave thanks that the creature seemed to be out of its misery. He gave thanks that the brethren had successfully completed their task here tonight. And lastly, Peredur thanked God that he had never become such a creature as that one had been.

52

Cavan watched from the edge of the crowd as Lord Muiredach escorted Tanwen away from prying eyes and ears. "You have news for me?" he asked.

"My lord," she began, but he tipped her head up and kissed her before she could say anymore. His lips were warm and welcoming. She melted into them, completely forgetting why he'd taken her aside in the first place.

"I can't have anyone wondering why I keep you to myself so often. The sorcerer, least of all." And he kissed her again.

"I am ever your servant, my lord," she said, smiling through her kiss. She dimly recalled a person she had once been who would have been insulted by his words. To be used in such a cavalier manner—her former self would have balked at that, but this new vampire self took her pleasure where she could. And Lord Muiredach's kisses were luscious and deeply satisfying. They carried on, walking. "But do you think claiming me this way is helpful, where Cavan is concerned?"

"I've chosen the lesser of two evils," he said.

Tanwen nodded. "He did tell me a few things."

"And?" he asked.

"And I saw some things."

"Are you going to make me drag it out of you? Because I might enjoy that a little too much—and you won't enjoy it a bit." He looked at her with a gleam of amusement, but it did not do much to reassure her.

"He whispered something during a fight between our Dengel and two of the brethren."

"Yes?"

"Cavan called forth...something..." She listened carefully to her memory of the scuffling through the forest. "There were more than one of them. Seemed to be small, like rabbits, or hedgehogs, but I know they weren't animals."

"You didn't see them?"

"No. He whispered the words as two of the brethren took down Dengel. As Cavan said, 'Not very honorable of them.' "

Lord Muiredach shook his head in agreement.

"As soon as they ran forward toward the fight, our vampire was able to throw off his attackers. Cavan's conjured spirits helped him."

Lord Muiredach looked back toward the others. Cavan had made himself scarce. "This is very good news. Very good news."

She put her hand to her throat. "He also choked me. Without using his hands."

"Did he?"

"My Peredur was there."

The vampire lord looked deeply into her eyes. She couldn't break away from that sensation, that pull to give him anything he desired. "Tell me."

She remembered the shock of seeing Peredur after all of this agony of waiting. After being turned in order to reunite with him, how could anyone ask her not to go to him? "I wanted to call to him, so he would know I was there."

"But Cavan prevented it."

Tanwen nodded.

"Your beloved is one of them, isn't he?"

She nodded again. Her heart pulled and twisted inside of her. Oh, how she would cry, if only she could.

"You must never go to him. You know that, don't you?"

She couldn't nod. That would be impossible.

"Never go to him," Lord Muiredach said, and a force she couldn't fight against pushed her head ever so slightly down and up, down and up. "You belong to us, now. You're part of my clan. We will fight for you, and you must fight for us."

Another emotion warred against her agony of loss. Relief at belonging to a clan. She knew how lonely she'd been within her own family for such a long time. Belonging felt so good. So good.

53

"That's a half dozen feedings in a week," said Melnak, his voice tight with frustration.

Bodies lay like heaps of sodden rags on the field, rain from earlier that evening still beading on their waxy skin. Peredur stood alongside the brethren, gazing upon the remnants of their cousins' feast as though witnessing a funeral pyre.

There was little left to identify them. A man. A woman. A few shreds of clothing.

The fishing village nearby had yet to discover the bodies. When they did, the elders of the village would recognize the signs. They would not mistake the killers amongst them as men or even animals.

Peredur felt the hum of purpose among the brethren as they set about erasing the blot of this scene from the landscape. The longer they could keep evidence of the rise of vampire feedings from detection, the better chance they would have to keep men from hunting down the monsters in their midst.

For this was the reason the Brotherhood been created. Left to their own devices, an overly exuberant clan of vampires could turn the entire surrounding population, leaving no food source and an ever-enlarging population to hunger for the blood of men.

In their turn, the men in the villages around such a transformation would raze the countryside, ridding themselves of nightmares that had become flesh. But the brethren had been called to prevent all of that.

Peredur hefted one victim's ravaged limbs while the others hauled their own part of the burden. They moved the bodies deep into the forest, entombing them in a natural crypt within a deep rock ledge. Brude and Vellocatus rolled large boulders to seal the burying place from the reach of scavengers and from the eyes of searchers.

"The local people will start to suspect," the Norseman said, looking grimmer than Peredur could have guessed possible for the most amiable of the brethren.

Nodding, Melnak backed away, already heading in the direction he'd chosen for himself.

"Meet at the cavern in two nights' time."

Before Peredur could blink, Melnak accelerated beyond the range of their vision. The amulet scar in Peredur's side flared with heat.

Sigbjorn gestured to Peredur. "Come with me, then." Gesturing after their departed brother, he said, "Rather keen to be rid of you, wasn't he?"

Peredur started to laugh, but the pain in his side cut it short. He hunched forward and followed Sigbjorn, ignoring the burning from his amulet scar, blocking out the image of the saint that rose up like a haunting.

54

Cavan was called to an audience with Lord Muiredach and five of his inner circle. Tanwen saw them gather and leave the cavern together. She knew what they would discuss. She needed some time to herself and struck out on her own.

Agitation spurred her to use her newfound speed to burst over here, fly over there. She went to the fishermen's cove, the scene of her very first feed. She went to the hut of the man who'd been saved by the brethren. Just the sight of the couple living their evening lives made her want to rip them into bloody shreds.

She took off before she could act on that irresistible impulse. Lord Muiredach and the others were hashing out a plan to rob the brethren of some of its numbers— most specifically her Peredur.

They said he was the most dangerous of them all. And he was the reason for her being here, the spark that set her true life on fire. She saw that the shadowy life she'd lived before being turned to vampire was laughable, really.

She wished she could warn Peredur somehow. The compulsion was partly out of gratitude for this new life, and partly because of that hold on her from her old self. It would never let go—her passion for Peredur.

Tanwen returned to the area that led to the cavern, but couldn't go any further. She thought of the vampire they'd watched during the altercation with the brethren, changing form into mist, into a bat and then a wolf. She looked down at her hands and imagined them turning into leathery black wings.

But nothing stirred inside her. She wanted so badly to be able to fly away from all this.

"A mouthful of blood for your thoughts."

She turned. Cavan stood only a breath away. She hated the way he looked so smugly at her. "Mmm," she said. "Blood sounds good. Where would we get some?"

"I know a place." He smiled at her as if he were the old Cavan and she didn't know he was a sorcerer with the ability to outfox even his mam.

She took his hand and they raced off, stopping on the outskirts of a village on the edge of a moonlit pasture. A shepherd lay sleeping on the ground, though his flock picked up their heads at their arrival.

"Shall we?" Cavan said, gesturing toward the sleeping form.

Tanwen put her hand on his arm. "I'd love to know something first." He turned to her, and Tanwen circled his waist with her arms. "Are you sure you want to know?" he asked.

"Would I have snuck off with you for a feed if blood was all I wanted?" she said.

Something flashed through Cavan's eyes, so quickly she didn't catch it exactly. "It may put you off of feeding if I tell you." He pulled her closer.

Tanwen wanted to pull back from that tug, but she allowed it, settling herself into a snuggle against his chest. If she wanted to know what was going on, it wouldn't come cheaply. "You must be pleased to be asked to a war council so soon after being turned," she said.

Cavan shrugged. "Lord Muiredach needed verification on a few matters."

"That's what I mean," she said, looking up at him. "Your arrival here was hardly met with trust, was it?"

Cavan shrugged again. "He is a prudent leader. I would do the same."

"You don't mind if they think you're dangerous?"

"If they didn't fear me, they wouldn't be worthy clan members."

"But they are, aren't they?"

"Worthy?"

"Yes. I like it here. I like it better than I ever liked being part of the village."

Cavan smiled and hugged her tightly. "I understand."

She did push out of his embrace this time, but not to avoid him. "We were so cruel to you," she said, looking into his eyes.

He swallowed, the pain etched on his face. This time he couldn't mask it quickly enough.

"Men are not so stupid as vampires allow themselves to believe. The villagers had a reason to fear me, just as our clan does. That's just how it is for someone like me."

"Do you like it here? In this clan?" she asked.

"I prefer to be where you are," he said with a disarming smile.

Tanwen felt for him suddenly. As a man he was never accepted, and as a vampire he was distrusted. "So what did they ask of you?" she asked.

"Hmm. Perhaps we'd better have our feed, first." He nodded with his head toward the shepherd, who stirred.

Tanwen wanted to say 'No, just leave him be.' She wanted to say, 'Tell me, you bastard!' She wanted to slam Cavan to the ground and force him to tell her what he held back from her—until Cavan's mouth opened and she saw his fangs gleam in the moonlight.

She turned to look at the shepherd then, who woke to see them gazing down upon him. His terror rose and filled the air, stirring Tanwen into a bloodthirsty frenzy. She didn't even know she leapt towards him.

There was only the joy of biting into his flesh. The fear-whipped blood tasted sweet, so sweet. Tanwen laughed with the delight of it.

She enjoyed the sight of Cavan's mouth coated in it. How she wanted to kiss the blood from his lips. Leaning forward, she did just that. The shepherd beneath them moaned as they plundered each other's mouths.

Cavan sliced into the artery along the neck. The spray was not as strong as it should have been, so it was easier to collect the blood in his cupped palm. Pressing down on the opened vein with the other hand, Cavan offered her the drink from his hand.

Tanwen gazed into his eyes. If she took this drink, would he relax his guard with her? She had to find out what the war council was about. Ever since she'd realized Lord Muiredach had sent her to spy on Cavan, and had enlisted Cavan to do the same against her, Tanwen needed every scrap of information she could get. She sensed she needed to stay one step ahead of both of them.

Leaning forward, she touched her lips to the side of his hand. He tipped his palm and poured the thick blood onto her tongue. It was still warm, though somewhat flat compared to sucking it straight out of the man, but she had to admit it was very sensual to drink from Cavan's hand.

She liked the way he looked at her. He didn't look arrogant as she would have supposed. No, he was very vulnerable as he watched her drink.

Tanwen tugged on his tunic, forcing him to let go of his hold on the shepherd's neck. Blood seeped, wasted into the grass as they tumbled together on the ground. She needed him to trust her. She would do whatever she had to do to get what she needed from him. If it gave her a diversionary pleasure in the meantime, so be it.

55

The tumult of voices drew them to the edge of the forest, where the inlet stretched away from the cover of trees. Someone struggled in bonds, fierce as a mountain cat. Peredur's heart grew heavy.

"They think they have their culprit." Sigbjorn shook his head sadly. "This is how it begins."

The village had decided. A hulk of firewood sat waiting on the beach. Glancing at Sigbjorn, Peredur watched the proceedings with ever-increasing sorrow.

Plans to break it all up began forming in his mind, but his brother felt the direction of Peredur's thoughts.

"We cannot," Sigbjorn said quietly, placing a restraining hand on his arm.

The amulet scar stabbed so fiercely, Peredur reeled as though struck. He clapped his hand over the scar and pressed hard.

Sigbjorn ducked, crouching to scan for attackers. Peredur shook his head, gesturing for the Norseman to rise. "There's no one," he said, breathless with pain. "It's the scar."

His brother stepped away from him. Peredur couldn't stand to see the worry in Sigbjorn's eyes, so he turned instead to the scene unfolding on the beach.

A woman screamed and ranted at the villagers. As she cursed them, Peredur was buffeted as though by hail. The amulet scar reached deeply, as deep as the spear that had pinned him to what should have been his last battlefield.

He tried to keep his mind on the fire licking at the edges of the ghoulish bonfire, but the pain scraped along his ribs, punctured his lungs, stole his breath.

The villagers couldn't hear his choked cry over the surf and the crackling of the flames. He flung himself down, convulsing mindlessly, unable to bear the white-hot splinters of pure pain splitting him apart.

Dimly, he saw the snowy-blond hair of his brother bending over him. "Peredur!"

Then another voice called his name.

Peredur.

The pain let up enough for an image to form in his mind. Saint Cittinus knelt, beseeching him from a prison of torment.

What is happening? Peredur asked the saint. From the beach he heard the woman's screams of terror turn to keening agony.

She is innocent, Cittinus said.

"Are you alright?" Sigbjorn asked, taking him by the arms to help him sit.

Her shrieking carried on the wind, raising the hair on his scalp. "We have to—"

The Norseman's granite-like arms pinned him where he sat. "No. We can't."

She lives, Cittinus pleaded. *She needs us.*

Peredur shoved Sigbjorn hard. As he scrambled to his feet, the Norseman tackled him to the ground before he got far.

"No, brother!" Sigbjorn said.

"What are you doing?" Peredur struck out, but Sigbjorn would not be bested. The woman's screams rose to a horrifying pitch.

She is innocent, the saint said. Pain flared high again along the phantom spear line inside him, taking

Peredur's breath away so that he stopped fighting Sigbjorn.

"We cannot stop this," the Norseman said, releasing Peredur. "This is their affair."

"We're supposed to stop them killing vampires, but we leave them to destroy each other – is that it?"

Sigbjorn sat back on his heels, panting. "We will take this news to the others. No doubt they will have similar stories to tell."

Peredur pushed through the pain to gain his feet. How it hurt to see the way his friend and brother withdrew from him. How it chilled him to see the image of the saint kneeling beside Sigbjorn, accusing Peredur with that stare.

The wind no longer carried the screams, only a disgusting smell amid the scattering smoke.

56

Tanwen curtsied deeply before him. "I am honored, my lord."

"Rise, dear one," he said, gesturing with an elegant hand. She stood and smiled gratefully, conscious of everyone's gaze upon her. This time he hadn't felt inclined to whisk her off to the edge of the forest. This time he called her before him in front of everyone.

Again he swept his hand, inviting her to stand at his left. Tanwen moved to obey, certain there was no shortage of females in their assembly who would want this honor. Well, they could all lose their beloveds the way she did, lose them to a brotherhood that existed to kill them all. They could be under intense suspicion as she was, held closer than a friend. They could all have it and more.

The throne room cleared of all except his war council. She noticed there was only one other female present, but she did not seem jealous – merely curious.

Cavan, of course, had remained behind. Tanwen noticed the other vampires now gave him a wide berth. He nearly stood alone in this tightly knit group. Her heart ached for him.

"I have asked Tanwen to join us this evening," Lord Muiredach said. "I trust this meets with everyone's approval."

A low murmur of support rose up. Tanwen gazed out at all the faces. She met their stares without apology. Some of them may have worked for generations before being invited to the war council. So be it. She had information that they needed...and didn't have.

One of the toughest of the vampires, Osfrid stepped forward. He nodded crisply. "My lord, Dengel has not returned to us in a fortnight."

Lord Muiredach rested his chin on clasped hands. He thought for a moment. "I have my suspicions, as I know you do, Osfrid."

"They have been more active since the arrival of the newest among them," another said. He and many others turned their gazes to Tanwen. It was hard to return their stares, but she did it.

"All of you are aware of the bond which exists between their newest brethren and our newest arrival," Lord Muiredach said. There was another murmur of agreement. "Tanwen has agreed to share her knowledge of our enemy. She has even agreed to serve, as needed, in our effort to stop him." He looked over at her, nodding for her to speak.

Tanwen stilled her nerves, took a breath and said, "His name is Peredur. He was my betrothed." She heard the tremor in her voice and waited until she was certain it would not return. "He was the most respected fighter in his war band. He is the last person you should want as an enemy."

The vampires muttered amongst themselves. One of them spoke up. "How is it that he has become one of the brethren when you have been turned to us?"

"He was one of them before I was turned," she said.

Osfrid faced Cavan. "And you summoned me to turn her," he accused.

Cavan retreated a step, but stuck out his chin. "I did," he said.

Osfrid looked back at the vampire lord. "Was I your pawn, my lord?"

Lord Muiredach smiled in amusement. "No. But you were his." He nodded toward Cavan.

Tanwen's heart leaped with fear for Cavan when the war council turned to study him. He backed up a few paces, but when no one advanced he lifted his chin in defiance. "She will play a significant role in the future of this clan." He gestured to Tanwen, and the war council turned again to stare at her.

Tanwen's emotions warred inside her. Her devotion to Peredur wanted to choke some sense into Cavan. At the same time her gratitude for all that Cavan truly had done for her, made her long to wrap him in her arms.

Lord Muiredach stood and held his arms out to embrace them all. "You see what we are up against. She has chosen a life with us even after being warned against it by her former love." Gesturing toward Cavan, he said, "He has done the unthinkable to one of our own in order to grant Tanwen her deepest wish. But that wasn't enough for him. He took it further. He forced our Osfrid to create yet another vampire – to turn Cavan who has now joined our clan. You were not just any man, were you?"

Cavan shook his head.

"No. He was a sorcerer," Lord Muiredach said. Another bout of muttering broke out. "And recall he was the first vampire to ever emerge from his turning sleep with all of his memories intact. This is what I am faced with. As long as I can trust him, he is a powerful weapon against the brethren who have held a painful sword over our heads. They've held it there forever, it seems."

Tanwen's heart beat fast. They were turning on him.

Cavan started backing up, but the war council pressed in on him. She slipped behind Lord Muiredach's seat but he had predicted her reaction. He was up out of his seat and in her path before she could blink.

Cavan bolted but was rushed by the other vampires. They clapped silver chains around his wrists, which halted him in his tracks. He pulled and twisted to escape, but the vampires tugged him forward and forced him spread-eagled to the ground before Lord Muiredach. Osfrid stood with his foot planted firmly upon Cavan's back.

Lord Muiredach yanked Tanwen in front of him so that she was forced to look at Cavan. "You claim you never knew he was a sorcerer before your turning," he said.

Cavan tried to look up at her, but Osfrid pressed down hard on his shoulders.

"That's the truth," Tanwen said, looking out at all the grim faces.

"Tell us more truths," Lord Muiredach said. "You met with this member of the brethren after he became one of them."

"Yes," she said. She watched as Cavan's wrists burned at the touch of the silver to his flesh. He writhed with the pain of it.

"Did he instruct you to turn? To become one of us?"

She turned to regard him. *"What?* No!"

"He didn't wish to plant a spy among us?"

Tanwen looked carefully into Lord Muiredach's eyes. She didn't see what she feared. He already believed her. This drama was for the benefit of his war council, that had their reasons to distrust her. She took a deep breath and faced them once again.

"He came to me after joining their brotherhood, which happened as he lay dying on the battlefield. He didn't even know they existed until they came for him."

"I'm sure we're all familiar with how the brethren are chosen," Lord Muiredach said.

"Well, what is it you want from me?" She dreaded their answer.

242 JULIA PHILLIPS SMITH

"How can we trust that he didn't come to you to enlist you in his campaign to wipe us out?" Lord Muiredach said.

"He came to say goodbye to me," she said. Cavan attempted to look at her again. Osfrid moved to prevent it, but a look from Lord Muiredach stopped him. Tanwen locked gazes with Cavan, seeing the pain it gave him to hear of her love bond with Peredur. If she tried to deny it, she would be suspect with the war council. If she admitted the full scope of their feelings, it would wound Cavan terribly.

"I was the one to beg him to make me into what he was, so that I could go with him. That's all I wanted, to be turned, to go with him, to be in whichever world he belonged."

"So this vampire at our feet – why do you suppose he helped you to turn?"

"I thought it was because he was my friend." She saw a bittersweet joy light up Cavan's eyes.

"This sorcerer you did not take for a sorcerer, not only helped you to turn," Lord Muiredach said, "but compelled Osfrid to turn him as well. Perhaps it is Cavan who helps the brethren, and not you."

Cavan laughed before he could think better of it. Osfrid drove his face down in the dirt. When he was let up, he spit and gasped for air, but still wore his dismissive smirk.

"What do you find so amusing down there?" Lord Muiredach asked.

"Why should I help the man who won the heart of her – the woman I love?" Cavan looked into Tanwen's eyes with a heartbreaking expression of surrender.

Tanwen's heart crushed when the war council members chuckled. She challenged them all with a fierce glare. "What is so funny about that?"

"How touching," Lord Muiredach said. "I'd laugh, but it's all so sad, really."

Tanwen nearly forgot the look he'd given her at the start of all of this. If he were being cruel to be kind, he seemed to relish the cruelty for its own sake. She twisted free of his grip. Looking over at Cavan, she tried to send him the message to lie quietly and say little. Then she knelt before the vampire lord.

"What must I do to assure you of my loyalty, my lord?"

"Are you in love with this sorcerer?" he asked.

"No, my lord. Not in love." She was glad she couldn't see Cavan's face.

He took a few steps toward Cavan. "And you. Are you in love with Tanwen? Even though she loves another?"

"You have already heard me say it."

Tanwen fought with herself to remain where she was. *Cavan, take care! Take care!* She heard a scuffle, heard Cavan cry out in pain.

"Say it so all may hear."

Cavan cried out again. Then, he forced the words out: "Yes, my lord. I love Tanwen. I have always loved her. I will always love her."

His words pierced her heart. She bowed her head with the pain of it.

"So it's safe to say you were not sent here by the brethren?" Lord Muiredach asked.

"No, My Lord," Cavan said. "I followed her here because I could not bear to live in the village without her."

She heard more rustling and scuffling. Cavan gave several small cries of pain. Tanwen started to turn around to see what was happening, but thought better of it at the last moment. Instead she waited until Lord Muiredach moved past her and took his seat once more. He caught her eye and gestured for her to rise and join him.

Tanwen did as she was bid. She looked everywhere but at Cavan.

"Does any vampire here challenge the presence of these two new arrivals in my war council?" Lord Muiredach asked.

No one made a sound.

The business of planning a search party to find Dengel began, as if the scene they'd just endured hadn't taken place. She waited as long as she dared. Then her gaze sought Cavan's once more.

When he stood, he looked crestfallen. She saw the silver burns had started to heal on his wrists and the members of the war council, who had given him wide berth, now stood as close to him as they would to any member of their clan.

Tanwen stole a quick glance at Lord Muiredach. He returned it easily. There were no apologies in his eyes. As lord of their clan, he must rule over this sorcerer or pay the price for his folly.

57

"What is wrong with him?"

Sigbjorn could not look Melnak in the eye. "I'm not certain. I've never known a brother to suffer such a thing." Everyone turned to stare at Peredur.

He remembered how it felt to wake that first night in the cavern, how they'd turned then to regard him. But that was when he'd been a stranger among them.

Now he was a part of them, had partaken of their blood, and they had tasted his. They had hunted together, feasted together, pulled one another from danger. He'd passed their trials and learned to be the salvation of lost souls.

Yet because he had tried to stop the innocent woman from dying horribly on the shore, suddenly he was an outsider again. He felt his brothers withdraw, even as they turned their warrior frames toward him. What could he do against that united show of force?

Anger burned as he took a few steps forward. Crouching at the ready somewhere inside him, the saint released a small tongue of lightning to lick Peredur's veins. He resisted the urge to double over, but his eyes squeezed shut with the force of it.

When he regained control of himself, Peredur saw his brethren gathered around him, their faces dark with suspicion. Gesturing roughly toward the scar, he said,

"He is here. Inside me." His voice trembled. "He burns me."

Melnak stepped forward, pulling Peredur's tunic aside to have a look at the mark which the amulet had left behind, the mark which was unlike any of the ones the saint had left to the others. "Looks no different than when I saw it last," he said, releasing the tunic.

"He's in here," Peredur insisted, indicating the amulet scar that lurked beneath his tunic.

"Our saint told you to fight our brother Sigbjorn?"

The Norseman once again looked away. Peredur felt the distance yawn and grow between himself and his closest friend – a new level of cruelty. "He told me that she was innocent," Peredur said.

"And after that, what did you tell him?" Melnak asked Sigbjorn.

"He knows we cannot interfere," the Norseman said. "He is not stupid."

"Yet he fought you," said Melnak.

"It was the saint!" Sigbjorn said.

"Why would he tell me to stop the villagers?" Peredur said, looking into the eyes of his brethren. He walked up to Melnak. "And why would you stand aside to let that woman die when it had nothing to do with her?"

"Do I look like Judgement to you?" Melnak said, moving nose to nose with him.

"Why did he stop me?" Peredur jabbed his hand toward Sigbjorn. The saint sent another bolt of heat through Peredur's veins, wringing a gasp from his lips.

Melnak reached out, seizing him firmly by the arms before Peredur could sag to the ground. "None of us has heard his voice, Peredur. Our instructions were given long ago, and passed down."

It was not that woman who deserved to burn, the saint inside of him said.

Peredur's body racked with searing heat, stiffening with screams that couldn't possibly give voice to what he was feeling, screams that Peredur turned into groans instead. Melnak released him as though he clutched a sword he'd grabbed up from a fire.

Sweat broke out over Peredur's body as he trembled with the force of the saint's heat. Cittinus' face appeared in their midst, though none of the others seemed able to see him. The youthful saint's gaze burned like the pain that roasted Peredur's flesh from the inside.

"When I came to you," Peredur said to his brethren, "you said you served the brethren. Serving ourselves is not the reason this Brotherhood was formed. She was innocent. It would have been easy to save her. I shouldn't have to explain this to you."

The saint's image rushed toward him, seemed to slam into Peredur's soul. His body rocked with the force of it.

Melnak, Sigbjorn and the others gazed in wonder at Peredur's ordeal. He felt so far removed from them, as though trapped on a far shore.

58

The search party returned without Dengel.

Tanwen watched the group of vampires as they approached Lord Muiredach. The females she conversed with kept talking, but Tanwen blocked their voices out. One member of the war council strode toward the throne room and tapped her on the shoulder to follow.

"Excuse me," she said to the others, but she did not wait for them to respond. She picked up her skirts and walking briskly to join Lord Muiredach. She brightened when she saw that Cavan was already there, speaking to a gathering of vampires.

Everyone found a place to stand as Lord Muiredach took his seat. He gestured for the leader of the search party to come forward.

A vampire stepped up and bowed. "My lord," he said.

"You have not located him."

"No, Lord Muiredach."

The vampire lord gestured for Cavan to come forward. He stepped up, his expression wary.

"Do you have a means of locating someone who cannot be found, sorcerer?"

Cavan quickly looked around, but when no one moved to take hold of him, he said, "I have several, my lord."

"May I impose upon you to use one of them to find Dengel?"

Cavan thought for a moment, then asked, "Is there a piece of clothing or adornment he would have left here, that I may hold?"

The vampires talked amongst themselves. One raced away and back in a few heartbeats. He held a long kerchief in his hand.

Cavan took it and handled it for several moments. He looked off into the distance as though he were listening for something.

Tanwen saw the hope and fear playing out upon the faces of the vampires. But Cavan's expression did not bode well for good news. He finally turned to Lord Muiredach and shook his head.

"You found nothing?" Lord Muiredach said.

"If he were still on this plane of existence, I would be able to feel it."

The war council muttered angrily. The vampire lord held out his hand for the kerchief. Cavan passed it to him with a brief bow.

Lord Muiredach looked at it with deep regret. "I fear Dengel has been cast into the true death by the brethren."

"Send them a message!" said one.

"One of theirs will pay for our loss!"

Tanwen felt their wave of anger like a hot wind. It blew over her and through her, until she wanted nothing more than to attack. But after the war council had whipped itself into a frenzy, Lord Muiredach held a hand up for silence.

"Normally, I would encourage you to take action." He laughed. "Normally, I would take the action myself."

The vampires laughed a dark laugh that made Tanwen long to see Lord Muiredach wreak vengeance. She looked over at Cavan, who gazed upon the war council with trepidation. He and his mother must have lived in fear of just this kind of mob. She pushed her way through the crowd to stand beside him. He looked at her when he felt her fingers brush his hand.

Tanwen didn't smile exactly, and neither did he, but she felt lighter inside.

Lord Muiredach held a hand up once more. "But that was before. We are in a different position now." He turned to regard Tanwen and Cavan.

She didn't want to hear what he was saying. At least part of her didn't.

"Now we are the grateful recipients of two newcomers to our clan. One of whom a certain member of the brethren will take a special interest in. Or at least, I imagine that will be the case."

Tanwen couldn't help herself. She thought of Peredur and wanted to warn him, wanted to race ahead of the plan that now formed here. Cavan grabbed her hand out of sight of anyone and squeezed.

She took a deep breath, and then another.

"And the other one...well..." Lord Muiredach said, "we can only thank Lucifer for him." He stood before Cavan. "Can you think of a way we could entice the newest of the brethren to come out and play?"

Cavan did not hesitate. "I can think of many, lord."

Lord Muiredach leaned in close and whispered, "Well I hope they all involve her." He gave Tanwen a bright smile.

"They do, my lord."

"Grand. We have a plan to pound out, then. Where are my best hammers?"

59

He ran.

He ran, but the voice of the saint would not leave him.

Where are you taking us? the saint asked.

"Stop it!" Peredur struck himself in the head.

I will be wherever you are. There's no use in this.

He stopped, closing his eyes, needing to block it all out, but Cittinus was there, too. "God help me."

The words had barely passed his lips when his bones and muscles locked up like stone. He tried to inhale deeply but his lungs would not respond to his command.

You ask Him now, the saint said. *Where were those words on the battlefield?*

Peredur tried to respond, but nothing moved. The rage he'd felt on that last day, his insistence on bargaining with his Maker, these memories flooded him so the saint could feel them as he did.

When you could have prayed to be taken to Heaven, what did you say instead?

He could hear it all again in his mind, the gurgling of the wound in his chest, the moaning of those who'd fallen all around him. *'God, I curse you!'* he'd said.

Using an inner force that Peredur could not prevent, Cittinus turned Peredur's body around. Peredur's legs moved both of them forward, back the way they'd come.

What are you doing? Peredur said in his mind. *Let me go!*

You asked for another life, Cittinus said patiently. *And He gave it to you. And He gave me to you.*

Peredur fought with everything he had, but he could not stop his own body from walking in the direction he did not wish to go. *Given me to you, you mean,* he said.

We must return to the brethren.

Why? Peredur asked. *They didn't listen to me. To you. She was innocent. I don't understand any of it.*

Look then, the saint said.

Suddenly Peredur no longer saw the night forest. He was in a sun-drenched courtyard in a golden desert. A line of a dozen ragged prisoners knelt before a centurion who held a bloody sword in his hand. Already laying off to the side were two headless bodies – the sand beside them drenched in blood.

"Swear allegiance to Caesar."

Cittinus gazed up, his dark eyes shining from an inward light. His face bore bruises, dried blood, dirt and sores, but it was Cittinus beneath it all. The broken youth rose up as straight as he could upon his knees, looked his executioner in the face and said, "We have none other to fear, save only our Lord God, who is in Heaven."

Glancing back for the nod from the proconsul, the centurion swung the sword back. The blade glinted white in the sun. When it made contact with the youth's neck, outstretched in prayer, the vision collapsed.

Peredur fell to the ground.

60

Tanwen followed several others from the war council along the coast until they made it to the still waters of an inlet. They kept a safe distance from the water itself, as any outcropping that brought them too close made them all dizzy and sick. But Cavan insisted he required water for this incantation to work.

They made their way down the steep slope to the beach. The dizziness rose. Lord Muiredach motioned everyone to stay as far back as they needed, but Cavan pushed on.

He walked directly to the water's edge, though he swayed and stumbled. Kneeling, he filled a leather sheepskin with water that lapped gently at his feet. Taking a moment to compose himself, he rose and rejoined them, his stride getting stronger the closer he got to them.

"Take the others to higher ground," Cavan instructed Osfrid. The vampire looked to Lord Muiredach for his cue, and at his nod, gathered the rest to a nearby hillock.

Cavan took Tanwen by the arm and sat her on a large boulder. He set up a shallow bowl at her feet and poured the water into it. A strong wave of nausea swept over her, and her head swirled. She could see Cavan fighting against the same thing, but Lord Muiredach held firm against it.

Pulling several small pouches from a larger sack, Cavan quickly worked to pour a measurement of this and a pinch or two of that into the bowl. He pulled out the short, thin stick he'd used back in his mother's hut and stirred the bowl's contents, whispering words over the bowl as he worked.

Tanwen's skin started to prickle. A breeze that seemed to emanate from Cavan himself whipped her hair in every direction.

Cavan stepped behind her and placed a hand on either side of her head, saying more incomprehensible words – louder this time. Tanwen felt even dizzier than before. She closed her eyes, but it didn't help at all. When she opened them again, all she saw were colors and lines shooting past her.

Then pressure from Cavan forced her to lean forward. She may as well have tumbled into a rushing river. Gazing down into the bowl of water, Tanwen saw that it acted as a window out of all this rushing and whirring. She looked into it with all her might, desperate to find something solid there. Her arms thrust forward to catch herself from falling, but Cavan held her and she stayed seated on the rock.

After what seemed like years, a face began to form in the inky depths of the bowl.

All the sounds of wind and falling stopped for her. Though her hair still swirled and her clothes flapped to and fro, she felt as calm as the still inlet. The face in the bowl was her beloved.

Peredur.

He gazed in confusion and wonder.

So many words leaped into her throat that not one of them found their way out. Tanwen reached forward toward that precious face, but Cavan's lips tickled her ear. "Don't break the surface of the water or the connection will be broken."

"What do I do?" she whispered.

"Just repeat after me," he said, and she nodded.

Peredur looked so stricken. *Hurry. Tell me what to say to him. Hurry!*

"My love," Cavan growled in her ear. Shivers ran up her spine. She repeated it, and it came out filled with Cavan's desire. For her.

Tanwen! It was him, his beautiful deep voice. But so full of longing. For her.

Why do you not come to me? Tanwen repeated Cavan's prompt.

Peredur's face lined with dismay. *You know I cannot. I know you do not come when I cry for you.*

His hand brushed his chest over his heart. He shook his head.

You have destroyed my happiness, Peredur. I shall never marry another. And you are gone.

He turned away. *You cannot be real.*

I am gone from my home. I'll never return there. I wish only for you, and I wander the world to find you. Where are you, Peredur?

He turned in every direction, clapping his hands over his ears. *Stop it!*

I shall haunt you as you haunt me.

Peredur turned back to face her, but blindly. *Where are you, then? Where do I find you?*

I'm on the northwest coast. A quiet inlet beyond the River Conwy. I will stay here until you find me. Hurry, my love.

He charged forward in their direction, and suddenly the connection was severed. Tanwen gasped with the pain of losing him.

Cavan released her, and she curled forward, needing so badly to cry but nothing came except a moan. So she moaned.

Lord Muiredach clapped Cavan soundly on the back. "Well done," he said.

"Your servant," Cavan replied.

"If you deliver this latest of the brethren to me, you shall be much more than my servant."

"My lord," Cavan said.

Tanwen sat up in time to see the last of Cavan's deep bow to Lord Muiredach. The clan lord offered his ring for Cavan to kiss. Cavan hesitated a moment, then went down on one knee, took Lord Muiredach's hand in his and kissed the ring.

Rage swept through Tanwen. How dare they barter for her as if she were not there? She may as well be back in her father's hut being made to take Rhodri as her husband. Tanwen jumped to her feet, desperate to run from here.

But the world tilted abruptly. Her face hit the sand and she blacked out.

61

He'd never foreseen anything like this for himself, never once imagined that someday he would go mad. Wasn't this madness – hearing voices, seeing visions, losing control of his own actions to an invader inside his body?

We cannot go to her, the saint said, turning Peredur's body back toward the brethren.

"I promised her," Peredur ground out between clenched teeth. With an effort that sent the sweat running into his eyes, he stopped the saint's movement of his body until they stood in a valley, surrounded by rock and scrub.

If you do this, it will change everything, the saint said again.

"Then let it change," Peredur said, and his body suddenly returned to him. The saint retreated. Finally Peredur could breathe as deeply as he wanted.

He was exhausted. He had no idea where to find Tanwen, where to begin looking for her. All he could think about was the blood he needed.

As soon as he sank his teeth into a slumbering man's neck, he knew what he needed to do. The hardy blood filled and repaired him, until he reached the point where he could sense the man's life force seriously weaken. He was almost unable to back away, to leave the man to the remainder of his life.

But the saint's fire burned the moment he tried to push a little farther.

Creeping out of the man's hut, Peredur sensed the presence of the brethren in the distance, yet he could not feel his beloved anywhere. Her heartbeat was something he couldn't mistake for anyone else's.

She must be farther away than he suspected. Though, if so, how could he have received that message from her?

In the end, Peredur and the saint made their way back to the others, who welcomed them without questions.

62

Tanwen sat in the council room listening to their plan to capture her beloved when he appeared to claim her. Cavan was, of course, deep in the thick of it. He was no longer cast to the side. Now he was their golden boy.

When she could stomach no more of it, she rose to her feet and swept from the room. She didn't bother to check to see if Cavan or Lord Muiredach noticed her leaving. She didn't care what they thought.

All she wanted was to get as far away from all of them as she could. Would she ever be shown how to transform into those other things? A wolf form would be so good right now. How she wanted to run and run and run on four swift legs. How she wanted to sink powerful jaws into something and rip it to shreds.

She didn't pay any heed to where she went. She was surprised to find herself back at the same inlet where Cavan had forced those terrible words from her lips.

Tanwen abandoned herself to the dizzy sickness and fell to the sand. Her true distress came at the realization that the words Cavan had squeezed from her had only been the truth.

Peredur *had* ruined her chances for happiness. Her heart cried for him every moment of every night. All the trappings of her new vampire life held a crazed importance to her because they distracted her from the pain of facing the loss of her beloved.

She crawled forward through the sand, sifting through it as though the grains could hold the touch of him. She actually did find the footprints she'd made, along with Cavan and Lord Muirdach some nights earlier. She howled at the injustice of it all.

Then she dug into the sand, flinging it everywhere, pouring it over her head. The minerals in the sand were comforting, as soothing as any warm bath had been in her human life. She wallowed in it until she resembled nothing so much as a ghost.

63

The knife tip bit as he dug at the scar, but Peredur was determined to be rid of him.

Remember your promise, the saint said.

"She needs me." Peredur sat tucked away from his brothers, deep in the cavern, deeper than he'd ever been. The echoing drip-drip of moisture rolling down the pillars of rock helped to muffle the sounds of his exertion.

On the night of your ordeal, when you hung in bonds before the tree – when you came for me, what did you promise?

Peredur glanced over. Cittinus crouched at his elbow, watching over the amulet scar with maddening acceptance.

"Didn't you know?" Peredur jabbed the knife deeply and dug, grunting with pain. "I have a history of disappointing people."

The saint faltered as the knife bit deeply. *You have never let down your brothers.*

"I haven't been with them very long. Just give it time." He flicked his wrist. The lump of flesh flew across the cavern to rest upon the gravel before it crumbled into dust.

Glancing all around him, Peredur saw only the cavern. He was alone with the pain he had given himself. No burning fire from the saint scorched his veins.

He laughed in exhausted triumph. Slipping off the rock upon which he'd braced himself, Peredur stretched out on the pebbly floor of the cavern. Minerals released their strength into his every muscle and joint.

It was going to be all right.

Now he knew Tanwen waited for him somewhere. She needed him. He didn't know how he'd been able to hear her voice or see her face.

But he was through with letting down the ones he loved. There had to be a way to make this right. There had to be.

64

This time when Tanwen swept from the cavern, she made certain Cavan was watching before she did. It wasn't long before he followed.

"Tanwen, stop," he said, but she did no such thing. "Tanwen!"

When he raced ahead of her and blocked her way, she wasn't surprised. Just annoyed.

"I don't want to talk to you," she said, which wasn't entirely true. Why else had she wanted him to follow her? She didn't know what she wanted. That was the real problem.

"You're having second thoughts about doing this. Aren't you?" he asked.

"I'm having second, third and fourth thoughts about it." She continued on her way, though she had no real destination. Only to get away from her turmoil.

"I know how you must be feeling," he said, catching up with her.

"No! You don't know the first thing about it!"

He grabbed her and swung her to face him. "Weren't you listening when Lord Muiredach forced me to tell the entire war council how I felt about you?"

Tanwen turned her face away.

"And I don't know anything about having my feelings thrown in my face?" he said.

She clutched his arms and looked deeply into his gray eyes, so bright with emotion. "Then you of all people should know I can't go through with this, Cavan! I can't feed him to you who wait like a pack of dogs to chew him up."

Cavan grabbed her just as roughly. "No matter how many times I remind you, somehow you always twist it back, away from the danger he means to us."

"Remind me? Don't you mean argue with me?"

He let go of her, panting with the effort of stopping words he wasn't saying.

But she clung to him still. "Why can't you take pity on us?" she said.

"On *us*?" he said as though she'd been sick all over him.

She released him and sagged to the ground, too miserable to plead with him any longer.

"Who ever took pity on me?" he asked. "How would I know how to show any to another?"

She looked up then, into his face and appealed to that scarred boy inside him. "You have already shown me such kindness, Cavan – you and your mam, both. That hasn't gone from you, surely?"

At the mention of his mam, Cavan jerked as though stuck with a knife. The look of complete vulnerability that crossed his face gave Tanwen a surge of hope. She crawled forward a few steps and grabbed hold of him, dragging him down to join her.

"You know why I agreed to be turned, Cavan. You *know* why."

Cavan shook his head and wouldn't look at her.

"It was for one reason. For *him*, and only for him."

"Please, don't."

"Cavan, you can't ask me to betray him like this! You have to help me warn him. He doesn't deserve— "

A long cloak brushed past them, and they jumped apart. Lord Muiredach looked down at both of them in amusement. "Come now. What could be so terrible? Not a lovers' quarrel, surely?"

Cavan hung his head for a moment, rising to his feet with as much dignity as he could gather. "No. Of course not." He held a hand out to Tanwen.

She had been so close to securing Cavan's help. Now she was less likely to stop this whole macabre reunion than she'd ever been. Tanwen used all the will she possessed to take Cavan's hand and get to her feet.

"My clan enjoys its entertainments," Lord Muiredach said. "Now, do try to remember you're both members of the war council, won't you?"

Tanwen nodded, unable to force a reply. Cavan simply clenched his jaw against the words he wouldn't let out.

Lord Muiredach swept a hand to indicate the path they were on. "Let's continue our stroll. The clan doesn't need to see any more, I think."

She took as deep a breath as she could. Peredur's face haunted her as she made herself walk alongside their lord. She listened to the vampires talk idly about insignificant things, and all the while the memory of Peredur charging to her during the final moments of her visitation took up all of her attention.

Suddenly the memory of her father's face rose up to replace Peredur's. It all came back so clearly. How stifled, how imprisoned she'd felt under her father's demands. She hadn't been a dutiful daughter when she'd lived as a maiden, and she was far from being a dutiful clan member under Lord Muiredach.

Her first days here as a vampire, when she'd had no memory of her life, had felt so free, so alive, so passionate. Now, as each memory surfaced, it all began to fall backwards into familiar territory.

Tanwen had lived as long as she meant to under these intolerable restrictions. Somehow she must work out a plan all of her own – one that would come into play the moment her beloved was in place for Lord Muiredach's hateful scheme.

65

The brethren worked silently, each to his own thoughts, readying their weapons for their next encounter with their cousins. None of them, except Peredur, could see the saint, who sat patiently at Peredur's side – the same side that held the scar, the same scar that had grown back the very next night.

Melnak kept glancing over at Peredur, who sharpened his blade with angry strokes of the whetstone.

"You feel up to this encounter?" Melnak asked, finally.

"I'll be fine." Peredur looked into the saint's eyes. Cittinus did not appear convinced.

Plunging his sword into the welcoming earth, Melnak grasped the pommel and looked off into the distance. "I don't know..." He gazed back at Peredur, his eyes bright with accusation. "You have been a riddle, of late."

"Are you worried that a warrior, one who knows how to fight, could be at all influenced by a saintly youth – one who only knew how to lose his head?" Peredur asked, while gazing pointedly at the saint.

Cittinus got to his feet, his face drawn with sorrow.

"Should I be?" Melnak asked, clearly *not* seeing the saint who stood directly between them.

"No." Peredur ignored the saint, returning his mentor's gaze, needing his brothers to believe in him.

66

Tanwen approached the hut with a mix of dread and desire. Tonight they'd plant the seed that would bring her Peredur to her at last. Or else they would compel his downfall.

Osfrid motioned for Tanwen to stay close behind him. As a rule, the vampires were solitary hunters but Lord Muiredach ordered Osfrid to take Tanwen along because Cavan needed her to procure certain items for the spell he would cast. Since she was to masquerade as a village woman whom the Brotherhood would soon encounter, the spell would be more potent if Tanwen collected what was needed.

She wished Cavan were here. Forgetting a step was more likely than not in Tanwen's distracted state. Her mind frantically wondered over and over how she would get to Peredur before the others did their worst.

Motioning for Tanwen to stay put, Osfrid stood before the closed door and called to the woman inside – but only with his mind. Tanwen heard the irresistible words and had to fight to stay put. A mere woman couldn't possibly resist, and she didn't.

She came to the door and pushed it aside, her face soft and radiant as though waiting for a lover. Osfrid gave Tanwen the barest of gestures to join him. She'd had to struggle to resist his earlier call. Answering this now was a floodgate of relief.

Tanwen crept up behind him and stared into the face of the mesmerized woman. She couldn't see or hear Tanwen, only Osfrid.

"Do you invite me inside?" he asked. She smiled such a warm smile, it aroused Tanwen to hunger in an instant. The woman stepped to the side and gestured for the vampire to enter her home. Tanwen slipped in on the other side of him.

Once inside, Osfrid took the woman into his arms and kissed her tenderly. She leaned back in his embrace, sighing with a pleasure Tanwen guessed was new to her...she seemed so overcome with feeling.

Osfrid backed her toward the bed, laying them both down. Tanwen's breathing grew heavy with the desire that filled the hut. The vampire stretched out over the woman's clinging form, his hands roaming everywhere at once. Tanwen's fangs grew hungry for blood.

The woman moaned a strange moan, filled with longing and fear. Osfrid reared back, then plunged his fangs into the sweet neck.

Tanwen snapped out of her lusty reverie. She dashed forward, pulling a cloth from the sack Cavan had given her. Osfrid wrenched his head to the side with incredible difficulty, his face lined with effort, but he spit the virgin's blood into the cloth that Tanwen held for him.

Still the woman was oblivious to Tanwen's presence. It was unsettling, as had been the wise woman's enchantment back in the village. Her hands trembling with the strangeness and the potent atmosphere in this hut, Tanwen rolled the blood-soaked cloth and tied it, placing it back inside the sack.

Next Tanwen positioned herself near to the woman's head. Osfrid rocked the former virgin back and forth as he took her. Tanwen's skin longed to be caressed; her body longed to join their rhythm. But Cavan required a snip of hair from this woman.

Tanwen forced herself to focus. She slipped a small knife from the sack and took hold of a lock of the woman's hair. Just then the woman tossed her head in abandon. The lock slipped from her fingers, but more of her hair fell over Tanwen's hands.

It was so soft and smelled so sweet. Tanwen buried her face in it, just for a moment. Before she knew it, her hands had crept up to stroke the woman's neck and shoulders, but Peredur's face rose up in her mind, his expression so wounded, so raw. Tanwen shook her head against the memories. She clutched the knife handle, determined to get what she needed so she might stroke her beloved once more – not this stranger.

A quick slice and the deed was done.

Tanwen stuffed the lock of hair into the sack along with the bloody cloth. Now it was just a matter of waiting this out so she could deliver the charms to Cavan.

She stood and walked away from the writhing bodies, no longer fettered by the power of their coupling. Clutching the sack of ingredients Cavan needed for his spell, Tanwen looked out into the night – already imagining the touch of her true lover.

67

It is time.

Peredur almost answered him, but didn't want his brothers to hear him talking to himself on the eve of battle. There was a woman in the next village over, whom it was said carried the signs of being turned.

He brought up the image of Tanwen that had appeared to him so recently, the one where she'd begged him to come to her.

If we go to her, it will change everything.

Melnak motioned them all to head out of the cavern. Joining the others as they set out at an easy run, Peredur's blood began to heat with the saint's fire.

No! he cried out in his mind. *You must allow me to fight! They will take us down if you don't let me off your damned leash.*

He focused on moving his own limbs, fighting the drag on his bones as though escaping the sucking mud of a hidden bog.

When you came for me, what did you promise? the saint asked again.

Peredur's vision of the saint's desert ordeal reared up in his mind. Saint Cittinus had been a starving, broken youth, standing up to the might of the Romans who'd conquered his homeland. He'd been given a simple ultimatum, and had answered it with unwavering inner conviction.

'Swear allegiance to Caesar.'

Cittinus had gazed up, dark eyes shining from an inward light. His face had borne bruises, dried blood, dirt and sores, but it had been Cittinus beneath it all. The broken youth had risen straight as he could upon his knees, looked his executioner in the face and said, 'We have none other to fear, save only our Lord God, who is in Heaven.'

He had not flinched from the blade as it swung to send his head flying across the sandy courtyard.

How could Peredur have insulted him by claiming to be the stronger of the two?

That broken, damaged youth had begged, 'I thirst' during Peredur's amulet trial. What had been Peredur's response?

The night forest raced by as he fought the saint to keep up with his brothers, on their way to fight for souls in the name of the Almighty.

'As God wills it,' he'd said on the night of his ordeal.

No sooner did the words echo in his mind, but the dragging weight upon his limbs released. Peredur shot forward into the night, filled with joy to hear nothing but his own breathing, his own footsteps, his own thoughts.

68

The war council, along with the most ferocious of the fighters, collected along the edge of the trees to await the arrival of their prize.

Tanwen walked toward the woman's hut like a bride bedecked for her husband. The woman herself lay pale and emptied of every drop of blood, tucked away in the shadows against a tree.

Cavan had layered the woman's appearance over Tanwen's own, using the blood and hair she'd retrieved for him. She felt the magic humming on her skin. It mimicked the excitement that flickered inside her as she entered the hut.

Pulling aside the blanket, she lay on the pallet, settling herself and enjoying the familiar sensations of her previous existence. She missed them, the simple joys of a real bed, a fireside for gathering around, the cooking pots...all the trappings of home.Laying here, it was easy to recall that frosty night in her father's hut when Peredur had come for her. It seemed too good to be true that at any moment he would come for her again.

She turned and stared at the doorway, forcing herself to forget the clan gathered in the night to take down her beloved. Tanwen had her own plan.

For it to work, she must keep her wits about her and hold on to her courage.

The minutes stretched into hours. Perhaps he would not come, this night. Suppose they had all prepared this celebration and no one arrived to partake?

69

Peredur could not keep the shadow of his sorrow from the brethren that evening. Sigbjorn finally asked him about it as they made their way into the forest to the west of the road. They headed toward the home of a woman in danger of being turned into a vampire.

"You must have had a certain dream yesterday," the Norseman said matter-of-factly.

If the Norseman had ripped all of Peredur's clothing from him without warning, Peredur could not have been more surprised.

Sigbjorn nodded. "I can see for myself. You don't have to explain it."

"Why have I not had one before this?" Had each of the brethren been visited by his former love, as Tanwen had called to him some nights past?

The Norseman shook his head and smiled his blinding toothy grin. "Have you ever been delayed in anything you've done here, Welshman?"

"I see," Peredur said. "I'm somehow advancing more quickly than expected."

Sigbjorn nodded.

"Again?"

"I did not have my first dream until after I received my scar, which as you know was not for a year and a half."

"I suppose you know what sort of dream it was then?"

The Norseman smiled his brilliant smile. "Is there any other kind that's worth remembering?"

Peredur stopped grinning and grew serious. Sigbjorn's joking didn't match the vision Peredur had received of Tanwen. "Was it a dream, truly? What I mean is, did you ever..."

"It never returns, Welshman. Be assured of that."

Peredur was certain now that Sigbjorn was referring to another kind of dream entirely.

"The main reason to lay with a woman, of course," the Norseman continued, "is to make lots of little babies, and that is not in the realm of such as us. Our passions run to blood now. You don't need this – " Sigbjorn grabbed his crotch. "To drain a man of his blood."

"I miss her, Sigbjorn," Peredur said, hating the tone in his voice but unable to keep the yearning at bay.

"Each of us has left behind someone we miss, Peredur. Sometimes some of us have several dear ones that are missed. The difference depends on which of the brethren you consider."

They both laughed, Sigbjorn clapping a hand so heartily on Peredur's back that he stumbled forward several steps. Peredur waited until Sigbjorn fell into step with him and they continued on silently for a while. Then another laugh escaped him.

They both pulled themselves together, walking a brief while before dissolving into snickering once again. Melnak dropped back from the head of the group to join them. One look at the two of them, and the Byzantine realized the subject matter. He didn't bother to say anything, just gazed meaningfully at both and disappeared to the head of their party.

Sigbjorn and Peredur made sure to avoid looking at each other as they followed the others through the forest. Their sharpest wits were needed for the holy task ahead.

Once they were crouching in the shadows, and it was clear that the woman's hut waited for them, all thoughts of dreams and saints fell by the wayside. Peredur took up position and waited for the signal from Melnak.

70

Tanwen stretched under the blanket, smiling even as she wondered why this woman had lived alone. No matter – she lived no longer. But Tanwen would always be grateful to her for granting her this chance at happiness with Peredur.

Then suddenly, with no warning and with the lightning speed they all possessed, someone was at the door. She forced herself to stay down, her heart beating with the frenzy of her joy.

But whispers filled the air, words that scraped along her spine like claws. Tanwen jerked, flinging the blanket off and hissing at the speaker of such monstrous sounds. The face that gazed upon her was not her beloved's. It was a stranger's.

No. No, this cannot be.

She shrieked with agony. Crawling along the ceiling, leaping to the furthest corner, she tried to stay out of reach of the fire of those words, but they licked her skin without mercy. In a burst of desperation, she shot toward the door.

Two vampires blocked her way. No, not vampires. Two brethren.

Peredur.

One was Peredur.

She nearly faltered. His complete lack of recognition and the look upon his face took her courage and dashed it completely. Then she remembered. The tingling on her face reminded her that she was not in her own guise.

The three brethren all reached for something that hung around their necks. Tanwen stiffened with pain. Waves of torment washed over her as white pendants shone their damage at her.

She fought them off like a deranged cat, hissing and yowling. She completely forgot about the vampires lining the forest's edge, about her disguise, about her plan to steal Peredur away from the tumult. There was no room for anything except the pain, the awful pain.

Then all hell broke loose.

The vampires charged from their positions along the tree line. Holding their pendants before them, the brethren turned outward and formed a circle around her.

No matter how dreadfully the energy from the pendants hurt, the vampires advanced, stirred to anger and frothing for payback.

Tanwen was spared the pain now that it was trained outward. She fought for breath, collecting herself, though she didn't have much time. Her new clan was bound to overwhelm these three brethren, and she couldn't bear to lose Peredur when he was just returned to her.

Strangely, she didn't sense fear among this trio of brethren. A little drop of doubt rippled her certainty that her clan would rid itself of these pests. She turned to stare at her beloved.

With all of her might, she used her newfound ability to influence, to turn his attention away from the advancing vampire horde. Yet Peredur's attention remained just as focused.

At last he sensed her attempt. He glanced back at her.

This was it. Tanwen's life – her human life, and now her vampire life – it all came down to this. This second. This heartbeat.

His green eyes turned to look at her. His gaze didn't see her, only saw the woman she appeared to be, but she appealed to the goodness that she knew burned inside of him.

"Save me," she called to him with the most haunting tone she could find. It was the sound of her heart breaking at the fear of losing him when he was so close. So close.

With one simple gesture, she brushed her hand along his arm. Then she burst through the tumult, ducking beneath the outstretched arms of the brethren and careening into the night.

71

Peredur broke the circle they'd created, hearing the snarls of the vampires as they converged on Sigbjorn and Brude. But Peredur couldn't do anything else but follow the woman they'd come here to set free. A force he couldn't resist compelled him to do it.

Swinging his sword, lunging, turning and dodging, Peredur hacked a path through the vampires, keeping the fleeing woman in his sights. The sounds of the battle retreated behind him as he gained ground and dashed to close the gap between himself and the terrified woman.

She was fast, fast as any vampire. He turned to fight off one vampire who gave chase. Knocking him down with the flat of the sword, Peredur fumbled for his amulet and spoke the words that sent the vampire into a writhing frenzy. Slamming his sword into its sheath, Peredur sped forward before the vampire could recover.

The woman was barely visible as she ran over the field toward the sea. Every step forward cost Peredur dearly. *What was she doing?* His head swirled, his limbs grew weak.

Then she darted a look back at him.

Something pierced his heart at her glance. How wild and terrified she looked, as if she were trying to run right out of her skin. Time seemed to stand still for a long moment as they locked glances. For a moment, he thought...he...but no, it must be the dream, the dream he'd just had about Tanwen that charmed him.

The woman broke free of his gaze, turning once more to the sea. He couldn't let her reach the waves. If she waded into them, he would be forced to watch her drown herself. But he could yet free her of the vampires' hold. He knew he could.

"Stop!"

She halted for a moment, then pressed on. His steps sank in the sand. His fingers fumbled for the amulet. He dropped it, though it still hung around his neck. Persisting, he stumbled forward. She was almost upon the wet sand. The white lines of foam crept forward, forward to claim her.

"In the name of God, I command you to stop!"

She jerked backward as if he yanked her with a rope. Turning, her fangs gleamed as she hissed at him.

Peredur shook his head to clear it. He raised the amulet before him, but couldn't remember the words he must use. He swayed, trying to focus on the woman whose image doubled and blurred before him.

She rushed him, then. With a leap, she kicked the amulet from his hand and pushed him to the ground. Snarling, ripping at his neck, she went for the amulet with more force than he anticipated, almost more force than he could block.

They fought for several agonized moments. She pressed him down into the wet sand so his strength sapped away from him. With a terrific blow, she swiped the amulet from its leather strand around his neck.

Peredur's strength evaporated with the loss of the amulet. It had held him up against the power of the sea. Without it he lay there under her snarling gaze, unable to lift a finger to defend himself.

The vampire grabbed hold of him and rolled them both over and over away from the waves. The farther away from the wet sand they got, the stronger he became, until he took control of the rolling, stopped it and pinned her down in the sand.

The vampire no longer snarled at him. Its face shimmered before him, and for a moment he thought he looked into his beloved Tanwen's face.

Is this how the devil fought? By using an expression of love in the guise of the woman he was forced to leave behind?

But this couldn't be a delusion. This must be truly her. Tanwen.

72

Tanwen nearly forgot that Cavan's enchantment made her face appear as the dead woman's image and not her own. The confusion in Peredur's eyes hurt her as much as that first news of his death – until she remembered.

"My love," she said. "It's me. It *is* me."

He reared back as if she'd hurled silver into his face. She saw her moment and squirmed into a sitting position. Reaching out tenderly, she touched his face. "I've come for you. I couldn't go on another day if I couldn't be with you. You know you feel as I do."

"Tanwen?" he whispered, his voice breaking.

She nodded, and if she could have wept with joy, she would have. "I've followed you here. To this life. You said it wasn't possible, but here I am."

Peredur's face fought to conceal so many warring emotions. His eyes shone with joy. His fingers brushed aside the hair from her face, but still he denied her truth and shook his head, *no*.

"Yes," she said, grabbing his hands in hers. "I'm real. As real as you."

"But you're a...you're a..."

"A vampire. As you are." She smiled.

"Not as I am! I am one of the brethren! I told you—"

"Yes, you told me. If I were, you'd have to kill me."

"Yes. That's right. I nearly killed you tonight!"

She shook her head. "You thought I was someone else."

He took her face in his hands, roughly this time. "Whose face did I see just now?"

"It was a woman we'd started to turn."

"Where is she?" he asked, looking back.

Tanwen grabbed him, forced him to look at her. "It doesn't matter. She's gone now."

"Gone?"

"They drained her. She's dead."

Peredur hung his head for a long moment. Finally he looked up at her. He looked so disappointed. Even horrified.

"Weren't you coming to free her from being a vampire?" she asked.

He nodded, unable to speak.

"Well, she's not a vampire. No need to worry about her. She's with God, now."

"You don't seem concerned about her," he whispered, as if he could barely get the words out.

Tanwen's hurt feelings returned. "Why are you so concerned about her?" she asked, pulling away from him.

"You used her." His eyes filled with pain. None of this was turning out the way she'd imagined it. It was all turning out wrong.

"I would do it again, to get to you, Peredur. I told you I would do anything to be with you – and I did all I could, and more."

He grabbed her by the arms and shook her. "And I told you I would have to *kill* you if you became my enemy."

"How am I your enemy?" she asked. "I am a vampire, and you are a vampire."

"You are not yourself, Tanwen. Melnak warned me there was danger in reuniting, and now..."

"How can he know how I was before? How I am now? I have never met him. He doesn't know me. He doesn't know how much I love you, or what I would do for you."

"Stop it!" He threw her down into the sand and reached for his amulet, but his hands groped at the empty space where it had been. A look of panic washed over his face.

She laughed at how ridiculous he was to be frightened. "Don't worry yourself over that," she purred, and her heart warmed when he relaxed as she rose to her feet. She moved to him as he knelt on the sand, taking his head in her hands and pressing his face into her stomach. He didn't resist her. He wrapped his arms around her, pulling her close, inhaling her scent, kissing her breasts through her robe.

Running her hands through his hair, Tanwen's heart swelled with the joy that had been delayed somewhat – but how could she blame him? How shocking it all must have been.

"We can run away from all of them," she said. "We don't need anyone else. We can go where they won't find us."

He stopped then, looking up at her. "Where would that be?"

She shrugged. "I don't know, but it's certainly not here. We should leave soon if we're to get away from them."

"I have taken a vow, Tanwen."

Disbelief at what he was saying froze everything inside her. The joy that spiraled into the night shattered. "Your vow is to me," she said at last. "To us."

He shook his head, climbing to his feet. "It's not as simple as that."

"No," she said. "Stop! Don't say it."

"I have a sacred purpose. Perhaps that's why I was born in the first place. Born as a man so I would one day join this Brotherhood."

"Peredur, don't."

"I told you when I came to see you, back at your father's house."

She put her hands over her ears and curled into herself. "Stop! Stop it!"

Peredur wrapped his arms around her, pressing his face against hers, whispering into her ear. "I tried to explain, but you wouldn't hear me. I told you why I needed to go on the raid against the Irish, and you didn't hear me then, either."

"It's all pride with you. None of it has anything to do with me."

"Tanwen, I love you. I love you more than I'll love anyone for the rest of my life. And that promises to be a very long time."

"Not necessarily," a deep voice said.

Tanwen and Peredur both turned to see a long line of the war council forming all around them. Lord Muiredach sauntered forward with an appreciative smile.

"I think your life span just shortened by a great deal." He stopped before them, reached out to caress Tanwen's face and blocked Peredur's hand as it tried to strike his away. In three vicious moves, Lord Muiredach kicked her beloved to the ground.

As Peredur moaned and struggled to rise, Tanwen looked up into the face of her vampire lord. She and Peredur had not been quick enough. They'd wasted precious time and now it was too late.

Too late.

73

A vampire guard fell upon Peredur, clapping silver chains around his arms and legs before he could recover himself. He writhed in their burning grip, helpless to stop the vampires from dragging him along the ground, up the slope, away from the sand and onto the grass.

He snarled and spit and kicked at them, as much as the silver chains would allow. Dimly he heard Tanwen crying, "No! No!"

The vampires crowded around him, shoving, kicking and yanking hard on the chains. The vampire guard handled the chains with heavy gloves that seemed to protect them. Peredur tried to keep fighting but the silver drained the strength out of him.

When he couldn't fight any longer, he knelt before the howling mob, chest heaving as he fought for breath. He glared up at the vampire leader who stepped before him, arms crossed.

"You have me," Peredur said. "Is all this necessary?" He used the last of his strength to lift his bound hands.

The leader gazed down at him in amusement. "Of course not," he said.

Peredur stared without wavering. He kept his hands raised even though he began to shudder with the strain.

The leader gestured to his guard with a quick nod of his head. "Oh, alright."

Peredur fought the urge to sigh his relief as the vampires unwound the silver from his limbs. Instead he kept his gaze trained upon the leader. Tanwen's voice filtered to him again. "Please! Please! Let him go!"

The leader looked up, as if from a reverie. "Where is she?" he asked.

A commotion beyond the crowd broke Peredur's concentration. The circle of vampires surrounding him parted, and Tanwen was dragged to her knees beside him, where she encircled him in her embrace.

Peredur gazed into her eyes. She was beside herself with worry for him. Wasn't she worried for herself? He took a deep breath and placed a protective arm around her. Facing the leader once more, he said, "How did you turn her?"

The leader looked as though he had to think about that for a moment. Then a sly smile spread across his face. "I believe you'll have to ask *him*."

An imposing vampire stepped into view. His expression toward Tanwen was very unfriendly. Peredur held her closer to him.

"I was summoned to her, to turn her," the vampire said.

Peredur glanced at Tanwen, who returned his gaze without refuting the vampire's words.

"Summoned," the leader said. "That's an unusual word to use. For a vampire, I mean. Are you certain that's the word you want?"

The vampire nodded.

The leader smiled an almost embarrassed smile. "That's the word we shall use, then."

Peredur noticed a slight flutter inside him, as though he'd swallowed a bee that stuck underneath his ribs where the scar from his initiation marked his skin. He nearly reached for his amulet, but remembered in time that Tanwen had ripped it from his neck back on the beach.

"I told you I would do anything," she whispered for his ears only. "And I did."

Peredur turned and looked deep into her eyes. His Tanwen still lurked in there somewhere. He could feel her trying to break free of the vampire she'd become, but he knew from his own self-discovery that his new allegiance to the brethren was stronger than anything he'd ever experienced. Stronger still was his bond to Saint Cittinus.

He remembered Melnak's words.

"How ever did you manage to summon a vampire to turn you?" the leader asked of her. She stiffened.

The leader reached forward and took her hand. Peredur held her tightly at first, but when it became obvious it was a tug-of-war he loosened his grip. Tanwen rose to her feet, though she tried to resist. She looked over her shoulder at Peredur but couldn't break the hold the leader had over her.

Peredur tried to rise but the vampire guard kept him on his knees. The leader gathered Tanwen beside him, tucking her hand through his arm. She looked at Peredur with panicky apology. A deep dread settled in the pit of his stomach.

The circle of vampires parted once more. A figure stepped into view. Peredur's breath caught in his throat.

"I summoned the vampire, my lord." It was the wise woman's son.

"At whose request?" the leader asked.

No one spoke. No one had to. It was all too clear. Tanwen gazed at Peredur, her apologetic look of a moment before, replaced by ferociously stubborn pride.

Peredur's heart couldn't ache any more than if she'd reached into his chest and ripped it out.

He looked away to Cavan and addressed him. "You did *this* to her?"

"I did this *for* her," Cavan answered. "More than you cared to do for her."

The buzzing sensation in Peredur's side intensified. He struggled to catch his breath and not disclose any weakness. "I warned her not to do it at all."

"Females aren't always the best at following orders," the leader said. The only female in this mob – exclusive of Tanwen – balked at his words.

"Come, ladies," he said, smirking. "I'm well aware you have little regard for the way males conduct business."

The leader placed an arm around Tanwen's waist and leaned into her with an easy intimacy. She looked uneasily at Peredur, begging him with her glance not to believe, not to hear.

"However, I do recall your presence at several meetings of this war council," he said to Tanwen, gesturing with an elegant hand to indicate the mob surrounding them. Gazing down at Peredur, he said, "You are a prize I am very pleased to win. I, too, will do whatever it takes to get what I desire."

The leader passed Tanwen to one of the guards, who took her far more roughly by the arms. Motioning for Cavan to join him, the leader said, "It seems you two know each other."

Cavan nodded. "We do, my lord. He is from my village."

Addressing Peredur, the leader said, "Do you recall this vampire from the time when he was a man?"

"He is Cavan," Peredur answered. "Son of the wise woman."

"Are you in love with Tanwen?" the leader asked Peredur bluntly.

All of sudden Peredur knew what he must do. Closing his eyes for a brief moment while he found his courage, Peredur met the leader's gaze.

"No," he said.

74

"What?" Tanwen said, while Cavan made a sound of disgust.

"Unpleasant news for her," the leader said with a sardonic smile.

"It shouldn't be," Peredur said, gazing at her. "I explained quite clearly where my loyalties lie."

The leader nodded. Turning to Cavan, he asked, "And you?"

"My lord?" Cavan asked, suddenly on the alert.

"Are you in love with Tanwen?" the leader asked.

Peredur's heart seized up.

Cavan appeared to struggle with a flare-up of rage. He forced himself to lower his gaze. "Yes, Lord Muiredach."

Lord Muiredach. So that was his name.

"Yes, what?" the vampire lord pestered.

"Yes, my lord," Cavan ground out. "I am in love with Tanwen."

"I know, I know," Lord Muiredach chuckled. "We went over all of this before." He gestured to the guard who held Tanwen to bring her forward. "And you? Whom did you say you loved when I asked you before?"

"I am in love with Peredur," Tanwen said, her voice thick with emotion. Peredur forced himself to look at her, to feel every bit of pain he deserved.

"Not this vampire," asked Lord Muiredach, nodding toward Cavan, "who did what could not be done...for you? Summoned one of us to turn you?"

"I am in love with Peredur," she repeated. "No one else."

"And you?" Lord Muiredach asked Peredur. "I ask again, to whom does your heart belong?"

Drawing himself up as straight as he could while on his knees, Peredur said, "My loyalties lie with the Brotherhood."

"How utterly predictable. So, there's no longer room in there," he said, stepping forward and tapping Peredur in the chest, "for *love*?"

Peredur met the gaze of his tormentor. "Not in the manner she would require. All of that is gone now. As you are well aware."

"Ah, yes. Your Brotherhood." Lord Muiredach chuckled. "You practice an infamous restraint none of us would care for."

The entire mob of vampires growled and chuckled in a manner that set Peredur's skin crawling.

"I suppose as you're still fairly new to the Brotherhood, you still haven't discovered that some things aren't as they were spelled out for you on first arrival," Lord Muiredach said. Flicking his finger, he called two vampires forward, the other female and a hulking vampire.

They looked toward Peredur with smiles of pity. Then the female began licking her way up one of the clan vampire's neck, kissing him deeply and hungrily.

Melnack's words burned in Peredur's brain.

Lord Muiredach squatted down beside Peredur. "There's none of this where you come from, I'd bet." Peredur looked at him with barely concealed contempt, which seemed to have no effect. "It gets better. I promise."

And with that, the vampire laid the female down on the grass, pushed aside his trewes and exposed a lie that cut Peredur deeply.

75

Tanwen looked past the two bodies undulating with unbridled sex, watching her beloved struggle to pull a mask over his own shattered faith. She should take comfort in the look in his eyes. He'd said he didn't love her anymore, that his cursed brethren were preferable to her, after everything she'd been through to get back to him.

But her love couldn't be crushed so easily. Even if he'd said those hateful words, she couldn't stop her heart from bleeding for him as he knelt there, forced to watch a pleasure his brethren denied him.

Suddenly his green eyes were watching her, green eyes filled with betrayal, filled with rage, with warning – with desire.

Desire. For her. She was certain of it.

That explained it. He'd been told he could no longer indulge in sex as a member of the Brotherhood. He didn't want his beloved to live without something so integral to love, with the expression of love.

Oh, Peredur. How I love your attempt to spare me. But you don't have to spare me anything. Here we can indulge as much as we like.

Lord Muiredach was whispering something to her beloved. Peredur looked away, trying not to listen, but Lord Muiredach sped to the other side in a heartbeat, his lips still moving, whispering, not giving Peredur any respite.

Her heart beat fast as she watched the vampires' bodies quicken their pace toward release. Her own arousal increased, her excitement almost unbearable at the thought that Peredur might still come around to her. She took a step toward him but was held back by the guard.

Tanwen glanced with annoyance at the one who restrained her, but the vampire met her gaze with desire. She felt his arousal and cursed her body for responding to it.

"No!" Peredur said finally.

The couple reached their climax to the cheers of the war council. As they peeled apart from each other, Lord Muiredach bared his fangs before Peredur.

"*No!*" Peredur cried again, struggling with renewed strength against the guard who held him.

The air filled with that hideous scraping against every part of her. She realized Peredur was speaking those hateful words again, even without that pendant he'd held out before him. The entire war council snarled and hissed against them and, as one, they turned toward Peredur.

She couldn't let them tear him to pieces. Tanwen shoved and pulled against her captor, and in the tumult from the words that filled the night with agony, she slipped away from his clutches. Crawling past legs and bodies, she threw herself across her beloved, though his words bit into her like beaks and talons.

"What are you doing?" Lord Muiredach said, his usual calm completely unhinged.

"What are you doing to *him*?" she cried.

Peredur stopped sending those horrible sounds into the air. She sensed a strange hum now that she was this close to him. She couldn't quite place it.

Lord Muiredach got to his feet and glared down at both of them. "He will join us, or he will die. The true death will be his. It's up to him." The vampire lord turned and gathered something from one of his guard.

Two vampires dragged Peredur to his feet, arms outstretched. Another cut Peredur's tunic from him, leaving him bare and beautiful. Tanwen lunged to stop them, but powerful hands stopped her. She twisted to get away, but when she saw it was Cavan holding her back, it took the fight out of her.

Lord Muiredach held a wineskin over Peredur's head, but when he tipped it, clear water streamed out. It ran in rivulets through Peredur's dark hair, over his face, dripping over his chest. Peredur tried to take a deep breath, but sagged in the vampires' grip instead.

She shook her head at this hideous display of revenge. *Not her beloved.* "Stop," she whispered. "Please don't!"

"You don't have to watch this," Cavan said in her ear.

"Help him!" she cried.

"I can make it so that you don't see what's happening," Cavan said as if he hadn't heard a word she said. "Just like with Mam."

"You are the greatest prize I could hope for," Lord Muiredach said to Peredur.

"You can stop this," Tanwen hissed to Cavan. "Can't you?" She jerked roughly so she could see into those gray eyes of his. There was hurt there, hurt that she should ask for anything on behalf of her beloved. But he, of all people, should know the limitations of her feelings for him. "You...you will...never turn me..." Peredur forced out.

The war council rumbled its distain. Lord Muiredach tipped the wineskin again, pouring more of the disorienting water over Peredur's head. He retched as though he would vomit, but nothing came out.

Tanwen grabbed Cavan's face and made him look into her eyes. "You say you love me."

"I do," he said. "I love you." The pain in his eyes reached inside her. His pain was like her pain. She was hurting him by asking him to save her beloved, but Peredur's gasps of shock behind her gave her the resolve she needed.

"You summoned the vampire for me. Didn't you?"

Cavan nodded, but he looked so lost.

"If you could do something like that, surely you can help him now?"

Cavan shook his head. She grabbed his face with even more desperation, even more tenderness.

"The full extent of your power isn't truly suspected by Lord Muiredach," she said.

Cavan looked past her at the vampire lord. She saw pride fill his eyes, then just as quickly he shuttered over it. He looked at Tanwen once more, while behind her she heard Peredur's stifled cries of distress.

She felt the same dreadful buzzing coming from Cavan as she'd felt beside Peredur. She looked down at its source, which lay beneath Cavan's tunic, over his chest.

"What's going on?" she asked.

Cavan's eyes filled with dread. "If I do as you ask of me, he'll truly be lost to you."

"What do you mean, Cavan?" She risked a look behind her. Lord Muiredach poured more water over Peredur, eliciting cruel laughter from the war council. Peredur writhed in their grip, moaning.

"You don't understand," Cavan said. "You think it's a simple thing, but my coming here, my being a sorcerer and a vampire..." He shook his head and laughed, the slightest edge of hysteria creeping into his voice. "You don't understand what will happen, Tanwen!"

A hideous gasp from Peredur made her turn in time to see one of the guard wrap a silver chain around

Peredur's throat. His skin burned beneath it, the water turning to steam. Lord Muiredach leaned forward, fangs bared once more.

"You must beg me for it," he taunted. "Beg! Beg to be made a vampire, a true one, not one of those abominations from the Brotherhood."

Peredur's eyes blazed his contempt, even as he grimaced in pain. He somehow found the strength to shake his head. Then his gaze found Tanwen across the space between them. Her knees nearly gave out.

She grabbed Cavan and said, "He needs my help."

"If you just let Lord Muiredach get on with it, Peredur will become one of us," Cavan said, gripping her just as tightly.

She craned her head to watch the unthinkable. Peredur shook his head again, protesting, "No!" as Lord Muiredach's fangs skimmed along Peredur's outstretched arm. Her beloved's mouth worked to form the words that enraged them so, that choked the air once again with breathtaking agony.

At the very same instant Tanwen felt the buzzing rise to a frantic pitch beneath Cavan's tunic, over his heart. Cavan winced and made to clutch it, but Tanwen grabbed hold of his hand. His gray eyes filled with despair.

"Is that what I think it is?" she asked.

Cavan nodded once.

"He needs it," she said.

"You're the one who took it from him!"

"Then I'm the one who should give it back." She tried to reach into his tunic for it, but Cavan fought against her.

"This will change everything!" he said, grabbing her hands. "Not just between you and him, or between you and me. For everything. For everyone."

"Tell me the truth, Cavan," she said. "Have you seen this? What's about to happen?"

Peredur screamed behind her. She looked again. Lord Muiredach held the same silver medallion he'd once pressed onto Cavan over Peredur's heart, pouring water on it at the same time. Steam rose as his skin blistered and sizzled.

She looked back at Cavan. He also watched what Lord Muiredach was doing, wincing at his own remembered pain. Cavan looked into Tanwen's eyes, and her heart soared with hope at the change she saw there.

He reached into his tunic, pulled the humming, buzzing pendant from around his neck and pressed it into her hands. It gave off an eerie blue light. It was heavy and it hurt her hands terribly to hold it.

She waited only as long as it took to grace Cavan with her look of gratitude. Then she took off at a run for her beloved.

Peredur opened his eyes in time to see her approach. Lord Muiredach and the others turned but could not stop the events which Cavan had forseen. Tanwen ran with all her strength into her vampire lord, knocking him off-balance. He dropped the silver medallion. In its place, Tanwen slapped the white pendant with its humming blue glow directly in the burnt circle created by Lord Muiredach's torment of her Peredur.

The moment it touched her beloved, a silent wave of destructive power knocked Tanwen and everyone else to the ground.

76

The torturous crush in the center of his chest gave way for a heartbeat. Peredur opened his eyes to see Tanwen thrusting his lost amulet toward his chest.

The throbbing in his side rose to an unbearable resonance. It joined the amulet's joyous singing over his heart. Peredur stood straight as a sword. The saint's power burst forth from him like a thunderclap, but there was no sound at all except that of the vampires landing in heaps at his feet.

That's when it all broke loose.

An energy bolt coursed through his body, turning everything in sight an eerie blue color. Peredur's hair whipped around, as if it were in a windstorm. Jagged lines reached out from his body like darting snakes' tongues. The scene before him fell away as he arose in the air.

Don't be afraid, the saint said inside his mind.

What is going on? Peredur asked without speaking.

This was foreseen.

What is happening?

The vampires are soon to be a greater threat. A weapon strong enough to keep them in check is required.

What do you mean?

Your brethren never saw me, never heard my voice, because I was not for them. I am for you.

Some of the vampires shook off the effects of the energy surge and struggled to their feet. His Tanwen got to her knees and looked up at him, her mouth open in awe. The wise woman's son crawled to her side, wrapped his arms around her and pulled a sacred wand from inside his tunic.

Twirling it around both of them, drawing a circle in the air that Peredur could see, Cavan recited words that ignited a bubble of light around him and Tanwen.

Peredur raised his arms above his head. The shooting lines of blue light that flicked from him grew thicker, collecting around his arms and hands. They seemed to draw more power from the heavens. He let the energy bolts grow as strong as he could bear.

Is this the right way? Peredur asked his saint.

Does it feel right?

It feels good. Peredur tilted his body so he could look down at them – the vampires trying to get away. The one who had been summoned, who had created a new vampire by taking his Tanwen into their life...he began to run.

Peredur brought his arm down as though he could grab hold of the vampire, but the blue lines of energy collecting in his arms and hands grabbed the vampire instead. In a burst of silver light, the vampire's skeleton stood out in stark contrast to the inky night. A howling screech broke the stillness. In a moment there was nothing left of the vampire but a pile of ash.

I killed him, Peredur said to his saint.

Yes. You are the weapon required.

What is happening to me?

It has already happened.

Two of the vampire guard rushed forward, arms raised, trying to grab hold of Peredur's feet with wild jumps.

They are defending their clan, Peredur said. *I would do the same if I were them.*

Very true.

Still Peredur kicked them both away, aiming his hands at them, incinerating them.

Their clan is a dangerous one, Saint Cittinus said. *For humans and the brethren alike.*

I mustn't let them get away.

No, his saint said sadly.

Peredur swept his arms to the left and to the right, reducing every vampire to cinders as they ran. At last there was only Lord Muiredach racing for the bubble of light that contained his beloved and Cavan within it.

"Let me in!" the vampire lord shrieked.

Cavan simply stared at him, while Tanwen looked up at Peredur. Lord Muiredach gazed around him, at his entire war council blowing about him in ashes. He got to his feet and faced Peredur, who hovered above him just beyond reach.

"You would have made me into one of you," Peredur said.

"Yes," Lord Muiredach said without apology.

"I would give you the same chance to join with me, if it were mine to give."

The vampire lord laughed bitterly.

"Would you join our brotherhood, if it were possible to do so?" Peredur asked.

"You know the answer to that," Lord Muiredach spat out.

"Yes. And as it turns out, the opportunity is not mine to give." Peredur stretched out his hand and threw the bolt of blue energy to wrap itself around the vampire lord. Lord Muiredach laughed again as his skull lit up the quiet night.

Then he was gone.

"Peredur!" Tanwen called from inside the bubble of light. Her voice was muffled, but it tugged heavily on Peredur's heart.

We must let her go, the saint said inside him.

I can't.

We must.

Cavan spoke the words that released the bubble. Now there was no light except the blue glow emanating from Peredur and the saint, and the faint stars hanging so high above them all.

Peredur watched as Cavan pulled Tanwen to her feet, watched as his beloved fought Cavan, screaming and hitting and pulling to get away.

I can't let her go, Peredur said.

We must. She has done her part in this. Now we must let her go.

Peredur's heart weighed all the heavier with the saint inside him, as he told the wise woman's son, "Take her. Go, now."

Tanwen's face froze in shock and disbelief at his words. Cavan used that moment of shock to drag her up over the rise and away into the trees.

I've hurt her, Peredur said. *I've hurt her and she saved me.*

She has done her part, the saint said again. *Now we must let her go.*

Peredur began sinking fast. Several figures ran toward him in the darkness as he hit the ground and crumpled in despair.

Strong hands helped him to sit up. Familiar voices coaxed him to open his eyes.

The blue light still glowed faintly in his chest when he looked down to see the amulet. It was seared into his flesh over his heart. Melnak knelt before him, his eyes brimming with confusion and worry.

Peredur brought his hands up to his chest, to the amulet glowing there. He smiled and said, "It's alright. He is here with me."

"Who do you mean?" Melnak asked, but Peredur could tell by the fear in his eyes that he already guessed.

"Our saint," Peredur said.

Melnak gazed at him for a long moment. Peredur could feel his mentor, his creator pulling away from him, and there was nothing he could do to stop it.

When Melnak and the other brethren knelt as one before him, bowing their heads before their new lord, the only thing Peredur could do was stand there along with his saint, their blue light shining into the darkness.

END OF BOOK ONE

COMING SOON FROM JULIA PHILLIPS SMITH
BOOK TWO IN THE DARK AGES VAMPIRE TRILOGY

AUTHOR'S NOTES

This story takes place in an era once known as the Dark Ages, which followed Roman Imperial rule and preceded the medieval period. Due to a longstanding lack of written historical documents or archeological artifacts, the Dark Ages were an apt term for a considerable time frame, about which mainly legend remained.

Technological advances have profoundly changed the way we think of this era. Knowledge of the preceding Iron Age now informs our understanding of the day-to-day rhythms of tribal life in Europe and Britain during this period. The era known as the Migration Period is now a much better term for the centuries falling between the cracks of Classical antiquity and the Middle Ages.

It does make for an irresistible setting for a vampire tale, however, especially since the following medieval period brought the Inquisition, with its rampant vigilance against demons, witches and devils.

Though this is a work of fiction, I have remained as faithful as possible to current research available on the era.

A note on several of the characters in this book:

One of the brethren is based on an actual historical figure, who married the queen of the Brigantes, Cartimandua. Vellocatus was a warrior who lived in the 1st century and served as the armor-bearer to King

Venutius. When Queen Cartimandua divorced Venutius following his rebellion against her forces, Vellocatus ruled beside her for over a decade. When Venutius staged a successful second uprising against his former wife, Cartimandua retreated with the aid of her Roman allies. However, Vellocatus disappears from historical record at this point.

The other character based on an actual person is the saint. Cittinus was among a group of early Christians beheaded in Carthage for refusing to swear allegiance to the Roman Emperor. The group of seven men and five women, all from North Africa in modern-day Algeria and Tunisia, were urged to renounce their belief in a problematic cult, on pain of death. None of them did so. Their final words to the court were recorded. Cittinus' struck me in particular: *"We have none other to fear, save only our Lord God, who is in heaven."*

There is nothing to indicate that this particular saint's bones were ever made into amulets. This is a fictional conceit of my own making. However, the veneration of bone fragments was already an ancient practice before the advent of Christianity, and it would not be hard to imagine someone either of faith, or with a sense of financial opportunism, gathering up some of the bones of this group of martyred believers for future profit. Traditionally it has been believed that the soul of a martyr was in such a heightened pitch of holiness at the moment of death, that the physical body's remains were charged with supernatural power.

I have included a brief glossary of terms at the end of the book to clarify the origins of each member of the brotherhood, whose homelands have undergone several name changes in the centuries since this story takes place.

Julia Phillips Smith
October, 2011

GLOSSARY

Members of the Brotherhood:

Melnak - Referred to as the Byzantine
Origin – Byzantium
Now known as Istanbul, in Turkey
Wladyslaw – Referred to as the Polanie and as the
szlachcic, a nobleman
Origin – Chwaliszewo
Now known as Poznan, Poland
Sigbjorn – Referred to as the Norseman
Origin – Agnafit, Svealand
Now known as Stockholm, in Sweden
Brude – Referred to as the Pict
Origin – Craig Phadrig
Now known as Inverness, in Scotland
Velocatus – Referred to as the Brigante
Origin – Stanwick
Now known as Richmond, North Yorkshire, England
Adalhard – Referred to as the Frank
Origin – Cenabum, Gaul
Now known as Orleans, France

ABOUT THE AUTHOR

Debut author Julia Phillips Smith is honored to add this special milestone to her arts industry background.

A graduate of Ryerson University's film program, Julia's previous writing credits include scripts for radio and television. She has donned various creative hats, including theatre stage manager, 3rd Assistant Director for an independent feature film, and editor for a TV documentary.

Julia lives on Canada's east coast with her husband and her mom. A longtime blogger, she invites you to visit A Piece of My Mind (http://julia-mindovermatter.blogspot.com/).

Also Available from Julia Phillips Smith
***Bound by Dragonsfyre* – Book One in the
Dragonsfyre Trilogy**